BLOOD ON THE COWLEY ROAD

A gripping mystery full of twists

PETER TICKLER

Detective Susan Holden Book 1

Revised edition 2020
Joffe Books, London

ISBN 978-1-78931-306-2

IN THE BEGINNING

The familiar figure was crossing at the pedestrian lights when Danny Flynn first spotted it. Standing outside the patisserie shop, looking in, he had been using the window as a mirror, to try to spot the man who he knew was following him. Flynn had been standing there for at least five minutes, stock still except for the occasional slight shifting of weight from one foot to the other. His eyes, however, had flickered ceaselessly from left to right across the glass, desperately trying to identify the stalker, until suddenly they had collided with the reflection of Detective Sergeant Fox. It wasn't the face that he recognized – that was largely in shadow – but the overall shape and size of his body and the way he carried it. You don't forget the person who deprived you of your freedom.

He resisted the temptation to jerk round and check he hadn't been deceived. Instead, he watched the man's reflection move across the road and turn right along the opposite pavement. Only then did he turn his head briefly to satisfy himself that he was correct, that the man who had been following him in the shadows was none other than that plain-clothes policeman who had entered that café on that terrible afternoon. He hadn't realized who he was at the time, in fact he'd barely noticed him come in and sit down. The bloody manager had been pissing him off. The cappuccino he'd ordered had been lukewarm, and there'd been dead weevils on the sandwich. But the manager insisted they were stray poppy seeds. Danny had lost his rag at that point. Not that he was later able to remember exactly what happened, but he did remember the pain as the copper bent his arm around his back and shouted at him to calm down. He'd ended up in Littlemore Hospital for six weeks as a result, so of course he could remember Detective Sergeant Fox.

Danny turned back towards the window. He watched with mounting anxiety as Fox's reflection stopped outside the music shop. Flynn had gazed into that window many times himself, admiring the guitars and drum kits. But how much could the policeman see in this light? Was he too using a shop window as a mirror? Was he watching him watching him? Inside Flynn's head the voice was persistent now and urgent. Run it was saying. Run while you can. Before it's too late. Run. But Flynn was rooted to the pavement. Because overriding all was the fear that if he moved first, if he, Danny Flynn, started to walk or run, then the policeman would see him, and follow him again, flitting in and out of the shadows, remorselessly, relentlessly, back to his flat, back to his home. And who knew what he would do then?

Quite suddenly, Fox moved on. He glanced briefly at the posters in the video shop window, walked a few paces further, then turned right and disappeared out of sight down James Street. Flynn emitted a gulp – but not of relief. The policeman had gone, yes, but where exactly had he gone? James Street was Danny's street. His address was technically Iffley Road, but the house in which he lived stood on the corner, and from his second floor window at the back he could – and often did – look right down James Street until it bent to the left out of sight. If he was in the Cowley Road, he always walked up James Street to get home. James Street was his patch. But what if the policeman was waiting? In the shadows behind a hedge. Or suppose he had taken up a position of surveillance in one of the upper rooms? Danny was still using the shop window as a mirror, watching the corner of James Street in case Fox should retrace his tracks, but his heavy breathing was steaming up the glass. He knew he had to get home. If he could just get home, then he would be all right. He could lock himself in, and he would be safe. He looked at his watch, and decided to wait two more minutes. When they had elapsed – and the large policeman not reappeared – he took three deep breaths, and set off across the road. An oncoming car had to brake sharply, but he didn't notice. Once over the road, he turned left as Fox had done, walked as far as Marston Street, and stopped. Then, he took another deep breath, turned right, and plunged fatefully into the darkness of Marston Street.

CHAPTER 1

Edith Brownwood paused at the pedestrian crossing, and looked right. Years of experience, plus one very close shave, dictated this behaviour. But it was not the car drivers that scared her. It was the cyclists. The bike riders of Oxford – she and all the members of her Tuesday morning coffee group were agreed on this – were a lawless and discourteous subspecies. Their core belief seemed to be that the streets belonged to them, and that by definition all the rules of the road were therefore irrelevant to them. Edith's view of the cycling fraternity had been brusquely reinforced three years previously, when a middle-aged man clad in yellow lycra had clipped her as she was stepping out off the pavement and had sent her tumbling onto the tarmac. She had been lucky on that occasion: just a few bruises. But at the age of 81 she was only too aware of her mortality. One fall, one broken hip, and she'd be in hospital, and then a home, and then a coffin. She'd seen it happen to her friend Brenda, and she was damned if was going to happen to her.

There were no cyclists hastening carelessly towards her. A red Mini was approaching, but it was slowing obediently down. She nodded in approval, and advanced cautiously across the road. Once on the opposite pavement, she turned left towards the city centre. She had walked some fifteen paces when she suddenly stopped, and turned her head to the right.

She knew this end of the Cowley Road intimately – so she knew almost without looking that something was different. That something was a blue circle on the wall of the car park, and on that circle there was something that looked like writing. She screwed up her face as she tried to work out exactly what it was she was looking at, but it was no good. Not for the first time, she told herself that she really must go to the optician. Her sight was getting worse. She advanced towards the wall, squinting her eyes, until she was barely a foot from it. The object of her attention was higher than her head, and she stretched her left arm up to touch it. It looked, now she was close up, like one of those blue, round plaques that they put up on the buildings of the famous. There was one of Dorothy Sayers on the wall of Christchurch Cathedral School. Only this didn't feel like one. They are metal, and this most certainly wasn't.

Puzzled, she opened her bag to look for her glasses. Maybe plaques were plastic nowadays. Everything seemed to be plastic nowadays. But what on earth was a plaque doing here? Famous people didn't live in car parks. Unless, it suddenly occurred to her, someone famous had lived here before it was a car park.

She had just got her glasses on when she heard a sound. It came from high above her, and it lasted barely a second, and it sounded like nothing she had ever heard before. Unless maybe it was a seagull in pain.

And then there was another sound, much duller, but much louder because it was much closer. Something had landed at her feet, so close she felt a sudden gasp of wind as it struck the ground. Dead close.

It took a few moments for her eyes to readjust from the plaque to the large object at her feet, and a few more for her brain to assimilate the fact that the crumpled brown object with protruding black things was a body. A woman's body. A woman in a long fawn mackintosh, black high-heeled boots, and shoulder-length brown hair.

Edith Brownwood felt herself wobbling slightly. She tried to tell herself to keep calm, but then she noticed two rivulets of red liquid emerging from under the woman's head, and creeping slowly across the pavement toward her.

And then she fainted.

DS Fox paused at the door in surprise. For several seconds he stared at the sign on the door – 'Detective Inspector S. Holden'. It must have been put there while he was away. He had known about the promotion – she had told him herself the day before he had gone on leave – but nevertheless he still felt surprised. He wasn't sure why. He knocked, and opened the door. DI Susan Holden was on the phone. From the sound of it, it was her mother again. Holden looked up at him, shrugged a smile, and gestured with her free hand for a drink.

'Coffee?' he mouthed. She nodded.

'No!' she said sharply down the phone, as Fox began to retreat from the room. 'I cannot come now. Nor am I responsible for my mother's behaviour. But I will come over as soon as I can. I cannot see what difference half an hour will make.'

There was a babble of noise from the other end of the mobile, but Holden pressed a button and it went quiet. It was at times like this that she envied people who smoked. She leant back in her chair and imagined the relief to be gained by drawing smoke deep into her lungs and then exhaling. Breathe it down in one powerful intake, then slowly let it and all the anxieties of the moment out. In, then slowly out. In, and out.

She had smoked her imaginary cigarette down to the smallest of stubs by the time Fox reappeared, a polystyrene cup in each hand. She beckoned him to the chair.

He was a big man: around six feet four inches tall, broad across the shoulders, and with a square face. When he stood or walked, he did so with a slight stoop, like many a tall man.

He had long arms that swung untidily from his shoulders, and his curly hair was a mixture of dark brown and patches of grey.

His surname had been a source of canteen banter from the very first day he took up the post of Detective Sergeant at the Cowley Office of the Thames Valley Police. This was no surprise, for anyone less like a fox was hard to imagine. A bear was the animal that came most obviously to mind for most people. A big cuddly bear. At first, that is. Later, people usually revised their comparison, for when push came to shove, he was more than capable of using his formidable bulk to great effect, and then comparison with a grizzly bear was more appropriate.

Detective Inspector Susan Holden, typically, saw him differently. He was for her a much smaller and more companionable creature – a dog in fact. Or, to be precise, a terrier: rough haired and showing signs of wear and tear maybe, but with a knack for doggedly (DI Holden smiled at her own pun) tracking down a quarry and never letting go once it was in his grasp.

They had worked together for nearly four years, and not once in that time had she had serious cause to regret their partnership. Once, she had had to suggest that his long dark coat might benefit from a clean, and she had long ago trained herself not to worry about the unruly nature of his hair, but for her those were mere bagatelles. What mattered was that, like any good dog, he was trustworthy, faithful and patient.

'Have a good holiday?' she asked once he was settled.

'So, so.'

'Only so, so?' she said.

He frowned slightly. 'I stayed with my sister for a few days. In Weymouth. Did some decorating.'

'Decorating! That was kind of you. But you are meant to relax on holiday, you know.' Her tone of voice was gentle, slightly teasing, designed to draw him out, but Fox wasn't prepared to prolong discussion of his leisure time. He slurped noisily from his plastic cup of coffee and returned them to the present. 'What's been happening here? Anything interesting?'

His superior smiled resignedly to herself. The one distinctly undoglike characteristic of the sergeant was a dourness that could easily and unexpectedly mutate into sulkiness, but that was something she could live with. 'Well, I could give you a blow-by-blow account of Mrs Holden senior's one-woman crusade against the world,' she continued cheerily, 'but seeing as it's Monday morning, and you have just returned from a decorating holiday, I'll spare you that.' She leant forward, elbows on the desk, hands pressed together as if in prayer. 'I've got a death for you to investigate.'

'A suspicious death, you mean,' he said, suddenly interested.

For a moment, Holden could almost see him wagging his tail, head cocked slightly to the side, a terrier begging to be let off his leash. 'Not really,' she said apologetically. 'Self-inflicted probably. A jumper.' She saw the eagerness in his eyes begin to fade, and tried to rekindle it. 'Actually, not so run-of-the-mill. It made the front page of the Mail on Saturday, thanks to the antics of some art student. Anyway, DC Wilson has got the details. He can provide support, but I want you to handle it. We can't afford any slips with the press so interested.' She got to her feet as she finished. 'Keep me informed. I've got to go and apply an emotional poultice to my mother's warden. Otherwise, we'll have another dead body for you to investigate before the day is out.'

'What time did you get to the car park?'

Ed Bicknell frowned, and pulled distractedly at the wisp of beard on his chin. He was a little over six feet, Fox estimated, but probably not more than eleven stones in weight. All skin and bone. The blond hair was obviously dyed, while the facial hair, which he had managed to grow, was tinged (naturally) with ginger. He wore the ubiquitous student uniform of jeans and a T-shirt; in his case the shirt was decorated with the faded but unmistakeable face beloved by chic revolutionaries – Che Guevara. When he spoke, his voice was local Oxford. 'About seven-thirty, or maybe quarter to eight. I overslept. Meant to get there earlier.'

Oversleeping was obviously something Bicknell was good at, Fox decided. When he and Wilson had rung the bell of his flat at 11.00 that morning, there had been some delay before the door had been opened by a befuddled-looking Bicknell dressed only in boxer shorts.

DS Fox had a pad in front of him, and he scribbled a note on it, though he did this more for effect than anything else. It was Detective Constable Wilson's job to take notes, while he put the questions. 'So what did you do then?' he asked.

'I put my plaque up on the wall of the car park. There are some steps that lead up to the first floor of the car park. I went and stood there and pretended to read a paper.'

'Why?' Fox said suddenly.

'Because!' Bicknell snapped. That was the question his father had asked only a month ago when he had gone "home" for the weekend. But, of course, his father, being his father, hadn't even pretended to listen to his son's answer. Instead, he had suddenly got up, poured himself a large whisky, and turned on the 24-hour news for the third time that evening. At least Fox appeared to be interested. He had leant forward, and his eyes were looking straight into Bicknell's face. Bicknell sighed, and then continued in a tone which suggested he was humouring a rather irritating small nephew. 'Because that was the point of the project. To see if people stopped. To see how many just walked past. To observe those that stopped. To photograph them. Unobtrusively. Isn't that what you police do? Watch people, take photos without them knowing, then use it all as evidence against them?'

If Bicknell's response irritated the Detective Sergeant, it wasn't apparent. Fox scribbled a few more notes in his pad, and continued in the same unemotional tone as he had started with. 'And one of the people you photographed was Sarah Johnson?'

Bicknell nodded.

'I'll need a copy of it.'

'I took three,' Bicknell said flatly.

'Three?' echoed Fox, his voice rising a semitone.

'The paper only printed one, but she was there quite a time, staring at the plaque.'

'How long?'

Bicknell pulled at his chin again. 'Maybe four or five minutes.'

'Did you talk to her?' Fox asked.

'What do you think? I was up the stairs, trying not to be noticed. Like the proverbial fly on the wall. I was observing people, not chatting to them to see if any of them were feeling fucking suicidal.'

'So, what happened after she moved on?'

'Not much. I took one or two more photos. It went very quiet. Most people just walked past without noticing. That's what happens. Either there's a group, and other people stop to see what is going on, or there's no one and everyone walks past without noticing. I was beginning to wonder if I shouldn't do something ... you know, intervene in some way to generate some interest when ... Christ, she just fell right out of the sky.'

Bicknell fell silent. Outside, a car backfired. Fox flinched momentarily, then asked a question. 'Did she make a sound – before ... when she fell?'

Bicknell considered this, raking back in his memory. 'There was a shout – a couple of seconds before she hit the ground.'

'What sort of shout?'

'Christ, what sort of question is that? A loud cry. Maybe terror, or maybe it was a war cry, giving herself courage to jump. How the hell should I know?'

Again Fox scribbled, but his eyes and attention remained focused on Bicknell's face. 'What did you do then?'

Bicknell gave an exaggerated sigh. 'I rang you lot, didn't I? On my mobile.'

'Then you took some more photos. Of Sarah Johnson, lying there dead on the pavement.'

'It seemed like an opportunity.'

'Did it now?' said Fox. This time his voice was louder, and harsh, and he was half on his feet. 'An opportunity for what? To make some money out of a wretched woman's death? A few sensational photos for the press.'

Bicknell leaned back, his eyes fixed unblinking on Fox's face. He smiled. 'Carpe diem, detective.'

'Carpe what?' Fox said, momentarily thrown off balance.

'It's Latin. Seize the moment. Carpe diem. Otherwise, detective, in this life you just get left behind.'

Fox stood up, straightened his back – it had ached since he had woken that morning – and walked over to the window. He looked down at the featureless strip of grass that masqueraded as garden and wished he was somewhere else, anywhere else. He wasn't fussy. Just not here. Not investigating the death of a woman whose answer to the problems of life had been to jump off the top of a six-storey car park.

'Can I see the plaque?' he said at last.

'It was in the papers,' Bicknell said. 'Didn't you see it?'

Fox ignored the question. 'I need the plaque, as evidence, and copies of all the photos you took that morning. You don't have a problem with that, do you?'

Bicknell got up and went over to the large desk sited under the window. He leafed through a pile of paper sheets until he found one he was happy with.

'This is a copy,' he said, placing it on the coffee table in front of Fox. 'I'll have to burn all the photos onto a CD.'

Fox looked at the plaque. It was a strong blue colour, with white writing. Paper card it might have been, but the first impression was strikingly realistic, even this close. It was no surprise that it attracted attention when it was up on the wall. No surprise that Sarah Johnson chose to stare at it for so long.

'When you put your plaque up, did you know that two people had jumped to their deaths from that car park in the last six months?'

'It was hardly a state secret, now was it?'

Fox's eyes were still on the plaque, as if scanning it might somehow bring him a blinding revelation. When that didn't work, he read it out loud: '26 April. Jo Smith stood here while contemplating suicide.' When he looked up, Bicknell had moved back to the desk and was turning on his computer.

'Who was Jo Smith?' he asked quietly.

'Jo Smith?' Bicknell snorted. 'Jo Smith was a figment of my bloody imagination. All right?'

Fox spun round with a sudden spurt of anger. Who the hell did Bicknell think he was? For a second he imagined the pleasure to be gained from punching the cockiness out of him. Fuelled by the thought, he strode over to the desk and leant with all the physical threat he could muster across Bicknell's personal space.

'Don't you regret what you did at all? Hasn't it occurred to you that it might have been your smart-arsed project that tipped her over the edge? That if you had bloody well stayed in bed that day, she might still be walking around Oxford today?'

If Bicknell was taken aback by Fox's burst of anger, he wasn't going to show it. 'If I did tip her over the edge,' he snarled back, 'so fucking what? Who are you to pass judgement, detective? How the hell do you know that she isn't better off dead than alive? Maybe life was, for her, just too bloody shitty to be worth carrying on.'

'And maybe she was just having a bad day,' Fox responded. 'Maybe if she had made it to the next day, she would have felt better.'

'Maybe you missed your vocation as social worker, detective.'

Fox stood up straight again. Again pain shot across his lower back, but he kept his eyes full on Bicknell. 'You're quite a cool bastard aren't you?' he said, his voice now under control.

'Look, detective, let's just get this straight, then you can stop trying to lay all this shit on me.' Bicknell's computer had come to life. He started to tap away on his keyboard as he spoke. 'She's dead, right? She chose to jump. Right? No one – unless, of course, you know any different – pushed her. She just climbed up to the top, looked out across the dreaming spires of sunny Oxford, and jumped. As a consequence, I got some great publicity – not to mention some cash from the newspapers. I've already had two galleries on the phone wanting me to exhibit my work. Sarah Johnson's death was the best thing that could possibly have happened to me. So if you want to know if I've any regrets, the answer is not many. If you want to know if I lie awake at night wondering if I behaved properly, I don't. Now, if you'll give me a couple minutes, I'll burn these photos for you. Then, if you don't object, I've got some phone calls to make. All right?'

CHAPTER 2

When the door of Sarah Johnson's flat was pulled back by a woman with brown shoulder-length hair, blue-grey eyes, slightly up-turned nose and a thin oval-shaped face, DS Fox felt as if he was seeing a ghost. He was a down-to-earth, sceptical man, but in the moment in which the door opened and he looked into the face of Anne Johnson, he was – however briefly – a believer. His logical approach to life should have prepared him for the facial similarity of the two sisters, but if less than an hour after scanning the blank features of a corpse in the morgue you come face to face with the living embodiment of that corpse, it would be easy for logic to get submerged by emotion.

'Yes?' Anne Johnson had been rung two hours earlier by DC Wilson, but she too was briefly nonplussed, primarily because she was expecting someone in uniform. Her first thought was that they were from the funeral directors, despite the fact that she had arranged for them to call round the following day. The taller, older man, certainly looked the part: he was wearing a dark suit, white shirt and plain tie under a long black coat, and his downcast expression seemed to her to be appropriate for someone in the burial business. It was this man who responded. 'Detective Sergeant Fox. And this

14

is Detective Constable Wilson.' He paused, still not entirely back in the logical world either. 'You must be …?'

'Anne Johnson,' she said hastily. She offered her hand, while wondering if this was appropriate for greeting a policeman on duty. 'Please, come in.'

While Anne Johnson got them a mug of tea, Fox sat on a distinctly tatty armchair and looked about the room. He would have liked to have wandered around, nosing around into every corner of the flat, to see what Sarah Johnson had liked to read, to eat, to dress in. What photos did she have in her bedroom? What was on her bedside table and in its drawers (assuming she had one and it had drawers). Were there pills for depression there? Had she stopped taking them? But somehow it seemed insensitive to do that until they had drunk tea together and talked about Sarah. Only then would he feel he could ask permission to look through the dead woman's possessions.

'So,' Anne Johnson said, after she had sat down and taken a sip from her mug, 'what do you want to know?'

'We are required to make a few enquiries, for the inquest. Just a formality, you understand?'

'You want to know if she was the sort of person who would commit suicide, you mean?' She spoke firmly, unemotionally, in a manner perfected at those wretched parent-teacher evenings that were one of the least enjoyable parts of a teacher's lot. How often had she sat opposite a pushy middle-class parent, calmly answering his or (more frequently) her overanxious questions. Not-so-little John or Victoria was invariably absent from these intimate public meetings – and always for some highly implausible reason – so pushy parent was able to lay it all out while the next pushy parent in line tutted noisily about the time everyone else was taking. Not that Miss Johnson viewed the slightly ponderous detective and his young sidekick as half as challenging as some of her parents, but the situation unquestionably was. If she could just treat this interview as a rather unexceptional parent-teacher meeting, then she felt she could get through it without bursting into tears and making a fool of herself.

'I suppose so,' DS Fox admitted. 'Yes.' He looked down as he spoke – almost demurely – thereby sabotaging her attempts to pretend that he was the archetypal parent from suburban hell. 'If you don't mind?' he added gently.

Anne Johnson took another sip from her mug. 'Sarah was always a bit up and down,' she said, and then immediately regretted it. What a stupid, stupid expression. And who was she to patronize her sister with such a trite description? She looked up from her mug at Fox. He gave a vague but encouraging grimace. 'Bipolar disorder the doctors called it,' she continued. 'Manic depression in ordinary language.' The words began to tumble out. 'Since she was about eighteen or nineteen. She went to Edinburgh University, had a breakdown her second term. She was sectioned and shut away in hospital until they had diagnosed her and worked out what drugs to pump into her. Then out she went into the community, stigmatized for ever – unable to get a job, a mortgage, anything that you or I would call a normal life.' She paused, and this time Fox intervened.

'When did you last see her?'

'Not recently.'

'Or speak to her?'

She took one, then a second sip from her mug. 'Look we weren't exactly best buddies. It was about three weeks ago. I try ... I used to try and ring her on the first of the month. Otherwise I knew I would never get round to it.'

'I see,' said Fox.

'Really?' Her voice was sharp this time. 'Personal experience is it? Got a sister like mine have you.' Normally, she prided herself on maintaining a detached patience throughout even the most trying of parent interviews, but somehow the bland 'I see' of this ponderous detective had had the power to blow away all her normal inhibitions of social intercourse. 'Because if you haven't, I don't see how the hell you can possibly see.'

Fox looked down, wondering if perhaps he should leave, and come back another time. But before he could come to a decision, DC Wilson exploded. Not literally, of course. He had been taking a sip from his mug of heavily sugared tea when Anne Johnson had launched her unexpected broadside. The small amount of tea that entered Wilson's mouth had immediately taken on a sinister life of its own, forcing itself into the unfortunate detective constable's windpipe. Wilson's windpipe – as is the way of windpipes in such situations – objected to this sudden intrusion of liquid, and after a short pause while Wilson fought for control and lost, the tea hurtled across the small table around which the three of them were seated and splattered unerringly on Anne Johnson's T-shirt.

'Bloody hell!' Fox rose to his feet, his face three shades darker than it had been.

'Sorry,' the wretched Wilson burbled. 'I am so sorry.' He too was on his feet.

Anne Johnson stayed firmly seated and laughed. Not the laugh of a woman at the end of her emotional tether, but rather the laugh of a teacher in control. A laugh – at once unexpected and incongruous, raucous in tone and then suddenly terminated – which Miss Johnson occasionally employed in class to bring her unsettled pupils back to heel. Fox and Wilson were both suitably perplexed. 'Do sit down,' she said in the calmest of voices. 'Please!' Wilson looked at Fox, Fox looked at Wilson, and in unison the two naughty schoolboys resumed their seats.

'I think it would be in all our interests to bring this meeting to a prompt conclusion.' Having gained control, Ms Johnson had no intention of relinquishing it. 'As far as I can see, we have established that my sister was a manic depressive. We have established that I have not seen her for some time, and have not even spoken to her for three weeks. So, obviously, I cannot help much vis-à-vis her recent state of mind. What I can add is that when I last spoke to her she seemed to be in good spirits. In fact, it was quite a relief

17

to me, because she had been very low earlier this year.' She paused, considering if there was anything else she wanted to say. 'I think that is about it,' she said eventually, 'but if you want to snoop round her bedroom, look inside the medicine cabinet, sniff her knickers, or do whatever it is that policemen do in these circumstances, then you have my blessing.'

'Thank you,' said Fox, meaning it. 'But if you don't mind, I do have a couple more questions – then we'll do our bit of snooping and go.'

She looked steadily at him, gave a slight nod of her head, but said nothing.

'Did your sister – do you know – keep a diary, or anything like that.'

'Yes.' The answer came instantly. 'It's in the little cupboard by her bed. It was on top of the cupboard when I arrived, but I thought it best to put it away.'

'Thank you,' said Fox, who had decided that politeness was the best approach. 'The other thing would be to ask you if you know of a man called Jake?'

Anne Johnson didn't have the opportunity to reply, because at that moment the doorbell rang. There was nothing polite about that, though, because it rang and continued ringing, as if someone had leant up against it accidentally and was pressing all their weight on it.

'Who on earth could that be?' Anne Johnson rose to her feet and moved towards the hallway of the apartment, while Fox surreptitiously rose behind her, and moved to the side so that he would have a full view when the outside door was opened. He recognized Danny Flynn immediately, but the man framed in the doorway had eyes only for Anne Johnson. 'You're her sister aren't you? Sarah's sister. She told me about you.' Anne surveyed the stranger with apparent calm – though a nurse taking her pulse at that moment would have noticed a considerable acceleration in its rate. The man had hair close-cropped almost to his skull and eyes that were never still. He wasn't tall, slightly shorter than herself, Anne judged, and he was skinny with it, a fact accentuated by the tight black leather jacket that he wore zipped up to his neck. On his hands, she noticed, he was wearing white latex gloves. 'Yes,' she said, 'I am Anne. Who are you?'

He ignored the question. 'They were following her, you know. Had been for weeks.' Suddenly Anne felt glad of the presence of the two detectives. The man was now shifting his weight from side to side, as if warming up for a slalom. Then he suddenly looked behind him to his left, then to his right, before sticking his hands into his jacket pockets and letting out a deep sigh. 'I told her to tell the police, but she just laughed. She was always laughing was Sarah.' Again he paused, and again he looked behind him to left and right. 'She should have listened. Now she's dead.'

'Hello, Danny.' Fox had moved forward and was standing by Anne's shoulder. He didn't think she was at risk. Danny was disturbing rather than dangerous, in his experience, but he felt it was time for him to intervene.

'You!' He almost hissed the word.

Fox tried to be disarming, without expecting Danny to be convinced. 'You all right Danny?'

'You've been following me.' His voiced was raised now, almost a shout. 'You've been following me again!'

'No I haven't, Danny,' he said with exaggerated calmness. 'I've come to speak to Anne about the death of Sarah, that's all. Just doing my job.'

'They did it!' He was hissing again now, and again he looked behind him. 'They forced her to jump. They forced her.'

Anne thought she could see a tear in the corner of his left eye. 'Who did?' she said. 'What do you mean?'

Danny raised his arm and pointed at Fox. 'He knows' he shouted, and then he was gone, down the path, out of the gate, and off down the street.

'Stop!' Anne said, and moving forward after him, but Fox was moving forward too, at her side, placing a restraining hand on her arm. 'Leave him!' he said sharply.

She turned and pulled her arm out of his grasp. 'Didn't you hear what he said?' The schoolteacher's poise had evaporated, leaving behind raw distress. 'Aren't you going to stop him? Take him in for questioning?'

'No,' said Fox firmly. He was standing across the path now. 'There's no need.' For several seconds he waited, unsure whether she might suddenly try and run after Danny herself, but eventually she gave a muffled snort and retreated back inside the flat.

'Danny is known to us.' They were sat down again around the square pine coffee table, and Fox had switched into patient explanation mode.

'And Danny knew Sarah, right?'

'Yes,' replied Fox quietly.

'And Danny said they forced her to jump.'

'Danny's paranoid.' It was Wilson who said this. Both Anne and Fox turned to look at him. If Fox was unhappy about his colleague's brusque interruption, he didn't show it. 'He always thinks he's being followed,' Wilson continued. 'By us – the police that is – or MI5 or MI6 or the CIA. You name it, he's been followed by it. So, if he thinks Sarah was being followed, then that's only to be expected.'

'Thank you, Constable,' Anne said icily. 'Very informative. I suppose I should feel reassured.'

'Perhaps I should stress that we aren't going to ignore Danny,' said Fox, trying to regain the initiative. 'We know where he lives. We know he is always in and out of the day centre. So we can always talk to him in calmer surroundings. But if I were you, I wouldn't place too much credence on what Danny says. Besides, there's no reason to believe that Sarah didn't take her own life.' He paused, then stood up. 'Unless, of course, you know something that we don't?'

It took the two detectives less than five minutes to complete their 'snoop round' the flat. They found Sarah's diary and an address book, various boxes of pills, but otherwise nothing that was of interest. As Wilson carefully bagged these items, Fox went and stood at the door of the kitchen. He felt, after the harshness of his last remark, that he ought to make some sort of amends. He waited while Anne Johnson finished drying up the mugs from which they had drunk their tea. 'Sorry about Wilson,' he said, gesturing towards the marks on her T-shirt. 'Drinking tea is not something they include on the young detective's training course.'

She folded the tea towel and laid it carefully over the back of the lone chair in the kitchen. The she looked up at him.

'You asked earlier about someone called Jake?'

'Yes.'

'Why?'

'Your sister had a mobile phone, and on the day she died, she tried to ring someone listed as Jake. Do you know him?'

'No,' she said. 'That is to say, I haven't met him. But he's a worker down at the day centre. Relatively new, I think. Sarah seemed to like him. I think she found him a good listener.'

'Thank you. I'll follow him up.'

'Right.' She paused, but only briefly. 'I guess that while you're at the day centre, you could follow up Danny at the same time.'

Fox didn't smile. Just nodded. 'Don't worry. I will.'

They continued to look at each other in silence – not aggressively, but neither was willing to be first to look down or away. Still looking at her, Fox called through to his colleague. 'DC Wilson. Are you finished yet?' 'Sir!' came the reply. Then the noise of something being dropped and another less respectful word fell from the lips of the Detective Constable. Fox frowned, but Anne Johnson merely grinned. 'So that's what they teach you at police school. How to swear colourfully while searching a suspect's house. I learn something new every day!'

'Sorry,' Fox grinned back. He was beginning to enjoy being with this woman. 'Actually, I think it's one of the optional courses. You can choose that one or tea drinking while interviewing witnesses and suspects.'

*

21

She stood on the doorstep of the flat, and watched as the two detectives made their way down the pavement. And as she watched, she smiled for a second time, a secret, comfortable and not entirely innocent smile. 'Cute,' she said to herself, as she turned back inside and shut the door. 'Very, very cute.'

CHAPTER 3

'So, where are we with Sarah Johnson?' said DI Holden as she finally turned away from the urgent e-mail she had been composing, and looked across at DS Fox and DC Wilson. The sudden question caught Wilson off guard. It was not that he had been dreaming (he was not given to that sort of thing), nor that he was thinking about his girlfriend (he didn't have one) or even his boyfriend (not his sort of thing). Rather he had been practising his observational skills on the new Detective Inspector's office. He had exchanged barely a dozen words with her in the six weeks since he'd taken up his post in the Cowley office. Most of the time he had been tagging along behind DS Fox or DS Roberts as he 'got to know the ropes'. Twice he had heard comments made about Holden – one respectful, the other distinctly sexist – but he liked to draw his own conclusions from his own observations. He had always been good at observing things; even before he was of school age, he had demonstrated a knack for finding items that his mother had lost at home. By the time he was eight he started to turn that observation towards people. This started shortly before the end of the autumn term, one in which his poor work (he was later diagnosed as mildly dyslexic, but not until he was half way through

Middle School) and worse behaviour had somewhat strained relations between him and his form teacher, Miss Turner, and his mother. After a difficult meeting at the end of school one Friday, he had felt relieved to be packed off to his grandma's house across town. But he had hardly curled up in the large musty chair in front of the television before his grandma marched in, switched it off, and stood over him with hands on her hips in a manner that made him shudder.

'So, young man,' she said, 'what has been going on at school? Your mother is at the end of her wits.'

'It's not fair,' he protested.

'It's not fair on your mother, young man,' she said firmly. 'That much I do know.'

'Miss Turner hates me,' the eight-year-old said plaintively.

'Does she now?' said the seventy-year-old, unconvinced.

'So does Mrs Wallace.' (Mrs Wallace was the classroom assistant.)

'Well,' his grandma said, taking a deep breath as she did so and bending down till her face was opposite his. 'In that case, what you have got to do,' and she poked him gently in the ribs as she said this, 'is make them like you.'

If the boy had had ears that could prick up, they would have pricked up. 'How?' he said. 'How Grandma?'

'What is Miss Turner's favourite colour?'

'Blue,' he said, without hesitation. 'She likes to dress in blue.'

'Does she wear jewellery?'

He paused, envisaging in his mind Miss Turner. 'Yes,' he said finally, 'she wears earrings. Little ones usually. But when we have a special day, she always wears long dangly ones. Once she wore a moon in one ear and a sun in the other.'

'And what can you tell me about Mrs Wallace?'

'Muck!' he said triumphantly. 'She likes white muck.'

For a minute the old lady was puzzled. 'Muck?'

'Yes,' he said. 'I saw it last week. She took a spray thing out of her bag, and I read the words "white muck" on its label.'

Wilson's grandma laughed. 'White musk. You mean white musk!'

'Why do you want to know, grandma?' he asked.

'Because,' she said, suddenly serious again, 'tomorrow we are going to buy them each a Christmas present that they will really like. And every time they use that present they are going to think about you and they are going to say to themselves, maybe that boy Colin Wilson isn't so bad after all.'

'So will they like me when they've opened their presents?' he asked.

His grandmother smiled. 'It may not be that simple or quick. But if you do as I say, we'll get them to like you, by hook or by crook.'

And so Colin Wilson began the task of Making His Teachers Like Him. It wasn't always easy, and it didn't usually involve giving presents (except on suitable occasions) but it did involve him making observations and then acting on those observations. When Miss Turner mentioned one Friday that her father wasn't very well, he made a Get Well card and gave it to her the following Monday. When she lost a parrot earring, it was he who found it under her desk. And when he once arrived early in class and found her already there, dabbing at her eyes with a handkerchief, he withdrew silently, shut the door firmly behind him, and stood on guard, refusing to let anyone else in until Miss Turner herself came and opened the door.

So the greenhorn Detective Constable who sat in the Inspector's office that morning was a man who had learnt to observe and notice both objects and people. He noticed that there was no picture on the rather bleak desk, and he wondered if that meant that DI Holden had no partner (or did she prefer not to advertise her private life). He took in the dark, discreetly striped trouser suit, the white blouse and the stud earrings, but drew no particular conclusions about her from them. He recognized the scent she was wearing, but couldn't quite place it. And, looking around the room, he observed that she had made no attempt to stamp her personality, her ownership on it. Was it just a matter of not having had time over the last week, or was it significant of something in the way she viewed work and her work environment?

'So where are we with Sarah Johnson?'

If Holden's words had taken Wilson by surprise, the same could not be said of Fox. 'We've interviewed the student Bicknell, and her sister, Anne Johnson. Bicknell claims not to have spoken to her, but he has given me copies of all the photos he took that morning, including three of her looking at his plaque.'

'And the sister?' queried Holden, with a hint of impatience in her tone.

'She confirmed that Sarah was a manic depressive. She admitted that she hadn't actually spoken to her for about three weeks, and hadn't seen her for some time, but she did say that Sarah had been in reasonable spirits three weeks prior to her death.'

'Three weeks,' Holden echoed. She pressed the first finger of her left hand on her forehead between her eyes, and shut her eyes briefly, trying to focus on this information. 'What do you make of that, Wilson?' she said, again catching Wilson off guard.

He blushed slightly. 'Well,' he said uncertainly, 'I suppose, given the cyclical nature of manic depression, highs followed by lows' – Wilson was feeling his way here – 'and given that this was three weeks before her death, it isn't at all inconsistent with her having jumped—'

Wilson's stumbling sentence was cut short by Holden. 'As evidence goes, it proves nothing. Quite right.' She turned now to Fox. 'What next then Derek?'

'I want to interview Jake. He's a worker at the day centre. She tried to ring him the morning of her death three times. He should be able to clarify her state of mind.'

'Good,' Holden said, nodding her head. 'Anything else?'

'Danny turned up at the flat when we were interviewing Anne.'

Holden looked puzzled. 'Danny?' she queried.

'You know,' Fox continued, 'mad Danny Flynn, from the day centre.'

'Ah, yes. Of course. What did he want?'

'He said someone had been following Sarah.'

The DI laughed, again catching Wilson off his balance. 'Sounds about par for the course, for Danny.'

'Yes,' admitted Fox.

'Nevertheless,' she said firmly, 'we do need to be sure that it was suicide.'

Anne Johnson's first reaction on seeing the place where her sister had plummeted to her death was to turn on her heel and run. But that would have been difficult. She had dressed up for the occasion – a white blouse, a discreet dark-blue skirt, and moderately high heels – and given that she had trouble even walking in high heels, running away was patently not a realistic option. A second complication would have been the extravagantly large bouquet of flowers she held in her arms. It had seemed such a good idea when it had first occurred to her. It would be some weeks before she could lay poor Sarah's body to rest, so to place a wreath of flowers at the site of her death had seemed an ideal temporary tribute. But now, standing on the dirty grey strip of paving stones at the base of the car park, it all seemed banal, pointless and even tasteless. The stunning bouquet seemed ridiculously over the top for this tawdry setting. Who was to say that by tomorrow morning someone wouldn't have nicked it for their lover or elderly mother, or that a drunk wouldn't have urinated all over it? And what was she trying to achieve with this bouquet anyway. To commemorate her sister's wonderful and fulfilled life? To celebrate the sensitive, supportive and joyful relationship that she and her sister had enjoyed? Without warning, her body shivered. Who the heck was she trying to fool? Her sister's life had been punctuated with mental health problems and mangled relationships, and she, Anne, had been only too ready to wash her hands of Sarah when things got difficult. And when she'd told the detective that she rang her sister every three weeks, well that hadn't actually been the truth, had it? God, what a selfish cow she was! These thoughts were followed by a wave of self-loathing that hit her with such physical intensity that she thought she was going to be sick. She bent over, propping herself against the wall with one hand while the other clung on to the flowers. She waited, willing herself to retch, but nothing came up, and gradually the feelings of nausea receded, until she was able to straighten herself up and breathe in a gulp of air.

But, although the nausea had gone, the sense of futility she had felt earlier was flooding back. Looking round, she realized that she didn't actually know where the body had fallen and lain. She'd studied the photos in the paper, and she had tried to listen to what the police had to say, but now that she was here, none of that was much help. Somehow she had assumed that there would be marks of some sort on the pavement, maybe a dark circle of something that she could identify as blood. Didn't the police use chalk to mark the positions of dead bodies, or was that only on television? Or maybe you had to be the victim of murder, not just a suicide, to attain that level of importance? But the only markings on the pavement were bird droppings – pigeons she guessed – and what looked like spatterings of yellow paint. (How did they get there?)

It was at this point that Anne Johnson became aware that she was being watched. She looked up to see a young man staring at her. He must have just come out of the car park, for he was standing two steps from the bottom of the concrete stairs that led down from the first storey of the car park to the pavement, some five metres from where she was. To her astonishment, she recognized him.

Her first words were softly spoken, addressed more to herself than to anyone else. 'Jesus Christ! You're him!' The young man must have heard – or possibly lip-read – her words, for he remained still, frozen to his step. Only his eyes betrayed agitation.

'You're him!' she said again, this time more loudly, and with the index finger of her right hand pointing directly at

28

his head. 'You're the art student in the paper? The bastard who pushed her over the edge.'

If Bicknell was startled by the violence of her words, he was not showing it. He looked at her for three or four seconds, before thrusting his hands into the pockets of his zipped jacket in a studied act of defiance. He then stepped forward down the last two steps, spun round and started to walk away.

'Stop right there!' Anne Johnson was at school again, her voice lancing across the playground, bringing bullies and bullied reluctantly to heel. Bicknell came to a halt, and after some hesitation turned around. When he looked up, he saw her as many younger persons had over the years. She was not a tall woman, but as she stood there, one hand firmly on her hip, the other casually holding her bouquet like it was a lethal weapon, he felt a shiver of something not so far removed from fear. He felt compelled to move towards her.

'I'm him,' he said, when he was half a pace from her. 'That is to say, I'm the student in the paper. But I don't push people off multi-storey car parks. So, I'd be very careful what you go around saying, lady.'

'I was speaking figuratively,' she said, looking straight into his eyes.

'Whatever,' he responded, holding her gaze. Ever since he had printed off those photos he had taken of Sarah Johnson, as live and dead, Bicknell had got to know her features in some detail. Now, like DS Fox before him, he found himself taken aback by the face of her sister Anne – the same straight brown hair, oval face, and slightly upturned nose.

'God, you are like her.' The words came out automatically, an unconscious reaction to his thoughts.

'Only on the surface,' she responded instantly. 'Underneath we're chalk and cheese.'

He nodded uncertainly. 'Right' he said, but wondered why she had been so quick to emphasize their difference.

'Did you talk to her?' she rushed on. Then paused, uncertain how to phrase what she wanted to say. 'Before she

… before she ….' The words stuck to the back of her throat, unwilling to be uttered. She tried again. 'When she was looking at your plaque. Did she say anything? Did you get an impression of how she was.'

'No!' he said flatly. She said nothing in return, merely did something with her face which made him realize that more was expected. 'I was taking photos, from a distance. Talking would have … have interfered with the experiment.'

'The experiment!' She tossed the words back at him, because it was easier to be cruel than generous. Easier to inflict pain that endure it. 'Well, that would never do. To interfere with the experiment.'

She had spoken loudly, loudly enough, she realized, for passers-by to hear. An old woman with a shopping trolley had stopped and was watching with fascination – Anne scowled at her until she resumed her slow progress – then turned back to Bicknell. 'Look, I need to lay these bloody flowers right where she fell. You can at least help me with that.'

Bicknell was floundering in unfamiliar waters. Policemen who thought they were tough was one thing, but this woman …. He sighed silently. Easier to go with it, wait for the storm to abate. 'It was over there,' he said, pointing.

She turned, and moved three paces, and placed the flowers gently on the pavement. 'Here?' She turned her face towards him, her voice now calm, wanting reassurance. He nodded. She turned back to the flowers, and maintained the position for some thirty seconds. A bus pulled past and stopped a few metres away. A young woman lugging a baby in one arm and dragging a folded carrycot with her free hand got off. She expertly opened up the carrycot with a single flick of her hand, put the infant in it, strapped it in, then walked past, looking with mild curiosity at the woman and her flowers. Finally, Anne Johnson stood up and turned towards the immobile Bicknell. 'Come on,' she said, 'I'll buy you a drink.'

As Detective Constable Wilson turned the corner and brought the unmarked police car gently to a halt, Detective Sergeant

Fox, who was seated next to him, wondered – not for the first time – what genius it was that had come up with the name of the Evergreen Day Centre. Tucked away in a cul-de-sac off the Cowley Road, the two-storey building showed few signs of lasting for ever and no sign of anything green. The overall impression it gave was of unutterable greyness; only the metal windows protected against this uniformity, but the white paint applied to them was not of recent memory. At least someone had decided to rail against this dank vision from the 1930s: a brightly painted board leant against the wall to the right of the double doors, bidding all comers 'A warm welcome to the Evergreen Day Centre' in a mixture of reds, pinks and blues (but curiously not a single splash of green). A group of three men, who stood smoking to the left of the sign, turned as one to survey Fox and Wilson as they approached. 'Who the fuck are you?' The youngest of the trio spoke loudly, and Wilson flinched involuntarily. Fox, however, merely smiled: 'Good morning to you, gentlemen. Is Jim Blunt around today?'

It was the oldest man who replied. He was a strikingly thin man, and had grey, wispy hair, and a smile which revealed teeth long overdue a visit to the dentist. He sported a faded tweed jacket, white shirt, and brown corduroy trousers. 'Do you have an appointment?' he demanded in an aristocratic accent. 'Mr Blunt is a busy man.'

'And so am I,' replied Fox, walking past the trio and pushing open the twin doors which served as the entry pointy to the hidden world of the Evergreen Day Centre.

'Well, well, well! If it isn't our favourite copper, Detective Fox.' The greeting from the squat man who stood in the middle of the room was every bit as mocking as had been that of Mr Tweed Jacket outside, but there the similarity ended. His hair was closely cropped, he wore a black polo style shirt, and black jeans, and his voice was pure Brummie. Where Mr Tweed Jacket was tall and thin, Jim Blunt was short and broad. The only common physical feature, Fox idly thought, was a total lack of loose fat anywhere on either man: Blunt was solid muscle, and Mr Tweed Jacket was solid skin and bone.

'We need a few minutes of your time please, Jim,' said Fox conversationally. 'This, by the way, is my colleague DC Wilson.'

Blunt flicked a glance at the uneasy young man standing at Fox's shoulder, but otherwise ignored him. 'Follow me,' he ordered, and led them through a door in the left-hand corner of the room. A short corridor took them to a small room containing two armchairs. He waved Fox to the dirty mauve one, and himself sat heavily down into the dirty red one. 'Shut the door, lad' he said, pointedly not looking at Wilson. Wilson did so, and took out a notebook.

'So,' said Blunt, 'I guess you've come about Sarah.'

Fox nodded, but said nothing.

'Can't say I'm surprised,' Blunt said suddenly. 'But then, in this business nothing comes as a surprise. Mind you,' he continued without any apparent logical connection, 'she'll be missed.'

'By whom?' said Fox quickly. 'Jake?'

Blunt frowned and pulled at a non-existent moustache. 'Why do you mention Jake?' he asked, looking straight at Fox.

'She tried to ring him the morning she died.'

Blunt pulled again at his invisible moustache, then nodded, apparently satisfied, and stood up. 'I'll send him through. But don't keep him too long. He's cooking lunch today.'

Fox held up his right hand. 'Just one more question for you. Would you say Sarah had been particularly low recently? I mean, we know she suffered from manic depression—'

'Your bloody label, not mine!' Blunt cut in angrily, and the colour of his face turned a fierce red. 'You're just like the doctors. Manic depression, bipolar disorder. Why is it that you want to stick fancy sounding labels on people with mental health problems. They're just people, with problems, right. People who need bloody help. Help they don't get

32

from their fucking families, help they don't get from their fucking fair-weather friends. That's where we come in. But we're just people too. We're not bloody miracle makers.'

With that, Blunt wrenched the door open, and marched out.

A minute later, a young man appeared at the still-open door, and announced himself as Jake Arnold. He wore a plain, mid-blue shirt, rust-coloured whipcord trousers, and a pair of blue leather lace-ups of slightly darker hue than the shirt. A twisted leather band was just visible on his left wrist, and an unconvincing smile crossed his face.

'We won't take much of your time,' Fox promised, once Jake was settled in the red armchair. 'We are just trying to establish the state of Sarah's mind in the period of time leading up to her death. For the coroner's report. We understand that you knew her quite well?'

'She used to come here a lot. So we saw each other then.'

'And outside the day centre? Did you meet up with her in your private time?'

Jake Arnold chewed on his bottom lip as he considered this question? 'Workers have to maintain a sensible distance between themselves and the members of the day centre.'

'Quite,' said Fox, nodding and smiling in what he hoped was an encouraging manner. 'But I imagine individuals tend to develop stronger relationships with one worker than another.'

Jake chewed again on his lip. 'Yes,' he admitted finally, 'I suppose Sarah did tend to turn to me rather than any of the others.'

'So you were friends really?'

'Yes,' he said with apparent reluctance. 'I guess we were friends. We used to go to the football together sometimes. She was a United fan.'

'So, do you have any idea why she might have killed herself?'

'Not really, no,' he said.

There was a silence while Fox waited for Jake Arnold to expand on this uninformative response. Wilson, who had yet to write anything in his notebook, noticed with interest that just before Jake spoke, his right hand pulled briefly at the lobe of his ear.

When Fox did finally break the silence, his voice had a much harder edge to it. 'You're not really being very straightforward with us are you, sir?'

'Sorry,' said Arnold nervously, 'I'm not sure what you mean.'

'Oh, dear,' Fox said with theatrical weariness. 'Have I got to spell it all out? On the morning of her death, Sarah made three phone calls. All those three calls were made to your mobile number.' He stopped talking, and waited.

'My mobile was turned off. I never spoke to her.'

'I see,' Fox said, taking a deep breath and wondering how hard it was worth pushing. 'In my book, that makes you rather unusual. Most people seem to keep their mobiles turned on all the time – on the buses, in restaurants, while they are waiting for their nails to dry. My sister even takes hers to the loo,' he lied.

Jake looked up then, and a flash of anger rippled across his feminine features. 'Are you saying you don't believe me? Are you calling me a liar?'

'No, sir' Fox said calmly.

'I kept it turned off because I was fed up with being rung up by Les Whiting. Les was my boyfriend, right. Was being the operative word. Only he kept ringing me up, hassling me, so I've been keeping my mobile turned off the last week or so. That's why Sarah couldn't get hold of me.'

He paused, slightly breathless, giving Fox the opportunity to lean forward confidentially. 'Still,' Fox said quietly, 'I expect she left a voice message?'

Jake Arnold chewed on his lip again. 'Yes,' he said, uncertainly. 'She just said she was trying to get hold of me.'

'But you didn't bother.'

'Look, I didn't pick up the messages until that evening, and of course I had heard about her death by then.'

When Fox spoke again, his voice was even quieter. 'Jake,' he said, 'The third phone call was over two minutes long. She must have said rather more than "Give me a call".'

Wilson, standing to the side, couldn't help but notice for a second time that Arnold's hand plucked again at his right-hand earlobe. 'She sounded a bit stressed,' Arnold admitted.

'Just a bit?' Fox replied instantly.

Arnold, who had been hunched forward, now leaned back. 'Very stressed. Very stressed indeed.'

'Did she give any clues about what might be causing her to feel stressed?'

'Jesus!' he said. 'What does it fucking matter? She was bloody abusive because I hadn't rung her back. Maybe, if my mobile had been turned on, maybe things would have been different. Maybe she wouldn't be dead. But it wasn't. And she is. But at least she's got some peace now.'

Anne Johnson and Ed Bicknell sat opposite each other in a poorly lit corner of the Moonshine pub and, for the first time since they had sat down, both fell silent. The overall impression given by the pub, Anne had thought moments earlier as she stood at the bar while waiting for a second round of drinks to be poured (Ed, rather to her surprise, had insisted on buying the first round), was one of drabness and 'couldn't-care-less-ness', a word she liked to employ at school sometimes when work and attitude fell short of her expectations. The heavy red drapes and upholstery, which in their prime might reasonably have claimed to be sumptuous, were now worn and dirty. Looking down at the stretch of seating just to her right, Anne had identified no less than seven large stains. Had the lights been more penetrative, she had little doubt that many smaller marks would have become apparent. The heavy pattern of the carpet helped to disguise some of the stains on it, but almost bare patches, where the pile had been worn down to the backing, could not be hidden. As she walked over to the table, she noted five cobwebs decorating the three windows which were in her view. She noted too Ed Bicknell, his eyes trained on her.

'Here you are,' she said placing a pint of Guinness in front of him, and sitting down in the seat she had vacated a few minutes earlier.

She took a long, slow sip from the top of her lager, placed it on the beer mat on her side of the table, and leant back. Bicknell's eyes followed her over the white foam of his glass, but he said nothing. She watched his throat pulse as he slowly lifted the glass towards the horizontal. She watched his head as it ever so gradually tipped backwards. Finally, when there was only white froth on the sides of the glass, he set it carefully down on the table and grinned. Anne looked away. Over to the right, a short woman with loose-fitting blue tracksuit trousers and pale, tight-fitting T-shirt – its colour was hard to determine in the warped light of the Moonshine – pulled unenthusiastically at a one-armed-bandit with her right hand, while her left hand held a half-smoked cigarette. A jangling noise signified a small win, but the woman showed no excitement beyond taking a pull at her cigarette. Anne, whose eyes had been focused on the large fold of stomach that separated the woman's trousers from her T-shirt, snorted audibly, and turned her attention back to Bicknell. His mouth, which had relaxed back into an emotionless slit, curved almost mechanically back into a smile. Suddenly, Anne felt irritated.

'Do you have to stare?' She leant forward aggressively, with the consequence that he flinched backwards so sharply that he almost fell off the little stool he was crouched on.

'Sorry,' he mumbled, once he had recovered. 'I didn't realize—' He tailed off.

'I find that hard to believe,' she said firmly. 'Very hard.'

There was a silence. Another jangle of coins from the direction of the one-armed-bandit announced another small win for the woman with the midriff bulge.

'Just to satisfy your curiosity,' Anne continued in slightly gentler vein, 'I'm a 36D.'

Bicknell blushed and looked down. Anne leant back as far as her chair would allow. She consciously sat up as high as she could and pushed her shoulders back and down as she remembered being ordered to do as a school girl by a martinet teacher called Miss Knight. As a child, it had seemed a bore, but once she had reached sexual maturity and discovered that sitting very erect had the effect of accentuating her breasts, it had become altogether more interesting. A gentle smile flickered across her face, and she waited for him to look up.

CHAPTER 4

It was about 10.45 on Thursday evening when Peter Mellor slipped out of Mill View Cottage in the village of Iffley, jogged gingerly down the hill with Gemma, his boxer dog, at his heel, and walked over the weir bridge. The two of them followed the narrow path as it swung sharply to the right, burrowing its way between the dark trees until it brought them to the big double lock gates. For two or three minutes, the man stood in the middle of those gates, looking down river into the blackness, where the Thames disappeared towards Sandford, and remembering a woman he had once known. Then, with a sigh, he turned round, called his dog, and started to retrace his steps along the path to the weir bridge. There he stopped, aware that Gemma was no longer with him. He whistled, then called her sharply by name. Gemma barked, once, then again and again. But she was not, as the man had thought, trailing behind him. She had, in fact, already crossed back over the weir bridge, and was perched on the edge of the bank, barking down into the shadows where the cold water spat and hissed.

'What's up, girl?' the man asked, but the dog merely barked again. The man walked to where she was and looked down to see if he could see what she could see, but the darkness was intense and unforgiving. Only as his eyes grew accustomed to the lack of light did the shape that was attracting the attention of his dog became apparent: a circular object that bobbed around on the surface of the water. 'It's only a ball!' the man said to his dog, trying to reassure himself as much as the distressed old bitch. 'Let's just leave it.' But then suddenly whatever it was that had been anchoring the object in the swirling current released its restraining grip. With a violent jerk, a man's body leapt up vertically out of the water causing Peter Mellor to shriek and his dog to yelp. For several moments it appeared to stand miraculously there on the water, before – almost in slow motion – it began to pirouette round like some grotesque ballet dancer. Finally it teetered, first backwards, then more savagely forward as it crashed face down into the darkness below. As one, the watching man and the watching dog turned and fled back up the hill towards Mill View Cottage.

At 8.45 the following morning, Detective Constable Wilson tapped on Detective Inspector Holden's half-open door.

'Morning Guv,' he said tentatively.

'What time of day do you call this?' Holden asked waspishly, without looking up.

'Sorry, Guv. I overslept.'

'And where the hell is Fox?'

'He had a dentist appointment first thing,' he said defensively. 'Broke a tooth yesterday,' Wilson elaborated. 'He was in a lot of pain.'

'Well, that's a bloody fine bit of timing,' Holden responded without sympathy.

'Yes, Guv,' said the hapless Wilson, still standing there half in the room and half out, and wondering what the hell had happened to make the DI so sharp.

Finally, she looked up and locked eyes with him. 'We have another dead body, Wilson,' she said. 'Fished out of the river at Iffley lock last night.'

Wilson's thoughts at that moment should have been straightforward, curious, and focused directly on this news.

And to give him credit he asked the obvious question: 'Do we know who it is?' But it was the first time he had been on his own with Holden, and the scrutiny he suddenly found himself under from her caused his thoughts to be anything but straightforward. He hoped it didn't show.

'Oh, yes,' Holden said with a thin smile. 'We do indeed. The gentleman concerned had a wallet stuffed full of ID information. Debit card, credit card, library card, Blockbuster card. You name it, he had it. Very helpful was our Jake Arnold.'

'Jake Arnold?' Wilson's whole face seemed to gape in surprise. 'Shit!'

Holden smiled, pleased at the affect her piece of news had had on the young man. 'As you so delicately put it, Constable,' said Holden. 'Shit!'

*

Ted Smith was a big man, with thinning grey hair and sideburns that might once possibly have looked trendy in the valleys of Wales, but not within recent memory. He had a stomach which betrayed a fondness for too much of his own beer, and a rather melodious, deep voice which took Holden quite by surprise. 'I've been expecting you lot,' he said, as he showed them into the Iffley Inn.

'We just need to ask you a few questions,' Holden said. 'Purely routine.'

'Of course,' he said eagerly. 'Fire away.'

'I understand the dead man had been in the pub. Perhaps you can tell us what you can remember about his visit.'

'Well, let's see. He came in about nine-ish. It was very quiet, don't you see, what with it being this time of year and a Thursday. So I was quite glad to see a new face. Hoped he might become a regular.'

'So you hadn't seen him before?'

'No, I don't think so. We've only been here three months, you know. Anyway, I pulled him a pint, and we exchanged a bit of football chat. His hat and scarf were in the Oxford United colours, so we talked about how rubbish they've been playing recently. Then Mick – he's one of my regulars – wanted another pint, so I had to deal with him and this boyo went and read the paper over there in the corner. Ten or fifteen minutes later he bought another pint, then he started chatting to this Yank tourist who had had a meal, and next thing was he was showing him how to play bar billiards. They must have had a couple of games, then the Yank said he had to be going, but he bought him a pint. So he sat drinking it over with the papers again. Then – I guess it must have been about ten o'clock – he brought his glass up to the bar, and I thought he wanted another pint, but he just wrapped his scarf round his neck, pulled his hat down tight on his head, and walked off without so much as a "Goodnight".'

'Did he eat while he was here?' Holden asked.

'No, only a bag of pork scratchings. I remember because he wanted a second packet, but we'd run out.'

'Did he appear to be OK? I mean, some people hold their drink better than others.'

Ted Smith rubbed his unshaven cheeks while he pondered this question. 'He seemed all right,' he said finally. 'I mean, he managed to play bar billiards without any problems. I keep an eye open for people who look like they might damage the baize, but he was fine. It was the Yank I was more concerned about. He looked as though he had never picked up a cue in his life.'

'So what happened after he left?'

'Well, we closed at the normal time. There was only Mick and a group of students left – it was bloody quiet really – and after a bit of tidying up, I went outside for a bit of fresh air and a fag, and that was when I saw all the lights up near the lock. So I walked up there and saw them pulling this body out of the water by the weir, and I noticed he was wearing a striped scarf. His hat was missing, but I was pretty damn sure he was the bloke in the pub, so I told one of the coppers there.'

'How come you were so sure?' Holden asked. 'Lots of people must wear Oxford United scarves round here.'

Smith snorted. 'Have you seen the scarf, Inspector?'

'No,' Holden admitted. 'We'll be doing that later.'

'Well,' he said with a sneer, 'when you do, you will notice that the scarf is not an official Oxford scarf. It is very obviously a hand-knitted job – blue and yellow stripes. He told me his mother made it.' He paused and gave a large leering smile. 'I reckon he was a right Mummy's boy, if you know what I mean. Still attached to the apron strings. Flapped his hands around like a seal on amphetamines.'

'Can we just stick to facts,' Holden said sharply, trying to regain control of an interview that had started to go into a spin, 'and relevant facts at that.'

'In my view it's a fact. He was a pansy, a poofter, a homo, call it what you will. And how do you know it isn't relevant? Maybe he looked in the mirror when he went to the loo. Maybe, he decided he couldn't stand what he could see in it. Maybe the beer had loosened his inhibitions, so he went out and jumped in the river.'

'Thank you, Mr Smith,' Holden said with exaggerated politeness. 'We will keep your theory in mind. In the meantime, I have just got one more thing to ask, then we'll be off. Did you hear or see anything after he left the pub? Any shouting from outside or anything?'

'No,' he said.

'You're sure? After all, it was pretty quiet in the pub. Maybe you—'

Ted Smith cut into Holden's probing with barely disguised irritation. 'Look you here,' he said in a Welsh accent that had suddenly lost its musical charm. 'I said no, didn't I. It's a simple word, and it has a simple meaning. So I'll say it once more. No! All right?'

When she was a seven-year-old, Dr Karen Pointer had wanted to be a magician. Now she was approaching her thirty-seventh birthday, something of that spirit lingered on. As the three of them stood around the shrouded corpse, she leant over, took one corner of the sheet with her right hand, and paused dramatically. For two or three seconds she waited, and only then, as if she was producing a rabbit from a hat, did she flick the sheet through the air with a flash of her wrist to reveal the naked body of Jake Arnold. Wilson, predictably, gave an involuntary gasp, while Holden, equally predictably, refused to react at all to the showmanship.

'I haven't, of course, had time to complete a full examination and to carry out all the tests I would want to—' Pointer began.

'Quite,' said Holden. 'We understand that fully.' She spoke with a brusqueness born of anticipation and impatience. Dr Pointer had rung her on her mobile just after Wilson and she had left the Iffley Inn, and had suggested that since there were some 'unexpected findings' in her examination of the corpse, Holden might want to pop along and have a chat. But now they had 'popped along', the good doctor was in no rush to reveal her news.

'So everything I say,' Dr Pointer continued carefully, 'is said only on the understanding that these findings are provisional and therefore are subject to revision—'

'Would you rather we came back another day?' Holden asked with ill-disguised irritation.

Dr Pointer smiled. 'No need,' she said. 'I think I can say with ninety-nine per cent certainty that Mr Jake Arnold was dead by the time he entered the river.'

'How did he die?' Holden asked, doing her best to sound unimpressed.

'From a blow to the back of the head,' Dr Pointer said before falling silent again. After the magician's opening, she was now going to make the Detective Inspector ask for every bit of information.

Holden had no option but to play along with her game. 'Any idea what sort of weapon the killer used?'

'Of course I've an idea,' Dr Pointer huffed. 'There's a long depressed fracture which suggests a long, thin but heavy implement – maybe some sort of metal bar.' Again she fell silent.

'Um!' said Wilson trying to get the attention of the two women. Holden looked at him with irritation writ large across her face. Pointer, noticing, smiled her widest smile at the young man and immediately promoted him.

'Yes, Sergeant?' she asked expectantly.

'I was wondering,' Wilson said awkwardly, 'if perhaps it might have been maybe like a metal spike that people use for mooring their boats. That's what we used when I was a kid and we went on a canal boat holiday.'

'You used them for knocking people on the back of the head did you?' Pointer said, her smile cracking into gentle laughter. 'Oh, dear!'

'The constable's suggestion seems eminently sensible to me,' Holden retorted. Like some protective mother hen, she flew to the defence of her young charge. 'Or perhaps,' she added caustically, 'you can come up with a better idea?'

Dr Pointer's smile retreated before this onslaught. 'It's as likely as anything,' she admitted.

'Can you be absolutely sure he was dead when he entered the river?' Wilson asked, emboldened by his governor's support.

Dr Pointer looked across at him, but this time without a glimmer of humour. 'Yes, I can be and indeed am absolutely sure, Constable,' she said firmly, demoting Wilson back to the ranks. 'I wouldn't say so otherwise. If he had entered the water alive, there would be water in his lungs. As you can see,' she said, with a gesture towards the long slit down the centre of the corpse, 'we have taken a good look inside, and in my expert opinion there is no doubt, even though we haven't yet had time to complete a diatom test. Which we'll make a start with now if you haven't any more questions.'

Holden gave a slight but unmistakable bow of the head towards Pointer. 'Thank you, Doctor. No more questions.'

*

As Wilson brought the unmarked car gently to a halt in exactly the same spot as he had some fifty-one hours earlier, he was surprised to see that there was no one outside the Evergreen Day Centre. 'Where's the smoking brotherhood?' he quipped as the three of them got out. 'Have they got some new bike sheds to hide behind?'

Both Holden and Fox had been silent throughout the short journey from the station. After they had met up with Fox at the station, Holden had given him a quick, but thorough briefing on developments, before they had set off on the short trip to the day centre. Neither Fox, still feeling somewhat morose after his dental treatment, nor Holden was inclined to talk. Holden sat in the back, trying to concentrate on the task before them, but she found her thoughts being drawn by some invisible and undeniable force back to her mother. Her beloved, bloody-minded, point-scoring, I-know-better-than-everyone mother.

'Why can't you take some time off to help me get organized?' she had demanded on the phone the night before.

'I've already taken four separate days off in the last two months,' Holden had snapped tetchily.

'Oh' came the wounded response, 'you're keeping a tally are you.'

'No!' she had retorted, although she was. 'It's just that I do want to take some proper holiday sometime. And besides,' she had added, playing her trump card, 'I've got a death to investigate.'

'A murder?' said her mother with sudden curiosity. 'How exciting!'

'Actually, a probable suicide,' she had had to admit.

'A suicide?' The disappointment was evident even down a not very good line. 'And suicide is more important than a mother's needs?'

It was at this point in the Detective Inspector's replay of her conversation with her mother that Detective Constable Wilson had brought the car to a halt and made his joke about smoking and bike sheds.

Holden lurched back into the present, unamused. 'Wilson,' she said sharply, 'this is not the place for jokes. Your task is to listen, take your lead from us, and, if in doubt, to keep your mouth closed. This is a murder investigation, not a day out to Blackpool.' With that, she nimbly exited the car and started off towards the Evergreen Day Centre, as if trying to shake off the pursing fury of her mother.

No one greeted them at the door, and only when she had pushed through the outer pair, and then the inner pair did she realize why. Based on past experience (well, only two visits in four years if the truth be told), she expected to encounter a roomful of people arrayed around a series of functional tables on a varied selection of plastic upright chairs and seen-better-days armchairs and sofas. The last time she had had to call in, there had been a group making non-religious Easter cards in one corner, a couple of men, encircled by an intense group of spectators, involved in a silent chess duel in another corner, while a third group argued noisily over a Scrabble board. This time, however, everyone present was seated in a haphazard circle, which Jim Blunt was addressing. He noticed Holden immediately, and held up a hand – whether in greeting or as a warning she wasn't quite sure.

'Well,' he said, looking round the members, 'I think this is a good time to stop. The police have arrived. No doubt they'll have more news of poor Jake. Obviously, I'll keep you all informed, but for now try to carry on as normal. I know that's going to be difficult, but as long as we support each other, we'll all be OK.'

Blunt led his three visitors into the same cramped room that Fox and Wilson had entered two days earlier.

'So,' he said, after he had shut the door and sat down, 'can you tell me any more about it. We've got a lot of very concerned members out there. Jake was popular.' He paused, but only to catch his breath, and before Holden could respond he had started off again. 'It must have been an accident, right? I mean you can tell if he'd been drinking too

46

much. It's just that someone asked if he'd committed suicide. And after what Sarah did, well, I wanted to be able to assure everyone that it was just an unfortunate case of too much drink.' Blunt dribbled to a halt, looking from Holden to Fox to Wilson and back to Holden, searching for reassurance.

Holden, who was sitting bolt upright, leant forward, her face wiped clean of emotion. 'I'm sorry to have to tell you that in the light of what the pathologist has told us, we are treating the death of Jake Arnold as neither an accident nor suicide. Jake was murdered. Last night, after leaving the Iffley Inn. I don't want to say any more about how it happened at this stage, but we have, of course, got to conduct interviews, here, today, which will obviously be disruptive for your day centre.'

'Shit!' Blunt spat the word out like a piece of sour fruit. 'Damn and hell!'

'Perhaps we can start with you. Then you'll be free to break the news as best you can. After that, I think we should interview all your other colleagues. While Wilson and I are doing that, Detective Sergeant Fox and you can draw up a list of members, and try and prioritize those who had a relationship, good or bad, with Jake. And of course with Sarah Johnson.'

Blunt, whose eyes appeared to have half shut, raised his head with a jerk. 'Sarah?' he exclaimed. 'You think Jake's and Sarah's deaths are connected? She committed suicide, right? So what possible connection—'

'I think nothing at this stage,' Holden said firmly. 'I keep an open mind, and try to consider all possibilities. And one of those possibilities is that the deaths of Sarah and Jake, who seem to have had at least a friendship, are in some way connected.'

Blunt's mouth was open. Twice he tried to say something, and twice he failed. Holden noticed the side of his neck pulsing like a steam piston, and she wondered if he was going to lose it. She couldn't see him crying – he didn't seem the type – but sometimes those who held themselves together most tightly could behave in unexpected ways. A third time Blunt moved his mouth, and this time words came out. 'Are you saying Sarah's death wasn't suicide. That she was murdered too.'

Holden leant back now, and gave a deep exhalation of breath. 'Sarah's death was most probably suicide. We can't be certain. But as far as your members are concerned, there is no need to alarm them by suggesting it wasn't.'

'Right,' he said, and gave a single nod.

'In a minute, I'd like you to go and break the news about Jake to them, but first I have to ask you a couple of questions.'

Blunt drew his hand across the top of his head. Wilson wondered if this was a nervous reaction. Holden waited deliberately for a few seconds before continuing.

'How did you get on with Jake?' she asked with studied casualness.

'Well enough,' Blunt said, but he made no elaboration of his answer. Holden looked at him carefully. She frowned. She too was in no rush.

'Well enough ... for what, I wonder?' She spoke softly, dreamily almost, looking up at the ceiling as she did so.

Blunt waited for her eyes to focus back on him before reacting. And when it came, it was a measured and assertive reaction. 'Just well enough. Nothing more, nothing less. I was his boss. I had to tell him off occasionally, and challenge him too. He was a bit idle, if you want my honest opinion, and sometimes he needed a metaphorical kick up the arse. Generally, he took it well. But we weren't pals or anything. It's not a good idea from my point of view to get too pally with colleagues.' He stopped talking, and again his hand passed unconsciously across his head.

Holden held his gaze, and for several seconds said nothing. Only when he adjusted himself in his chair, and his hand for a third time flew low across his almost hairless head did she ask the obvious final question. 'Where were you last night? Between eight and eleven o'clock?'

'In my flat. Watching a DVD, until I fell asleep in the armchair.'

'Can anyone vouch for that?' Holden asked evenly.

'No,' said Blunt firmly.

Holden smiled. 'You appreciate that we have to ask'

Blunt smiled back. 'O yeah, detective, I've seen it on the TV!'

Holden waited until he was almost out of the room. 'One last final question, Mr Blunt, if you don't mind.'

He stopped and turned. The smile was still plastered across his face. 'That's what they all say, isn't it? Who do you model yourself on? Frost, Morse, or maybe you're more of a Columbo. Just missing the crumpled raincoat.'

'What was the DVD?'

'Why? Are you into films?'

'For the record, Mr Blunt.'

'Coen brothers. *The Man Who Wasn't There*? They got the wrong man. You'd like it.'

The two workers whom Holden interviewed (with Wilson silently taking notes) turned out to be very different from each other. Her first thought when Tim Wright walked into the room and folded himself into the chair which Blunt had previously occupied was purely sartorial. 'Nice shirt!' popped instantly into her mind, but fortunately not out of her mouth. But she couldn't make the thought disappear. The fact was that it was a nice shirt. Never mind that it didn't look as if it had ever come even close to contact with an iron. Or that the blue and white stripes would have looked more at home under a dark suit than above a pair of mid-blue jeans. Holden felt immediately irritated with herself, but Wright had already started to speak.

'Such a shame about poor Jake,' he was saying, in a soft public school voice which matched all of Holden's expectations. 'Not exactly my sort of chap, but—'

Holden cut in, the striped shirt already firmly relegated to a metaphorical bottom drawer. 'What exactly do you mean by that?' She spoke sharply, and Wright's eyes blinked in sudden alarm.

'Well, you know,' he said, trying to buy time. Holden found her eyes becoming fixated on his Adam's apple, which contorted itself like some alien intruder trying to burst its way out of his neck. 'Like different backgrounds, different expectations, different styles of dressing, different in so many ways.' This time Holden let him peter out.

'He was gay, yes?' she said finally, but in a tone of voice that suggested she was making a statement more than asking a question

'I believe so,' Wright replied warily.

'I suppose that would have put him at risk from some people?' Holden continued.

'We are very hot on homophobia here,' Wright replied, this time in a more confident tone, though Holden couldn't help noticing that he was unconsciously twiddling the wedding ring on the third finger of his left hand. Or was it unconsciously? 'Very hot on discrimination of all kinds. Anyway, as a motive for murder, I do wonder if you're barking up the—'

'Motive!' Holden spoke sharply, angrily, jumping in before he could finish his wondering. 'Ever hear of queer-bashing?' she demanded. 'Ever seen the body of a man kicked to death because he was gay?'

Wright's ring-twiddling went into overdrive. He looked down and made no reply. Only when he looked up again did Holden continue. 'I have. He didn't have a face left when we found him. My colleague found his eyeball – his left one I think it was – several yards away in the gutter. Imagine how hard you have to kick a man to do that. And when they'd finished kicking him, one of them took out a knife and … well, I expect you can imagine the rest.'

Wright had gone pale, a rather sickly non-colour, and Wilson, who had stopped writing, was fast revising his assessment of his boss. Holden meanwhile leant back in her chair and watched. Wright, whose breathing was now heavy and noisy, pulled a puffer from his pocket and took two deep sucks on it.

'Do you want a glass of water?' Holden asked without sympathy.

Wright looked across at her and shook his head. 'I'll be fine.' Slowly his breathing calmed down, and a semblance of colour returned to his features. 'Do you mean that Jake had been—'

'No,' said Holden quietly. 'No mutilation. Just a cracked skull. You may have rules here. But I was trying to point out that not everyone plays by the rules. Killers certainly don't. Which is why we need your help. Are you aware of anyone here who didn't like Jake? For any reason.'

Wright ran his hands down the front of his shirt, as if he was suddenly aware of its creases. 'Look,' he said, 'I can't say everyone liked him all the time. It's the nature of the work that you have to draw boundaries, and if people try to cross the boundaries you have to stand up to them, And then, of course, for a while at least, they don't like you. Jake was quite a gentle man, tried to get on with people, but he didn't shirk his responsibilities. When he had to be, he could be very unpleasant. I always felt safe when he was around.'

'Any recent incidents that you can think of? Anyone that he might have upset recently?'

'I've just had two weeks on holiday. So, the answer is no.'

'OK,' Holden said with a shrug, as if deciding that there was nothing more to be gained. 'But if anything occurs to you, when you've had time to reflect, do let me know.'

'Right,' he said, and then stood up. But he didn't turn towards the door. A frown emerged from behind his eyes. 'Perhaps, I should mention one thing. He split up with his boyfriend a few days before I went on holiday. It was fairly acrimonious, I think. Not that I know much about it.'

'Do you know the boyfriend's name?' Holden was leaning forward now, her affected indifference now discarded.

'Les. Les Whiting, I think. Like the fish.'

'Boss,' said Wilson, as soon as Wright had left the room. 'That ties up with what Jake said.'

'Explain,' Holden said tersely.

'When DS Fox was interviewing him, he asked him about the phone calls that Sarah Johnson had made to his mobile, and he asked how come he kept it turned off so much, and he said – that's Jake said – that he kept it turned off because he had split from his boyfriend and he, Les, kept hassling him. So it all ties up.'

'Thank you, Wilson,' Holden said, and she turned a smile upon her slightly flushed detective constable. 'A brownie point for you!'

'Jake was in the wrong job.' Rachel Laing uttered this judgement as soon as she had sat down. 'Nice guy, but he'd never have lasted.'

If Holden was surprised by this blunt opening statement, she gave no sign. She was experienced enough to know that death, especially unexpected and violent death, affected people different ways. The morning after her own father had been obliterated in a three-car pile-up on the A34, her mother had gone to work as if nothing abnormal had happened, said nothing to anyone in the office, and only rang her, Susan, to tell her after she'd come home, watched the six o'clock news, and helped herself to a small sherry. Rachel Laing was big boned and broad hipped, wore clothes so nondescript you barely noticed them, and oozed matter-of-factness from the pores of her skin. 'It's not a happy-clappy world. The people who come here have pretty shitty lives and problems. Some cope, some don't. Some survive, some end up dead. Like poor Sarah Johnson. You have to be tough if you're going to last in this environment, and like I said, Jake just wasn't cut out for it. Nice guy and all that, but—'

'A nice dead guy, Ms Laing,' Holden interrupted, distaste apparent in every syllable she uttered. 'Just to clarify things, we aren't here to assess how well Jake Arnold was suited to working in the wonderful world of mental health. We're here to find out who the hell killed him. So maybe we could stick to that.'

'So what do you want to know?' Laing spoke without emotion, as if unaffected by Holden's outburst, though the ghost of a smile drifted across her face. 'If I know who the killer is?'

Laing never received an answer. Even as she was saying 'who the killer is?', there came a sound of shouting from beyond the closed door, followed immediately by a thud and the splintering of wood as the door exploded open. Two figures burst into the room, the first a very flushed Danny and just behind him an equally red-faced DS Fox, his hands already turning palms-up in apology.

'Danny!' exclaimed Laing, who had risen to her feet. 'Whatever's the matter?' Wilson, dropping his notebook, stepped forward, but Holden – startled, but still seated – lifted a hand and raised her voice. 'Stop! Everyone!'

Rather to her surprise, everyone did stop, and before they could start again she addressed Danny.

'Danny. I think we may have met once before, but in case you don't remember, my name is Susan. I am in charge of the police investigation into Jake Arnold's death. Do you think you might be able to help?'

Danny looked back at the woman sitting unruffled in the battered red armchair. She was wearing dark trousers and jacket, and a plain white blouse. Her hair was dark and short, short enough to reveal a small silver stud in each ear. She looked efficient, organised, in control, yet the tone of her voice was soft and gentle, reminiscent of cooling breezes on a hot summer's day.

'Why don't you sit down?' She was gesturing towards the mauve armchair that Rachel Laing was now standing next to. 'Rachel was just about to go, and if you'd rather, my colleagues could go too.'

Danny looked round the small room, at Laing, and Fox and Wilson. He walked two paces over to the window, and looked out of it, then across to the door, where Fox moved to the side. He looked down the short corridor for three or four seconds, before shutting the door firmly. 'They can stay,' he said, and moved back to the mauve armchair. He sat down with care, perching himself on the front. As if ready for what, Holden wondered. Flight or fight?

'It was my fault.' Danny spoke quietly, almost as if talking to himself. 'My fault, all my fault.' Holden, leaning forward, watched him as she may once as a child have watched a trapeze artiste walk the high wire in the big top. Her breathing seemed to have been put into abeyance as she waited to see if Danny would maintain his balance. He was rocking now, only just perceptibly, but rocking nevertheless.

'Why do you think it was your fault?' Holdens's words were as hushed as his. She hoped they sounded soothing and encouraging.

'Cause it was,' he said, still rocking.

'Danny!' she said, her tone slightly raised. 'You've got to tell me more than that. You've got to explain why.'

'Why?' he said, his voice rising to match hers. 'Because if I hadn't smashed his car in, then it wouldn't all have started.'

'It was you who smashed Jake's car in?' Rachel Laing broke in, astonishment apparent in every syllable of her question.

Holden looked up sharply. She said nothing, but the glare she gave and the aggressive manner in which she drew her two fingers from left to right across her lips, were a clear enough message to Laing to shut up. Holden turned back to Danny, but he seemed not to have registered Laing's interruption.

'Do you mean you crashed his car?' she asked.

'No!' he exclaimed. 'I don't drive. I saw it parked outside Sarah's flat late one night. It's an old green Mini. Occasionally he'd bring it here. Anyway, I just smashed it. I broke the windscreen and the driver's window, and the headlights, and then I did a runner. I shouldn't have done it, cause that's when it all started.' He was breathing heavily now, and Holden noticed a couple of beads of sweat on his now flushed face.

'All what started?' Holden purred.

'Well, that's when Jake started to be followed.'

Though the casual observer – and certainly not Danny – would not have noticed any change in the smile on Holden's face, behind it the raised hopes were suddenly extinguished.

She wondered how she could have been so stupid to expect anything else. With Danny, there was always someone following, so of course there was bound to have been someone following Jake, as there had been someone following Sarah, as no doubt Danny had been followed all the way from his room to the day centre that morning. Not to mention yesterday. Or the day before.

'How do you know he was being followed?' she asked, but her questions were now on autopilot. Only, unlike an airliner, they were going nowhere.

He frowned, as if puzzled by the question, then after a few seconds smiled. 'It was obvious,' he stated. 'Obvious!'

'It's not obvious to me,' said Holden, her autopilot betraying signs of irritation.

'You didn't know him,' he said calmly. He was still smiling, not at Holden though, but at his hands. He held his left palm open, and with his right he traced a pattern on it – a figure-of-eight, Holden reckoned – first one way, and then the other. 'I did. And from that day, he was different.'

'How do you mean, different?' Holden asked.

Danny looked up from his hands, but he was still smiling, almost beatifically. Holden was reminded of a picture of a saint that had adorned a notebook once given to her by her Aunt Ida. 'Different like two identical apples,' he explained, and his hands traced smooth patterns through the air as if he was a priest standing before the altar. 'One apple is green and shiny, and when you bite into it, it tastes like the best apple you have ever tasted, like the one your dad picked off the tree that day he took you to the fair and you sat on his lap down the helter skelter. And the other apple is green and shiny too, but when you bite into it, the flesh is soft and brown, and in the middle is a long black worm that has gorged itself so full that as soon as your teeth reach it, it explodes like a landmine of bitterness inside you. That was what Jake was like after I'd smashed his car.'

Holden leant back. She had turned the autopilot off, but the feeling that she was wasting her time was growing by the second. She looked back at Danny's grinning face, and then up at the looming figure of Fox. Her eyes sent out a SOS, and he dutifully responded.

'Can you give us a description of this man that was following Jake?' he asked.

'A description?' Danny replied with puzzlement in his voice.

'Yes Danny,' Fox said firmly. 'How tall was he? What colour hair did he have? Or was he bald? What was he wearing?'

Fox paused, but Danny made no reply. His right hand was tracing patterns on his left hand again, but the movements were faster than earlier, and jerkier. 'You did see him, didn't you Danny?' Fox pressed. Again there was silence. Danny's right hand began to slow down, until it stopped moving altogether. There was a slight shrug of the shoulders, and a single muttered word: 'No.'

'In that case,' Holden smiled, 'I don't think we need to ask you any more questions, Danny. But thank you. You've been very helpful,' she lied.

As Danny got up from the chair, Holden motioned to Laing to stay. She waited until Fox had closed the door before asking her question. 'So what is your take on all of this, Ms Laing. I gather you know something about the vandalizing of Jake's car?'

'Who doesn't here? It was the big day centre news when it happened.'

'And when was that?'

Laing shut her eyes briefly as she tried to focus on the detail. 'About three months ago, I should reckon. But you can check that in your records. Jake reported it to the police because his car was so damaged. But until just now, I had no idea that it was Danny who did it. Will you be prosecuting him for it?'

'I'm not sure there's a lot of point,' Holden said with a slight shrug. 'Not now that—' Her sentence dribbled to a halt. 'Look,' she said, 'what really matters here is not who smashed Jake's car. It's who killed him. Why did Danny smash up his car? Did Danny hate him enough to smash his head in too?'

Laing took a noisy intake of breath, then released it as if warming up for some imminent physical effort. 'When Danny smashed Jake's car, it was parked in Marston Street, right outside Sarah Johnson's flat. This took place roundabout 11.00 o'clock at night. It caused some friction between Jim Blunt and Jake when it became apparent that Jake had been visiting Sarah Johnson, and Jim thought he was overstepping the boundaries.'

'But Jake was gay?' Holden said.

'Yes!' She almost snorted the word. 'Sure he was gay. No one was saying he was sleeping with Sarah, but being round at her flat, and being there late at night – well, it suggests a degree of friendship that was well ... some would call it unprofessional. But personally, I would call it bloody stupid.'

'And what about Danny?' Holden said, determined to steer the conversation in the direction she wanted it to go. 'If he was jealous enough to smash up Jake's car, then he must have been very fond of Sarah?'

'Yes,' Laing said again, this time with something close to a sigh. 'I would say he was very fond of Sarah. Devoted. Like a puppy. Always ready to make her a cup of tea, or nip down to the Londis to get her some cigarettes. But she kept him at a distance.'

'But she didn't keep Jake at a distance?'

For a second time Laing sucked air in and out of her lungs while she pondered her response. 'In my judgement, her relationship with Jake was at an altogether deeper level than hers with Danny. She both humoured and used Danny, but Jake—' Laing paused and resumed again her deep breathing, in, out, in, out: 'Jake she needed. And on Jake she became, I fear, dangerously dependent.'

'And Danny became very resentful of this relationship, did he?' Holden pressed.

'I would say so, yes.'

'Would you say he hated Jake?'

'Hated him?' She leant back into the chair, and looked up at the ceiling. Unconsciously, she pursed her lips, before lowering her gaze until it met Holden's. 'Hated, as in hated him enough to have killed him? I think not. Disliked, yes. Hated no.'

'Really?' said Holden, a note of scepticism in her voice. 'I'm surprised that you should be so naive, given that you work with people. You must know how things can grow and grow. Small resentments can become large resentments. Large resentments can turn into jealousy, which can turn sooner or later, if not checked, into hatred. And hatred can lead to murder.'

'If you say so,' said Laing, in a voice which said quite clearly that she didn't share the detective's gloomy assessment of human character. 'Is that all?' she said, 'because if it is I ought to be getting out into the centre and helping the others.'

'Of course,' Holden said, accommodatingly. She rose to her feet to indicate the interview was over. 'Thank you for your help.'

Laing rose slightly awkwardly to her feet, suddenly feeling conscious of her own bulk. If she had been honest with herself, she would have acknowledged that she resented the rather trim figure that the Detective Inspector cut opposite her. With a curt nod of the head, she turned towards the door.

'Just one last question,' Holden said as the other woman's hand grasped the door handle. Laing turned, but said nothing. 'I was just wondering,' Holden said, as off-handedly as she could, 'whether maybe Jake was bisexual?'

Laing smiled, then uttered a single dismissive laugh. 'All I can say is, he never came on to me.' She laughed again. 'Thank God!'

CHAPTER 5

'Damn!'

Martin Mace was normally a dab hand with his hoe. He was a solidly built figure – just 5 feet 8 inches in his bare feet – and had once been solid muscle, the result of a ferocious commitment to a bodybuilding regimen. But three years of long-distance lorry driving had taken its toll, steadily turning solid muscle into less than solid fat. His hair was short and flecked with grey, and he sported on the back of his neck a tattoo of an ox and the letters 'OUFC', which reflected a lifelong commitment to Oxford United. But despite appearances, once he picked up his hoe and started to address the weeds that were a constant threat to his allotment, he became a man of subtlety and even grace. Like a ballet dancer spinning and pirouetting round the stage, the head of his hoe would flit between the rows of runner beans and carrots, amongst the Cos lettuces and the beetroot, and around the pyramid of canes up which his sweet peas were growing (his Granddad has always grown sweet peas on his allotment and so did he), and deftly but mercilessly it would destroy all interloping weeds. Sometimes, Mace would undertake this task even when no weeds were visible to the naked eye, for he found the very process of wielding his hoe both comforting and therapeutic.

But that Friday afternoon, the therapy was not working.

'Damn!' His dancing hoe had stopped still, as if appalled by the enormity of what it had done. It lay paralyzed in the soil, some three inches from the severed stem of a runner bean plant. With a single movement it had sliced carelessly through this green tube and terminated the life of those many green beans above that drew their life from it.

The hands which held the hoe tightened and stiffened. The knuckles turned white. And from somewhere above, Mace's mouth repeated the same simple word in ever-increasing crescendo. 'Damn! Damn! Damn!'

It had been a disturbing afternoon for Mace. He had gone to the Evergreen Day Centre to attend the Anger Management group which ran every Friday at 3.00 p.m. He had missed the previous session because of a traffic jam on the M40 just south of Birmingham. As a self-employed lorry driver, he could to some degree order his working life to fit in with his own needs. When the Yellows had been playing at Shrewsbury two Tuesdays previously, he had managed to arrive at the ground at 7.00 p.m. precisely, time enough to park his loaded lorry, grab a pie and chips from a local café, and join his mates in the away fans end just in time to catch the players finish their warm-up routines. Normally, he could be back in Oxford early on a Friday, in time to attend the anger management sessions which his GP had recommended, but a pile-up of two lorries and four cars last Friday had brought him and several hundred other vehicles to a two-hour halt. The odd thing was that when he did finally get back home, he found he was frustrated at missing the session. It was odd because he had started the course reluctantly. He had expected his doctor to offer him some pills to calm him down when he had finally plucked up courage to attend surgery, but instead she had warned him that pills might affect his ability to drive. She had then suggested that if he was serious, then he should attend the anger management group that she knew was due to start at the Evergreen Day Centre. So he had gone, promising himself that after one session he'd be able to tell himself that it was all a complete waste of time and not bother again. But on his arrival he'd discovered that one of the people leading the session was Jake Arnold, and so when the following Friday came round he found himself going along so as not to upset Jake. And then the following week he had gone along because – not that he would have admitted it – he wanted to. But then there was the crash and the missed session, and then today he had got there ten minutes early only to be greeted by chaos, and by news that had hit him like a left hook to the solar plexus. Jake Arnold was dead. More than that, Jake had been murdered. He was told about it by Rachel, who ran the group with Jake, and a tall plain-clothes copper with the humour and charm of an undertaker presiding over the funeral of his own mother.

'I'm sorry,' the detective had said without sounding as if he meant it. 'This may be a bit of a shock, but we need to ask you a few simple questions.' The questions had started with the mundane – full name, address, telephone and mobile numbers – and had then moved on to the slightly more creative.

'You first met Jake Arnold when you started this course, did you?'

Mace had been tempted to agree, but with Rachel sitting there he decided a lie was an unnecessary risk. He didn't know if Rachel knew anything about him and Jake, but she might do. 'No,' Mace said. The copper looked up with sudden interest, but said nothing, waiting for Mace to expand on his single word response. 'Jake was a fan of Oxford United, like me, so we'd seen each other at games. We weren't mates or anything, it's just that at away games you all get herded together. So when I came along to this course, well, we recognized each other, didn't we.'

'So you sort of knew him, but you weren't mates?'

'Yes!' Mace said, and then 'No!' Again the copper fixed him with an expression that was intended to convey that (a) he wasn't a man to be messed about with and (b) he was happy to sit here all day asking questions until he got replies that he was satisfied with. 'Look,' Mace continued, conscious that he wasn't handling this very well. 'What I mean is that I knew him by sight, but I didn't actually know him until after I came here, to the group.'

'So you got to know him since?' the copper suggested eagerly. 'You must see him at every game?'

'No. Not every game. I don't see him at home games, for a start. I always go to the Oxford Mail stand, he probably sits in the South Stand. And he doesn't go to all the away games either.'

'Did you see him at the last away game?' The copper was relentless. 'Where was it, by the way?'

'Shrewsbury. The Tuesday before last. Nil bloody nil. We played rubbish, but so did they. Jake and me had a chat at half-time.'

'About what?' the copper broke in quickly.

'About the football. What the fuck else? Hardly the time or place to discuss how I was getting on with my anger management, now was it?'

'Just one more question,' the copper had said then. Mace had felt relieved when he'd said this because inside he could feel himself getting more and more pissed off with the questions and the bloody copper's attitude and even with Rachel standing there with her mouth closed for once, but her eyes taking every fucking last thing in. 'Breathe deep!' He could almost hear Jake say it, which in the circumstances was a right stupid thing to be almost hearing.

'I need to ask you where you were last night,' the copper was saying. Mace tried to compose himself. 'I went to Lincoln in the morning. I got back about four o'clock,' he said as calmly as he could. 'Had some food. Went to the allotment. But it started to rain soon after I got there so I went home, watched the telly for a bit, and went to bed about 9.00 p.m. I had to be in Grimsby by 8.00 this morning, so I had to be up very early.' He stopped, waiting for a response. The copper frowned, scribbled a few notes on his pad, and grunted. 'OK, that's all.'

The interview was over.

At much the same time that Martin Mace was contemplating his hoeing disaster, and less than half a mile away from where he was so doing, Detective Constable Wilson was striding the towpaths of southern Oxford in search of a murder weapon. Not that he expected to find a blood-coated implement lying abandoned in the bushes by the side of the river. But he did hope for confirmation of his theory that the weapon used had been a mooring spike. He started his search in Iffley. He parked his car in the village, then walked down the sloping side road that led to the lock, precisely the route that Peter Mellor had taken with his dog the previous night. He paused for a few moments at the weir where Jake Arnold's body had shot suddenly into Mellor's view, and stared down into the water as if waiting for inspiration to rise fully formed from its swirling waters. With a shake of the head, he moved on, across the lock gates, then turning north. He soon passed the Iffley Inn on his right, but he had no interest in revisiting it, and his stride lengthened as his eyes spotted a narrowboat moored a couple of hundred metres up ahead. A middle-aged man dressed in navy blue slacks, polo shirt and nautical hat was busy checking his moorings, and it took only the most casual questioning from Wilson to elicit the information that they had only just arrived, having spent the previous night at Wallingford. He pushed on, slowing briefly at Donnington Bridge in order to read its undergraduate graffiti, but then accelerating northwards, swinging with the river first left and then right, until suddenly before him there lay, as at any time of year, a spectacular view right up to the Head of the River pub, lying in its much favoured and highly profitable position by Folly Bridge. Wilson stopped and for a moment took in the view. On the right stood college boathouses, lining the river in a strict regimental rank, while opposite them – and little more than fifty metres from where he was standing – stood the university boathouse in solitary isolation. But it was not at these that the young detective was looking. He had fished these waters as a boy, and the buildings were remarkable to him only as the background to memories of fish that he had landed and fish that got away. Wilson was looking for moored boats (narrowboats or small cruisers), but surprisingly, given that it was sunny and the weatherwoman had promised a very pleasant weekend, there was none to be seen. A cyclist's bell jangled unconvincingly behind him, but before Wilson could turn and look, the cyclist was past him, up and over the steeply humped footbridge in front of him, and away past the university boathouse, long hair flapping in the wind. Wilson did not follow. The bridge's purpose was to allow pedestrians (and cyclists of course, it being Oxford) to cross a small tributary which entered the River Isis at this point, and it was along the southern bank of this waterway that Wilson now began to walk. This was not a path that was well used, and he walked with care. And with anticipation. Because a few hundred metres along the tributary, where it looped round to go under the Donnington Bridge Road, he knew he would find the boats of several river dwellers, and there he reckoned, with a bit of luck, he would find someone missing a mooring spike. As luck would have it, he never got that far. He had walked for barely a minute before he came across a narrowboat almost hidden from view behind a densely foliaged hawthorn bush which was flanked on either side by two graceful willows. As narrowboats go, it was short, fewer than sixteen metres in length Wilson reckoned, and perched on its roof, sipping something from a mug, was a small bald-headed man in dirty brown T-shirt and jeans.

'Good evening!' Wilson said cheerily. The man looked up, nodded briefly, and said nothing.

'Sorry to disturb you, sir,' Wilson continued, this time brandishing his ID card in front of him as a matador might brandish his cloak at a bull. 'Detective Constable Wilson. No need to be alarmed, but we had some reports of thieving locally, and I just wanted to—'

The dwarf-man laughed. 'Ah, you've got a very nice soppy class of yob in Oxford, haven't you? Very genteel indeed!' He took another sip from his mug, then waved it in the air in a manner that made Wilson wonder if it didn't contain something a bit stronger than tea. 'Now in Birmingham, they smash your windows. In Leicester they throw all your clothes into the river and smear shit on your bedding. But in Oxford, posh city of dreaming spires, all they steal is a mooring spike, but only one mind you not two, because they wouldn't like your boat to float off down the river now would they.'

'When was this?' Wilson tried unsuccessfully to keep the sense of excitement out of his voice.

'Big case, for you, is it?' the man chuckled. 'Catching the man who stole a mooring spike.'

'When?' Wilson said, this time sharply. 'I need to know when.'

'Last night. When I was out getting some supper.'

'Can you be more precise?' Wilson pressed. 'Please.'

The man scratched his head in an exaggerated fashion. 'Well, let me think. I must have left the boat about 7.15, maybe a bit later. I walked up to the main river, then up to the town, and had a pie and chips and peas and a couple of pints in that pub by the bridge, and then I walked back. Must have got back to the boat maybe a bit after 9 o'clock. The stern was out across the river. And the mooring spike was gone.'

Wilson inspected the area where the mooring spike had been. The man had replaced it with another ('I always carry a spare'), but if Wilson had hoped to find some object carelessly dropped by the murderer when he removed the spike, by now his luck had run out. Five minutes later, having declined a cup of tea but taken the man's name and mobile number, he set off back towards Iffley, softly whistling as he went. He felt sure that Susan – that is to say Detective Inspector Holden – would be very pleased with him. He did hope so.

'Nice flat you've got here,' Holden said brightly, keen to avoid jumping straight into questions. She walked three paces across the spacious minimalist room, and took in the wide sweep of the river through the large picture window. It was 8.30 on Saturday morning and, directly below, a flotilla of mallards made its way from left to right across her vision, down river. 'I wish I had a view like this,' she said with feeling. She herself lived only a few hundred metres away as the crow flew (not that crows are often seen traversing Grandpont), but the view from her flat (the bottom floor of a two-storeyed Victorian terraced building) was merely of other terraced houses. Les Whiting lived on the third and top floor of a relatively new development of flats close by Folly Bridge. Holden remembered them being built, and remembered, too, envying those people who could afford to buy them.

'Thank you, my dear,' Whiting said. 'Kind of you to say so, though I prefer to think of it as an apartment. The word flat has such, such—' He paused, and ran his right hand through his streaked hair while he tried to conjure up the precise word he was looking for. 'Such uninteresting connotations. Don't you think so?'

Holden smiled. 'Thank you for seeing us. I appreciate you've got a gallery to run, and I guess Saturday is a busy day for you, so we'll try to keep it short and then—'

'Please!' said Whiting, waving her to a halt. 'I could hardly refuse to help the police with their enquiries, now could I? But before we get down to business, how about a coffee? Espresso, cappuccino, or Americano? Or I've got a very nice jasmine tea, or a selection of herbal infusions.'

'Cappuccino, please,' said Holden, impressed by the choice.

'Black coffee for me,' said Fox uncompromisingly, refusing to be drawn into the world of fancy hot drinks. 'With three sugars,' he added, before slumping heavily onto one of the two white sofas.

Whiting smiled the indulgent smile he often had to employ in his gallery in the High Street when customers tried to knock down his prices. 'Three sugars it is,' he said softly, turning towards the archway that led through to the kitchen.

'Sorry,' said Holden, 'but could I use your loo. Bad planning as my mother would say, but it's—'

'Woman's stuff?' Whiting interrupted. 'Don't you worry,' and he tapped his nose with the forefinger of his right hand. 'Mum's the word. Follow me!'

She followed, but he stopped in front of the door lavatory, blocking her way. 'Just to get this out the way,' he said firmly. 'I know Jake was bonked on the head, and I know he was fished out of the river. That's enough for me. More than enough. Are you with me?'

'Of course,' Holden said quietly. 'I understand.'

'Well, I hope that orang-utan of a colleague does too,' he said moving to the side. 'Anyway, I'll leave you to it.'

'Thank you.'

Five minutes later and they were sitting down around a low rectangular table which consisted of aluminium tubes of varying diameters and a sheet of glass. Holden took a sip from her cappuccino, and then waited for Whiting to take one from his.

'I'd like you to tell us about your relationship with Jake,' she asked.

Whiting took a second sip, before carefully placing his cup and saucer on the table. Fleetingly, his right hand touched the small silver cross hanging around his neck. 'He came into my gallery about six months ago. That's Bare Canvas, in the High Street, in case you're interested. Anyway he asked a lot of questions, but he didn't buy anything. You soon get a feeling when someone comes into the shop whether they are curious, or serious, or just trying to avoid the rain. He turned up again later that week, just before I was due to shut up shop, and we ended up going out for a drink. Well, to cut things short, we got into a relationship.' He paused again, and picked up his cappuccino, but this time just cradled it in his hands.

'Did he move in with you?'

'Not permanently. He'd stay over most weekends, and sometimes midweek, but we both liked our personal space.'

'And when did you split up?'

He lifted the cappuccino up close to his lips, but made no attempt to drink from it. 'Three weeks ago,' he said quietly. Holden thought she could detect a tear straining to form in the corner of his eye. 'Three weeks yesterday, to be precise.' There was another pause. Holden waited. 'He'd been seeing someone else.'

'Seeing someone else,' Holden echoed, a question mark almost visibly attached to it.

'Buggering someone else, if you prefer it, ma'am!' He spoke forcefully now, all nostalgic emotion now put firmly on hold. 'Not my scene. Wanting a bit of space is one thing. Fucking someone else on the side is quite another.'

'So it was an unpleasant break-up, was it?' It was Fox who said this, causing both Whiting and Holden to turn towards him. Holden frowned with irritation, but Whiting seemed unflustered.

'Have you ever had a relationship that went down the tubes, Detective?' He paused, giving Fox an opportunity to reply. But Fox said nothing. 'The ends of relationships are never, in my experience, pleasant. Never. In the case of Jake and me, he betrayed me, so of course I hated it. Briefly, I hated him. So I gave him his marching orders. But life is too short to dwell on things that don't work out. So if you are implying, as I think you are, Detective, that our break-up was so acrimonious that I decided to bash the cheating bastard over the head and then drop him in the river to make sure, then let me tell you that you have got it wrong.'

Whiting now raised his cup, which had been hovering uncertainly between his mouth and his lap all the time he was speaking, and took a long and noisy slurp from it.

'We have to be suspicious of everyone.' Holden spoke softly, almost apologetically, irritated as she was by her colleague's heavy-footed intervention. 'It's virtually part of our job description. I'm sure you must realize. And while we are on difficult questions,' she continued, plunging on while she had an opportunity, 'I might as well ask you now where you were on Thursday night. Please!'

To her surprise, Whiting smiled. 'Oh, Inspector,' he said, 'How reassuring this all is.' He placed the not yet finished cappuccino cup on the table, and leant back in his chair. He placed his fingers together, as if he was about to demonstrate to them that old rhyme that Holden suddenly remembered from school. 'Here's a church and here is a steeple, open the doors, see all the people.' But the fingers stayed still, as did his eyes which surveyed Holden as a chess player might stare at his adversary, immediately after making a move.

'First you do, well if not the good-cop, bad-cop routine, then at least the nice cop, miserable sod cop routine, and then even as I am in mid-cappuccino you slip in the "Where were you when the victim was murdered?" question. Of course, I knew it was bound to come, and of course like all good suspects I have an alibi that no one can vouch for.' He paused, half-smiling, forcing a response. But surprisingly it came from a suddenly good-humoured Fox.

'If you could just tell us what your unprovable alibi is, sir, then I can, like a good Policeman Plod, record it in my notebook, so that we can come back another time and try and trip you up on the details.'

'Sergeant!' Whiting almost bounced vertically in the air in his delight. 'How nice of you to enter into the spirit. Now let me see.' He paused – overdramatically in Holden's view – until he felt he had got sufficient audience attention. 'It was a migraine. I felt it coming on as I was on the bus home, so as soon as I got in I made myself a cup of jasmine tea, took two painkillers, and then took myself to my lonely bed. All very inconvenient, I know.'

'And no one phoned?' Holden asked firmly. 'No one rang the bell?'

'I unplugged the phone, didn't I.' Whiting's tone was flatter now, as if the seriousness of the situation was beginning to seep under the surface bravado. 'If anyone rang the doorbell, I didn't hear. I was in never-never-land almost as soon as my head touched the pillow.'

'You have a mobile?'

'Who doesn't? But I turned that off too. Obviously.'

'Why obviously?' Fox interrupted again.

'Bloody hell, haven't you ever had a migraine. Cause if you had, you wouldn't ask such a stupid question.'

'I specialize in stupid questions,' Fox responded evenly. 'I'm a stupid plodding, sergeant, and I ask stupid bloody questions.'

'Well, bully for you!' Whiting laughed.

'Perhaps we can focus on Jake,' cut in Holden, who was getting a little suspicious of Whiting's manner. His lover of recent time lay dead in the mortuary, yet here he was playing to his audience of two with a will. 'You may not have killed him, but someone did. It was a nasty, violent, deliberate act. Someone out there disliked Jake very much. So as Jake's close friend, maybe there is something you know that we ought to know. And if so, now is the time to tell us.' She paused, and added: 'If, that is, you want us to catch his killer.'

Whiting held up his hands theatrically, but then dropped them as if having second thoughts. 'Sorry. Point taken.' For a few seconds he shut his eyes, raising his right hand to his mouth. Then he opened them again and looked straight at Holden.

'Do you know about Jake and Jim Blunt?'

'Know what?' said Holden, her ears metaphorically pricked.

'Well, I guess Blunt wouldn't have mentioned it, and I doubt any of those self-seeking workers who fawn around him would have wanted to rock their cosy little boat.' He paused, looking for some sort of reaction from Holden. Like an actor, he seemed to crave the oxygen of audience approval, but the Detective Inspector had no desire to indulge him. 'Perhaps you can get to the point, sir!'

'The point, my dear, is that Jake put in a complaint about Blunt. A formal complaint. To management.'

'A complaint about what?' Holden said evenly, still refusing to cooperate with Whiting's game.

'He said that Blunt had bullied him. In supervision.'

'In supervision?'

'They had one-to-one supervisions every three or four weeks. Privately, in a room. So it was the ideal place for Blunt to bully poor Jake. No witnesses, you see.'

'Assuming that Blunt was bullying him.'

'Well, of course he was bullying him! Why on earth should Jake have lied about it?'

For several seconds, Holden said nothing. On the face of it, Whiting's loyalty to his ex-boyfriend, was convincing, even impressive. Jake had cheated on him, and that had hurt Whiting. Hurt him enough to end the relationship. Yet here he was taking Jake's side.

'Okay,' she said uncertainly, feeling her way. 'Let us assume, just for the sake of argument, that Blunt was bullying Jake. Now, that's hardly a motive for murder.'

'Why the hell not!' Whiting spoke sharply, his voice leaping an octave. 'He's a right bastard that man. I wouldn't put anything past him.'

Some four hours later, Martin Mace was pushing his way through the crowd of football fans in the garden of the Priory pub. Oxford were playing Bristol Rovers. Not quite a local derby, but it was a rivalry with history. Two men (Little and Large to their mates) sat at a small round table by the low wall that delineated the edge of the pub's official limits. There were six pint glasses on the table, two of them already empty, and two only half full. Mace was late.

'Hurry up, your miserable bastard. It's nearly your round already. Honestly, you move bloody slower than Julian Alsop, and let me tell you that ain't a bloody compliment.' Al Smith was 6 feet 4 and rising, with a body frame to match. Even sitting down, his physical bulk was obvious, and his voice cut a swathe through the babble of noise.

On another day, Mace would have given as good as he got, but on this occasion he slumped heavily down onto the empty stool, nodded at the smaller man, and picked up one of the glasses of Guinness.

Sam Sexton, a short, skinny man with a dark swirl of hair and at least three days of stubble, slipped unconsciously into his role of peacemaker. 'Leave him be, Al. He's had to drive to Grimsby and back today. It's enough to piss anyone off!'

'Fucking Grimsby,' Smith snorted. 'I hate bloody Grimsby. The only good thing about that hole is the fish and chips.'

'You all right, Martin?' Sexton asked. Mace had drained his pint, and was pulling the second one towards him. He ignored the question, and began to drink again, only stopping when the glass was two-thirds empty. He carefully placed the glass down on the table, then leant forward. For the first time since sitting down, he looked at his two friends. Each of them leant forward.

'Jake's dead!'

For several seconds, the three of them remained silent, while all around the chatter ebbed and flowed. 'They reckon he was murdered!' Mace continued.

'Fuck!'

'Murdered?'

'Some bastard whacked him over the back of the head, then dumped him into the river. They fished him out at Iffley Lock.'

'The poor bugger!' Sexton said.

'How did you find out?' Smith said, his voice no longer booming.

Mace had anticipated this question. He hadn't told either of his friends about the anger management group – he could imagine what Al's response would have been – and he didn't want to tell them now, but he did want to talk about Jake.

'I was down near the Evergreen Day Centre,' he improvised, 'where Jake works, and there were a couple of police cars outside. So I knew something must be up, and this guy started to tell me that one of the workers had been found dead in the river—'

'I'm not fucking surprised,' Smith said, his voice louder again and harsh. 'He was bloody asking for it if you ask me. Bloody pansy.'

'No one deserves to be murdered,' Sexton said quickly.

'Don't call him a bloody pansy,' Mace snarled. 'He was OK. I liked him.'

'Liked him, did you?' Smith leered across the table. 'Liked him a lot, did you?'

'Leave it out, you guys,' Sexton said plaintively. 'Martin,' he said, trying to steer the conversation to safer water, 'when did this all happen?'

Mace raised his glass and drained the rest of its contents. Then he put it down, belched and leant even further forward. 'Suppose, just suppose the person who killed Jake knows?'

'Knows what?' Smith replied, his voice now much quieter.

'About last May.'

'Don't be fucking stupid,' Smith said aggressively, but his voice was even quieter. 'How could anyone?'

'Suppose Sarah didn't jump?' Mace continued, ignoring him. 'Suppose she was pushed.' He paused, picked up his glass, realized it was empty and put it down again. 'Suppose she was murdered too.'

'You're just guessing, Martin!' Sexton said.

'Suppose,' persisted Mace, 'suppose that just this once, I am right. What then?'

'You've as much chance of being right as Paul Wanless has of lasting 90 minutes,' Smith laughed. 'Now, are you going to get your round in before the game fucking starts?'

CHAPTER 6

Susan Holden emerged slowly into a state of semi-consciousness and emitted a low groan. She never had been good with alcohol, and the three glasses of uninspired Chardonnay consumed in front of the TV the night before had left her with a low-grade headache. She had drunk it while watching The Graduate. She had seen the film before, but when the alternatives were Match of the Day, a third-rate reality TV show, a film starring Sylvester Stallone, or a fuzzy Channel Five 'investigation' into sexual problems, a youthful Dustin Hoffman was going to win out every time. In actuality, she had struggled to stay awake throughout, but she had been determined to see the end – that was the best bit – where Hoffman escapes from the church with the bride (not his, of course) and grabs a lift out of town on a bus full of bemused onlookers.

The upshot of all this was that she had gone to bed somewhat inebriated, totally exhausted, and without drawing the curtains. As a consequence, on Sunday morning the grey intrusive light of an unpromising day had slowly prodded and cajoled her into a state of, if not wakefulness, then at least one of fitfulness. She had resisted its summons, pulling the duvet up over her head, but even the duvet could not deaden the sounds of her father's clock. It sat in splendid isolation on a small table in the short space outside her room which masqueraded as corridor. Ding dong, dong ding, it rang, and then repeated itself, before beginning to chime out the hour: boom, boom, three, four. Holden found it impossible, even in her semi-conscious prostration, not to count the hours as she had loved to as a child. Seven, eight, nine. Then silence. Then: 'Shit!' Holden rolled to her right and scrabbled around on the side table until her hand found the alarm clock. She picked it up and squinted at its digital face. 09.01. She was late.

It took her five minutes to shower and brush her teeth. Then three more to dress and two more to find her handbag, which had mysteriously secreted itself under the sofa (fortunately a trailing handle gave it away). All of which meant that by the time she was ringing the No. 6 bell at Grandpont Grange ('Luxury accommodation for the older generation'), she was only 15 minutes late.

'Had a late night, my dear?' beamed her mother. Susan Holden, who was expecting a verbal barrage on the importance of punctuality and the neglect of the elderly by the younger generation, was taken completely off guard. The woman looked like her mother. She dressed like her mother. She was even wearing her mother's favourite perfume.

'Lucky you,' the imposter continued. 'If I were twenty years younger, I'd be out there clubbing with you!'

Holden, who at the age of 32 considered herself long retired from the clubbing scene, grinned at the improbable thought of her morphed mother and herself at the Park End. 'Mmm, I smell coffee,' she said, as she pulled her shoes off in the hall, and placed them tidily in the corner.

'It's been ready for ten minutes, actually,' her mother said firmly, as if to remind her daughter that she had not had a personality change.

'Sorry I'm late.' The words came out automatically, and the Detective Inspector was a little girl again, failing to meet the expected standards.

'Doesn't matter,' said her mother, though of course it did.

'Wow!' Again the response was automatic, but this time it was genuine. Holden was standing, her mouth literally gaping, in the doorway to the kitchen diner. Since she had last been to see her mother four days previously, the room had been transformed. The avalanche of objects that had emerged from the packing crates had disappeared. A few prized objects were on display, but chaos had been replaced by an almost minimalist order. The table was covered with a crisp white cloth, and on it were laid two places. Two glasses of fruit juice had been poured out, four croissants lay neatly on a central plate, and a selection of miniature packets of cereal stood neatly in line, recalling special breakfasts of childhood. Holden felt herself going gooey round the edges.

'Sit down,' her mother instructed, and she did. They ate in verbal silence, broken by the crunching of cereal, clinking of utensils, and the rustle of newspapers. It had always been the rule in the Holden house that you could read the paper at breakfast on Sundays, but never on other days, because meals were social events. Quite how and why this rule had been instituted, Susan had never discovered. Of course, her mother bought the *Sunday Telegraph*, which her daughter had long since rejected, but Susan found looking through the colour magazine a far from pleasureless task, and she even made a couple of mental fashion notes – a smart new dress and some shoes to match were promoted silently to the top of her list.

'So where would you like to go today?' daughter asked mother as she finished her second mug of coffee. She had promised her a trip out earlier in the week, by way of a placebo for not being able to help more with her move, and Wallingford, Henley and Thame had all been discussed then.

'I nearly rang you,' her mother purred, 'but then I decided it would be a nice surprise. Guess what. We've been asked out for lunch.'

'That's nice,' her daughter replied.

'After church,' added her mother.

'Church?' her daughter exclaimed, amazement apparent not just in her tone of voice, but every aspect of her features. This reaction obviously pleased the alien who had clearly taken up residence in her mother's body. A smile of triumphant delight erupted across the width of her face.

'St Marks, in Marlborough Road. You've been living here for two years. You must know it.'

'Only from the outside,' her daughter admitted.

'Well, in that case its high time you went to a service.'

Her daughter peered across the table, and a smile began to spread across her face too. 'Have you been bitten by the God bug, mother? Been born again. Because from memory you only go into churches for Christmas, weddings and funerals.'

'Doris asked me. Mrs Doris Williams. It's her who asked us to lunch. Lives on the next floor. She's been a great help. Got her fifteen-year-old grandson to help me sort out this place, put things in the high cupboards, and some in the communal storage room. I think the least we could do is go to church with her.'

And so it was that DI Susan Holden and Mrs Jane Holden (widow of five years) went to their first service together since the funeral of the late Mr John Holden.

That evening, Susan Holden circumspectly poured herself a small glass of wine from the now depleted bottle of Chardonnay, tipped the remainder into the sink, and then consigned the bottle to her green recycling box. Then she sat at the kitchen table, and tried to form a conclusion about what had happened in church. Not the service itself, though she'd found it both very different from what she'd experienced as a child, and rather invigorating too. But after the service. Immediately it had finished, she found herself being engaged in earnest conversation, first by a young woman – well mid-twenties, anyway – and then by a retired man with a grey bread, a bad taste in ties, and an archetypical twinkle in the eye. Clearly, being Christian didn't preclude gentle flirting with women half his age. When he was buttonholed by a tall, thin young man wearing a brightly striped T-shirt and an anxious frown, Holden found herself suddenly alone amid the babble of voices which signified that the members of St Mark's were 'sharing fellowship' with a will. She was looking around, wondering where her mother was, when suddenly she felt someone touch her shoulder. She turned.

'Hello, there!' The speaker was a short man, short enough that she found herself looking down on him. He wore jeans, trainers and a dark blue jacket zipped up to his neck. There was a sheen of sweat on his face, and Holden couldn't fail to notice the rather unpleasant smell that emanated from him.

'I know you,' the man said.

'Oh?' said Holden, trying to place him.

'You were at the day centre on Friday. You're a police-woman aren't you.' He pointed at her, not in an aggressive manner, but as he might have at other times have pointed at a flower or bird he had just recognized. 'Have you arrested anyone yet?' he continued. 'For Jake's death?'

'No,' she said. 'We haven't.'

'Do you have a prime suspect?'

Holden smiled, and wondered bleakly why Doris or her mother couldn't suddenly appear at her shoulder and rescue her. 'I'm afraid I can't talk about the case.'

'Don't you want to question me?' His finger had now turned and was pointing directly at his own chest.

Again she smiled, and gestured with her left hand (her right hand still held her mug, not yet emptied, of weak tea) around her. 'In church?'

'Why not,' he replied instantly. 'The perfect place. For the truth. For confession.'

With the tiniest shake of her head, Holden abandoned all hope of rescue. There was only going to be one way out of this. 'Is there something you know? Something you want to ... to confess?'

'Me?' The man laughed. 'Not me. Jake. It's Jake's confession you need to know.'

Holden, despite all her reservations about the man in front of her – he hadn't yet told her who he was – felt a surge of interest, even excitement. 'Did Jake tell you something?'

'Yes, he did.' The man's left hand moved up and grasped the zip of his jacket. He pulled it down two or three inches, then up again, nervously. 'On Thursday. About 4 o'clock in the Cowley Road. It can only have been a few hours before he was killed. He must have just come out of the day centre. I'd gone and bought an *Oxford Mail* at the corner shop. He was standing outside, smoking a cigarette. That was odd, cos I'd never seen him smoke before. I asked him if he knew when Sarah Johnson's funeral was. She was the woman who jumped from the top of the car park. Perhaps you know about it.'

Holden made some sort of encouraging noise. 'Yes, I do, but carry on. What did Jake say?'

'He said something very odd. I thought it was really odd at the time and the more I've thought about it, well, the more I got worried about it. You see, he said he didn't know when the funeral was because there had to be an inquest, and I said wasn't it terrible that she got so depressed that she jumped, and then he said this. He said, maybe she didn't jump. And I said what do you mean, and he said something like, well we can't be sure it was suicide. And then he said that he had to be going. And he walked off down the road. That was the last I saw of him.'

'Did Jake say why it might not be suicide?'

'No. That's all he said.'

'You're sure?'

The man's hand came up again, and like some remotely controlled weapon, pointed at her, aggressively this time. 'Of course I'm sure. I've got a good memory for detail. Just you remember it.' And with that, he had turned and walked away.

Sitting there on the sofa, her glass of Chardonnay in her hand, Holden tried but failed to come to a conclusion about this encounter. The man's name, as Doris had confirmed, was Alan. He was a regular face at the 10.30 service, though beyond that she wasn't too sure. He often came along to the Wednesday morning communion and the drop-in lunch which followed it. He didn't appear to have a job. 'I expect he's on benefit,' she had said. 'Probably can't hold down a job.' She had pulled a face as she said this, and then – Holden had decided – immediately regretted it. 'Still,' she had added quickly, 'isn't it marvellous how he comes to church.' Then with a broad smile, as if to demonstrate the generosity of her spirit: 'The Lord moves in mysterious ways!'

He does indeed, Holden said to herself, as she brushed her teeth. A day that she had expected to spend humouring her mother had turned out ... extraordinary. There was no other word for it. To begin with, her mother had been nice! She had gone to church. She had, even more extraordinarily, found herself enjoying it. And she had met a man who might have been one of the last people to talk to Jake Arnold. The only problem was to know what on earth to make of his evidence.

Wilson pulled the car up outside DI Holden's terraced house in Chilswell Road at 7.23 a.m. He had been surprised both to receive a call from her the previous night and by the instruction that he should pick her up from home no later than 7.25 a.m. No explanation. Just a curt set of instructions followed by a slightly less curt 'Good Night'. Leaving the engine running, he got out of the car, only to see that Holden was already out of the front door. He got back in, turned the radio off and waited for her to get in. 'Morning, Guv,' he said.

'Morning Wilson. Now, we'll take the scenic route to the office. Down the High Street if you please.'

Again Holden offered no explanation, and Wilson, learning fast, drove without question. It was only when they had crossed Magdalen Bridge ('Look at the mist, Wilson. Perfect backdrop for a murder mystery'), entered the ('second exit on the roundabout, Wilson') Cowley Road, and ('left here into the multi-storey, then keep going right to the top') turned into the car park that things began to become clear to Wilson. 'This is where—'

'Yes Wilson,' Holden said in a tone that implied that it was too early in the morning to be making statements of the obvious. 'This is where Sarah Johnson plunged to her death.' Wilson flushed, and tried to concentrate on getting to the top.

He had barely brought the car to a halt before Holden was out of her seat and marching across the empty tarmac to the concrete wall that ringed the top storey. Wilson turned the engine and side lights off, and hurried after her. Holden was leaning over the wall, looking down.

'Why have we assumed that Sarah jumped, Wilson?'

Wilson frowned. 'Well, everything points to it, I suppose.'

'For God's sake Wilson! Everything! Everything? Don't flannel. What are the facts? And,' she said, and then paused, 'what are mere assumptions?'

Wilson gulped involuntarily, and tried to think. 'She was depressive, Guv.'

'Says who?'

'Says her sister. Says, I mean said Jake. She went to the day centre because of her mental health problems, didn't she?'

'So she must have jumped?'

'Not must. But there were the phone calls to Jake the morning she died. He admitted she sounded very stressed. And then there was that student with his plaque about suicide.'

'True,' Holden conceded. 'But how can we know that someone didn't just push her over the edge. How do we know she wasn't murdered?'

'Look at the wall,' Wilson said. 'It's what, four feet high, maybe a bit more. It wouldn't be easy to push someone over that against their will.'

Holden stepped back from the wall and looked at it as if seeing its bulk and ugliness for the first time. She frowned, much as Wilson had shortly before. 'OK, Wilson. Maybe you're right. But I want to try something out. Just climb up on the wall and sit facing me?'

'Climb up?' Wilson said with an air of alarm in his voice.

'Yes, Wilson,' Holden said, her voice sharp and hard. 'Climb up on the bloody wall. Now. And for God's sake get a move on.'

Wilson looked at her uncertainly, but one look at her face convinced him that now was not the time to confess to a fear of heights.

'Look,' she continued, suddenly back into a gentler, coaxing mode. 'There's an old milk crate over there. Use it as a step, there's a good chap.'

Wilson breathed deeply, walked over to the green crate, picked it up, and moved back to the wall. Trying not to think of what was over the other side of the wall, he put all his concentration into the task: placing the crate firmly against the wall, testing his weight on it, then stepping up and pulling himself slowly up onto the top of the wall. He realized as he was doing it that the wall was wider that he had thought, and suddenly sitting down on it didn't seem quite like sitting on the edge of a precipice.

'There,' said Holden, still coaxing. 'That wasn't too bad. Even for someone who doesn't like heights.' This comment took Wilson completely by surprise, and it showed clearly across his face.

'In your file,' Holden smiled. 'And don't worry, I'm not going to make you stand up. I can't afford to lose a third of my investigation team at one stroke!'

Wilson smiled uncertainly back. If she was trying to get him at his ease, she had at least partly succeeded.

'Oh, look. I think your shoe lace is loose. Let me tie it up.' She moved forward and bent down to where his feet dangled. 'Keep still,' she said. For several seconds her hands untied and then retied the lace of Wilson's left hand shoe. Then she looked up at Wilson and smiled, her hands gently resting on his shoe. 'Now, before you get down Wilson, I want you to think about this moment in time. I want you to picture it in your head. You sitting up on a wall seven storeys above a very solid pavement. You didn't want to be there, but you are. You are relaxed. You are off your guard – somewhat. You are anxious, but only because you don't like heights. You are not anxious about me. I am your boss. I can be trusted. Yet my hands are on your shoe. At any moment, as I was tying up your shoe laces – they weren't undone, by the way – my hands could have tightened on your shoe, and I could have pushed upwards with all my strength, and by now you would in all probability be lying dead on the pavement below. But fortunately for you, Wilson, I am not a murderer, so you can now carefully get down off the wall and drive me to the office.'

'Sorry, Wilson.' They were driving along the Cowley Road, and Holden was wondering if she hadn't perhaps gone a bit far. 'I'm not a sadist, at least not normally. But I want you to think. Think hard. Outside the box, as well as inside. The chances are that Sarah did jump. Voluntarily. A suicide. Pure and simple. Only suicides are never pure and rarely simple for the person involved, I imagine. I just wanted to demonstrate that there are options. If someone wanted to get Sarah up on that wall, they could have. They might, for example, have said they wanted to photograph her there, against the Oxford skyline. She might have been flattered by the suggestion. They might have helped her up, held her shoe to give her a leg up, but after giving her a leg up, they could have given her a push. Goodbye Sarah.'

'I'd like to try and take stock of what we know.' It was some half an hour later, and DI Holden was addressing her small team in her office. It felt more cramped than it had the previous Monday morning, not so much because Wilson was there as well as Fox, but more so because a large free-standing noticeboard, which had materialised along the Oxford Road side of the room, cut off much of the natural light that would otherwise have come in through the window. In the middle

83

of the board was a large head and shoulders photograph of a smiling Jake Arnold, surrounded by four slightly smaller ones, each showing his dead body from a different aspect. To the left was a single picture of Sarah Johnson; like Jake she was smiling, though to Wilson's eye the smile was more forced than natural. He was struck more by the darkness round the eyes, and sense of sadness emanating from the whole. Or was that him projecting his own feelings. He wasn't sure. She was wearing round her neck a small heart-shaped locket on a fine gold chain, and he wondered who had given it to her. Was it a recent gift? Or was it, he suddenly thought, a gift from herself to herself. He did hope not.

'Jake Arnold died sometime last Thursday evening, after leaving the Iffley Inn. He left there at about 10.00 p.m. according to the barman, and his body was spotted in the river by the lock round about 10.45 p.m. He had been hit over the back of the head with a heavy instrument, hard enough to be dead before he entered the river. The weapon used might well have been a mooring spike.' She paused, and took a sip of coffee. 'Wilson. The mooring spike?'

'Yes, Guv. On Friday afternoon, I came across a man with a narrow-boat moored up that side estuary that leads from the main river down toward the western end of Donnington Bridge Road. He had lost a mooring spike the night before.'

'Lost?' Holden cut in sharply.

'Well, no, not lost,' Wilson fumbled 'Stolen. Apparently.' Wilson felt his assurance seeping away. He looked across to Fox for reassurance, but the slight smile that flickered across his face was anything but reassuring.

'When, precisely, Wilson?' Holden spoke each word separately, a pause in between each, asserting her authority over her young charge, but the tone of voice was softer, and she finished with a smile that was designed to encourage.

Wilson consciously paused, trying to compose his thoughts and his words. 'While he was out getting his supper. Roughly between about 7.15 and 9.00. Though he didn't seem too sure of time.'

'And how long would it take a person to walk from there down to, say, the Iffley Inn?' Holden asked.

'Fifteen minutes, I'd say, but you could do it quicker if you wanted.' Wilson replied.

'So what do you think, Fox?' Holden turned to her Detective Sergeant now, as if to reassure him that although she might be giving Wilson a lot of attention, when she needed the wisdom of experience, Fox was very definitely her man. 'Is this a premeditated killing or a casual one?'

Fox pursed his lips while he pondered the question. 'It could have been premeditated. The man – or woman – nicks the mooring spike and wanders off down the river. He could walk along the river bank, as long as he had some means of hiding the mooring spike. They are quite long, so maybe a sports bag or something like that. If he knew Jake, he would have known Jake lived in east Oxford. He could have waited for him to come along the path. It would be very dark. However …' Fox paused and took a slug of coffee. 'There is an alternative scenario. The mooring spike could have been stolen by a casual passer-by. Maybe a yob who fancies a bit of vandalism. Maybe he's had a few drinks. He wanders down the river towards the Isis, sees Jake mincing along the towpath, and before you know it he's whacked him over the head, and knocked him into the river. He throws the spike into the river too, and then gets the hell out of it.'

'So which of those do you fancy Wilson?' Holden said.

Wilson nervously smoothed the side of his hair. 'Well, I suppose, either,' he said with obvious uncertainly.

'Make a choice,' Holden interrupted brusquely. 'Based on what we know. On the facts.'

Wilson smoothed his hair again. 'Premeditated!' He spoke firmly now. 'The time factor definitely points that way. The latest it was stolen was 9.15. Probably earlier. Jake didn't leave the pub until round about 10 o'clock. Would a vandal really have taken three-quarters of an hour or more to cover a distance that would normally take a fit man only fifteen minutes? And there have been no reports of any vandalism taking place on Thursday evening. I checked with the duty officer this morning.' Wilson paused, now looking his senior officer full in the face. She nodded.

'I'm glad to see you're thinking, Wilson. For a moment back there, I was beginning to wonder—' She trailed off, and now in turn took a sip at her coffee. Then she looked across at Fox.

'Well, Fox. Marks out of ten for Wilson's analysis?'

Fox looked back at her. 'Well, Guv, in the circumstances, I think I'd give him a nine.'

'Nine? Why nine?'

'We don't want him getting big headed now do we, Guv?'

Holden shook her head gravely. 'Certainly not, Fox.'

'So, team, who's our prime suspect?' Holden asked the question as if asking a class of five-year-olds what the capital of Uzbekistan was. There was no immediate answer. Outside, a particularly noisy lorry, piled high with scrap metal, rumbled up the incline of the road, heading for the ring road.

'What about Blunt?' she suggested, unwilling to wait.

'Well worth an interview,' Fox said, 'based on what Les Whiting told us, but my instinct is that Danny is a more likely killer—'

'Why?' Holden responded sharply. 'If Jake's complaints had been upheld, Blunt's job, even his career is in jeopardy. He looks a tough bastard to me, so when Jake complained he was a bully, maybe he decided to get his retaliation in first.'

'Like I said,' Fox admitted, 'he is worth an interview, but Danny is the key, in my book.'

'Why?' Holden snapped again. 'Because he's a nutcase? Because if that's your criterion, there are plenty of suspects down at the day centre.'

'Because he is linked to both Sarah and Jake. He was devoted to Sarah, and he didn't like Jake. Jealous maybe that Sarah relied more on Jake than himself. So when Sarah tops herself, he blames Jake for letting her down and—'

'Wilson, what do you think?' Holden said sharply, still in combative mode. 'Which of them should we target?'

Wilson swallowed. 'This may seem like a cop-out, but why not target them both.'

'Both of them?' Holden asked out loud. Then she laughed. 'Is your father, or even your dear mother, a politician, Wilson? Because if so, you've clearly learnt a thing or two from them.'

Fox chuckled. 'Nine out of ten again, I think Guv.'

The idea had first formed in his head just after the school secretary rang back. 'Hello,' she'd said in a tone which exuded briskness, 'St Gregory's School here.'

'DC Wilson,' he'd said. He had intended to continue with some pleasantry, but Miss Hegarty was steaming remorselessly forward on her mission to connect her head teacher and the Oxford police without hindrance or delay. 'Please wait, while I put you through.' Wilson waited several seconds while Miss Hegarty's mission encountered some invisible hitch, but in that interval the idea materialized, like some speck of grit. One moment the eye is fine and unnoticed, the next there is a speck in it which you can't not notice. And like all respectable specks of grit, it resolutely refused to be dislodged by a metaphorical rub of the eye.

Wilson had first rung St Gregory's fifteen minutes earlier. Once he had explained his requirements to Miss Hegarty, she had promised to call back as soon as the head was available. In the meantime, Wilson had determined to get a firmer grip on the evidence, such as there was, of the death of Sarah Johnson. He had retrieved the case folder from Fox's meticulously tidy desk. The Detective Sergeant had 'popped out' to the chemist, to get himself some painkillers for his still-sensitive teeth, although Wilson had his theory – with little firm foundation, if truth be told – that his superior had developed an interest in the recently separated Doreen, who served behind the counter there. Wilson took the folder and looked through its sparse contents. His attention was immediately drawn to Fox's interview of Ed Bicknell. Reading it through, he felt immensely irritated – as he had while witnessing the interview – with the laid-back, upper-middle-class self-confidence and indolence which emanated from every pore of Bicknell's body. He wasn't anti-student as such, Wilson told himself, but how could a man get up at 11 o'clock in the morning and still think the world owed him a living. He, Wilson, knew that only hard work, bloody hard work, would get him anywhere in life. And besides, what sort of man was Bicknell that he could view the suicide of a woman as nothing more than an opportunity to gain money, publicity, and professional advancement. Wilson pushed the folder away, in disgust, not just with Bicknell but with himself, too. He was meant to be looking into whether Sarah Johnson's death was suicide, not jumping to a whole set of half-baked conclusions. He gave himself an almost physical shake, as a dog might after scrambling out of a river, and he reached for the CD onto which Bicknell had copied his photographs. He picked it up, inserted it into his PC, and took hold of the mouse.

The photographs were in chronological order, with a date and time on the bottom left-hand corner of each picture. He began to flick through them, spending a second or two on each one until he came to the first photo of Sarah Johnson. 8:42:33. About twenty minutes before she jumped or fell or was pushed to her death. He sat and examined the image. She was standing looking at the plaque and her face was fully in profile. She was wearing a fawn mackintosh, mid-calf in length, and below it jeans and black ankle boots. For several seconds Wilson studied the picture. One part of his brain, a part not concentrating on the image of Sarah Johnson, became aware that outside the room, down the corridor, there was a sudden running of feet. He ignored it, and clicked onto the next picture. Another one of Sarah Johnson, but this time two other persons had joined her. She had turned her head towards them, but this had caused shadow to fall across her face. Was she talking to the man or woman? Wilson could see only their backs. The man was dressed in a mid-blue denim jacket and somewhat lighter jeans. The woman was dressed in a dark jacket and skirt, and a white line around the neck suggested a white blouse too. Office clothes for her, more casual for him. Separate people or a couple of some sort? Wilson wondered. How easy would it be to track them down? Not impossible, despite the photo showing only their back views. Was she perhaps walking to her office in town as she did every day? Was he perhaps a student with less regular habits. But even if they could be found, what could they remember that would be useful?

Outside the police station, in the car park, a siren was turned on. Wilson registered the fact, but again discarded it as irrelevant to him. Then there was another noise, much closer to home. He stretched out a hand and picked up the phone. 'Hello,' a female voice said. 'St Gregory's School here.' In the several seconds it took Miss Hegarty to connect her head teacher to the Oxford police, the idea which was to plague Wilson for several days came into existence. Tiny, as yet barely formed, but nevertheless unquestionably there.

'Dr Adrian Ratcliffe, here,' a voice said tersely. 'Head teacher of St Gregory's. To whom am I speaking?'

Wilson winced at the grammatical precision of the question. 'Detective Wilson,' he replied, taking a split-second decision to obscure his own low ranking. 'Oxford Police, sir. It is very good of you to ring back so promptly.'

'What do you want,' Ratcliffe cut in, 'precisely? I do have a very exacting day in prospect, so if we could just cut to the chase.'

Wilson made a face down the phone line. 'We are just trying to complete our investigations into the death of Sarah Johnson.'

'Terrible thing,' the head teacher broke in. 'Such a terrible thing.' Wilson could almost see the man shaking his head as he spoke. 'Poor Anne, her sister, was quite distraught. You aren't wanting to speak to her, are you? I do hope not, because I have given her compassionate leave. No other family you see. I expect she is across in Oxford now, sorting out Sarah's flat. I suggest that you could always try contacting her there.' For someone who had a very busy day in prospect, it was surprising, Wilson reflected, how Dr Adrian Ratcliffe, Header Teacher of St Gregory's, appeared to have time to talk. It wasn't as if he, Wilson, had yet had the opportunity to ask a question yet. 'There must be so much for her to do,' Ratcliffe was saying. 'I had to do it for my mother. There were six large bin bags of clothes alone to take to the charity shops, let alone anything else. But doing it for a mother is one thing. That is somehow natural, part of the order of things. But to do it for your sister when you are in your mid-thirties, well that is just … just terrible.'

'So,' said Wilson, taking the opportunity offered by the lull in Ratcliffe's monologue, 'I suppose Anne is the sole heir and beneficiary?'

'Well, I imagine so,' said the busy head teacher. 'I'm pretty sure there's no other family. But you can always ask Anne herself. As I said, she's probably in Oxford.'

'We've already spoken to Anne,' Wilson said firmly.

'Well, why didn't you say so?' Ratcliffe exclaimed, 'instead of letting me rabbit on. Anyway, if you have spoken to her, why are you ringing me up?'

'When investigating, sir, it is important that we get corroboration where we can. The coroner prefers it.'

'Ah, ha!' Down the other end of the telephone call, in the office of the head teacher of St Gregory's, it seemed that the penny had suddenly dropped. 'No wonder you were so pleased for me to rabbit on.'

Wilson was feeling very pleased with how things were going, but of course he wasn't going to say so. 'Actually, sir, we just want to firm up on the details of the day of Sarah Johnson's death.'

He paused, and, in the city of Reading, Ratcliffe paused too. Two men silently taking stock. Waiting for the other to make the next move.

'Such as?' said Ratcliffe, back in terse mode.

Wilson tried to sound off hand. 'Well, for the sake of completeness, sir, can you just confirm that Anne was at St Gregory's on the morning of 21 September.'

'One moment.' Again the terse response, followed this time by nearly a minute's silence before Ratcliffe spoke again: 'Anne has a first lesson on a Friday. Then two periods off, then lessons before and after lunch. And she runs a gymnastics club after school, in the sports hall.'

'I appreciate that that is her timetable, sir,' Wilson said firmly, 'but that isn't what I asked for.' Wilson now had a definite sense that Ratcliffe was being less than straightforward. 'What I wanted to confirm whether Anne was in school as per her timetable. And if so, what time did she arrive at school?'

'Well,' said Ratcliffe with a sneer in his voice, 'I am not sure I am going to be able to give you precise details about when she arrived and so forth. We aren't a police state here you know.'

'Wouldn't she have taken a register of her class, first thing?' Wilson retorted. 'And if so, wouldn't she have signed it? As far as I am concerned, and as far as the coroner is concerned, that would be more than adequate evidence.'

'Just wait,' Ratcliffe said. 'I'll check.' Wilson smiled. No doubt Ratcliffe would take his time over the checking process, but that didn't bother him in the slightest. The head bloody teacher was rattled. The supercilious git! The wait turned out to be almost two minutes, though Wilson wasn't counting. In fact, his attention was focused again on the picture displayed on the PC monitor, picture number two of Sarah Johnson. The idea which had slipped into his mind while he was first waiting to speak to Ratcliffe was now making its presence felt. Could it … could it possibly be?

'Sorry for the delay.' It was Ratcliffe, and the tone of voice was suddenly breezy. 'You were right! I checked the register and I've had a word with the school secretary. The details of that terrible day are very fresh in her mind. Apparently Anne didn't make it to her first lesson. She had problems starting her car. Mr Ford took her place, as he had a free period, and she was in school in time for her lesson before lunch. So that would have been by 11.30 a.m. Of course, it was during that lesson we got the phone call about her sister. Now, does that about cover it, Detective?'

'Thank you,' said Wilson. 'That covers it very well. For now.'

'You look bloody pleased with yourself.' It was only five minutes later, and DS Fox had returned from the chemist and had sat down at his desk to see his young colleague smiling almost beatifically into space. 'Don't tell me the Queen has gone and invited you to her next garden party!'

Wilson laughed. 'I've just had an idea, that all.'

'An idea!' said Fox dramatically. 'Well knock me down with a feather. Detective Constable Wilson has had an idea. Are you going to share it with me, then?'

'No,' said Wilson, more firmly than he meant to. 'At least, sir, I'd rather not do so yet, until I have checked out a few things. It might be nothing.'

'Ah, the detective constable's idea may be nothing!' Fox laughed, but his heart was not in it. He got up and walked over to the corner of the room, where he switched on the kettle. 'I hope these bloody painkillers do the trick.'

Meanwhile, some thirty miles away at St Gregory's School, Reading, Dr Adrian Ratcliffe sipped at the cup of coffee that Miss Hegarty had brought in. For several seconds, he frowned. Then he picked up the telephone receiver and began to punch in a familiar set of numbers. He waited for the call to connect, and for someone, after two rings, to answer.

'It's me,' he said.

'Yes?' came a rather irritated reply.

'I'm afraid I've got some bad news for you.'

CHAPTER 7

Martin Mace brought his lorry abruptly to a halt, pulled the handbrake on, and switched the engine off. Then he leant back in his seat, shut his eyes, and blew a deep breath of air through his nostrils. He stayed there several seconds, eyes shut, and motionless except for the gentle rise and fall of his upper frame. The 6.15 start hadn't been especially early by his standards, but he felt remarkably tired. If he'd had a heavy weekend, he could have understood it, but following the goalless draw on Saturday he hadn't felt like going out and getting hammered with Al and Sam, and on Sunday he'd slept in a bit, watched the football highlights on Sky, met up with Sam for a single pint and a roast dinner at the Cricketers, and then spent the afternoon tidying up the shed on his allotment. OK, he hadn't slept that well on Saturday night or Sunday night, what with thinking about Jake, but he ought to be feeling brighter than this. Maybe a coffee would wake him up. The dirty white caravan some thirty metres in front of him didn't exactly sell itself very eloquently, but he knew from past experience that the coffee here was one of the best. He turned to pick up the *Daily Mirror* off the bench seat to his left when his mobile rang. He picked it up, looked at the display panel, and wondered who it might be. No one his phone recognized, that was for sure.

'Hello, Martin Mace here,' he said, trying to sound perky and professional. 'How may I help you?'

No one replied. Mace listened intently, but beyond the crackling interference that denoted a poor connection, he could hear only silence.

He spoke more loudly. 'Hello! Who is that?'

Again there was crackling, then a second or two of real silence, then a voice. 'Is that Mace? Martin Mace?'

'Yes,' he replied, speaking loudly and with exaggerated care. If this was someone offering him work, he didn't want to lose it.

'Martin Mace the lorry driver?'

'Yes, that's right. Can I help you?' He spoke eagerly, too eagerly perhaps. He only had three days of driving lined up this week, and two the next. He needed more.

'Martin Mace of Oxford?'

'Yes.'

'Martin Mace who lives in Meadow Lane, Oxford?'

'Yes.' But this time Mace's voice was quieter. Something about this caller – he wasn't quite sure what – was unsettling. He waited for a reply, but none came. Only anxiety came, creeping across the airwaves, out of the earpiece of his mobile, and down into his stomach like some invisible alien virus. And anxiety was closely followed by anger and aggression.

'Who are you?' He spat the question noisily into his mobile.

'Five hundred pounds.'

The anxiety receded. A job. 'You've got a job for me?'

'That's right. This is what I want you to do.' The words came out slowly, deliberately. 'I want you to go to the bank, withdraw five hundred pounds, and give it to me.'

'Is that you Al? Because if it is, let me tell you it ain't very bloody funny. You're pissing me off.'

'Listen!' The word was shouted down the line so loudly that Mace gave an involuntary start. 'Because you are pissing me off, Mister bleeding Mace. This is serious. Deadly serious.

94

I know you, and I know your dirty little secret. I know what happened on May the fifth, and I know that if you don't get the money today, and leave it wherever I say, then I will be telling the police about it too. Do you understand?'

A shadow passed across Mace's cab, as a large freighter from Poland pulled past, bumping and grinding over the uneven surface, as it sought a parking placing beyond the caravan.

'Do you understand?'

Mace nodded his head, as if his questioner was directly in front of him. 'Yes,' he said quietly, then more loudly, 'Yes.'

Mace waited for a reply – for some sort of instructions – but all he heard was a click as the caller hung up. Beyond the caravan, the Polish freighter rocked to a halt as its air brakes were applied. Mace watched as its driver climbed down, walked back towards him along the side of his lorry, and then turned right towards the bushes, where he proceeded to straddle his legs and urinate. Mace sat unmoving, his face transfixed. The man pulled at his zip, turned, and looked up, suddenly aware that he was being observed. He lifted his right hand, thrust a V-sign defiantly at Mace, and walked back round his lorry and past it, until he reached the caravan.

Mace, all thoughts of coffee abandoned, placed his mobile back into its cradle, connected up his seat belt, and turned the key in the ignition.

'He looks a bit rattled,' Holden said to Fox as they pulled up in front of the Evergreen Day Centre. She was referring to Jim Blunt. She had rung up and warned him they wanted to come round and speak to him about Jake, and even though they were three minutes early, he was standing outside the front with two other men, ostensibly smoking, but in reality, Holden reckoned, watching. Before the car had come to a halt, he was moving forward towards them, waving a welcome. Gone was the studied insouciance of Friday, when he had made them wait while he addressed his day centre.

'He's probably feeling guilty,' Fox said in a matter-of-fact tone.

'Of what?' Holden asked.

Fox turned the engine off, and turned to look at her.

'Of what?' Holden repeated. 'He can wait,' she added, her eyes indicating that 'he' was Blunt, who had now stopped, rather awkwardly, in front of the car.

'When I was staying with my sister, we went out in the car one morning, to get some more paint. She was driving, and we were going along the main road when she suddenly said "There's a police car behind us." "Yes", I said to her, "so there is, and there's also a policeman sitting in the seat next to you!" I remember that I laughed. But you know what she did, she pulled into a bus stop about fifty metres in front of us, so that the police car would go past. I was going to laugh again, but one look at her face stopped me. "You probably think I'm silly, Derek," she said, "but I can't bear being followed by a police car. I feel I must have done something wrong, broken the speed limit, jumped the traffic lights, or knocked down an old lady without noticing. Even though I know I haven't, I still feel guilty." '

Holden released her seat belt, and finally acknowledged Blunt's presence with a brief wave. Then she turned her face back towards Fox. 'What sort of creatures would we be if we never had feelings of guilt? Nothing more than animals, I guess.' And with that, she opened the car door and got out.

Blunt took them not to the small room with the dirty arm-chairs, but to a slightly larger room that served as his office. The centre of the room was taken up by a large desk that had clearly seen better days. It was in its turn dominated by the usual para-phernalia of computer, monitor, keyboard, mouse and printer. The only other item on the desk was a nest of three wire filing trays, the top one of which was marked 'In', the middle one 'Pending', and the bottom one 'Out'. It was behind this defensive wall that Blunt now sat, after briefly waving his visitors to a pair of red plastic chairs on the near side of the room.

'So,' he said, nonchalantly, and looking at Holden, 'what was it you wanted to talk to me about?'

Holden turned and gave a brief nod of her head to Fox. She had no intention of giving Blunt an easy ride. And as she and Fox had discovered from experience, one of the best ways to start that process was to confuse the interviewee over who the interviewer was.

'I'd have thought you would have guessed, sir,' Fox said firmly.

'Guessed?' Blunt said cautiously.

'Well, you being an intelligent sort of man, sir.' He spoke calmly, quietly. He paused, then smiled. 'And, of course, with the sort of history you've got—'

'Look,' Blunt said with irritation, 'I have a day centre to run, so I don't have time to play guessing games.'

'And we have a murderer to find, sir,' Fox said evenly, 'so we don't have time to waste, and that's why I am hoping you will cooperate sir.'

'Of course I'll cooperate,' Blunt blustered.

'Like you did on Friday?' said Holden, briefly entering the fray and forcing Blunt's attention to her.

'What do you mean?' Blunt replied, suddenly uncertain.

'On Friday,' Fox stated, again forcing Blunt to switch his attention and gaze, 'you stated that you and Jake Arnold got on well enough.'

'Did I?' Blunt said.

'You also said he was a bit idle and occasionally needed the proverbial kick up the backside.'

'Sounds about right,' Blunt acknowledged.

'But you didn't mention, sir, that Jake had made allegations that you had bullied him.' Fox stopped, looked evenly at Blunt, and waited for a response. Blunt looked back at him, but said nothing. For several seconds there was silence, until Holden broke in.

'Were the allegations true?'

'No!' Blunt snapped the word back.

'But they were damaging, to you, I imagine,' Holden continued. 'On the no-smoke-without-fire basis.'

'It was his word against mine. I've been running this centre for three years. He's been here a bare six months. Who are they going to believe. Him or me?'

Fox liked interviewing with Holden. They worked together well. He liked the fact that she didn't take over, and he found that he could tell instinctively when it was his turn to talk, and when his turn to shut up. 'Tell us about how you came to leave the army, sir. You were only there three years, which doesn't seem that long, really.'

The change of direction appeared to throw Blunt off balance. He looked hard at Fox, then back at Holden. The colour that had flared up just before now receded as quickly. Fox, scenting a breakthrough, pushed a little more.

'I understand you got into a fight, and you made such a mess of the guy you were fighting that he ended up in hospital. Or maybe it's something you prefer not to discuss publicly.'

But Fox had misjudged his quarry. Blunt leant back in his chair so far that it rocked up on its back legs. Then he smiled.

'I left the army with a clean slate. In fact, my CO gave me a glowing reference for Civvy Street. He liked the fact that I stood up for myself. The guy came at me with a broken bottle. I stopped him. The fact that he ended up in hospital for two months was his look-out, not mine. He got what he deserved.'

'Did Jake get what he deserved, do you think?' Fox said, with an edge of anger in his voice.

Blunt stood up suddenly. His face was red again, and his hands, Holden noticed, were clenched. 'End of interview,' he snarled. 'My army career has nothing to do with Jake.' He pointed the forefinger of his right hand aggressively at Fox. 'If you want to make any more insinuations, Detective, you can do so in front of a solicitor. Right?'

'No need for that,' Holden said mildly. She sat unmoving in her chair, refusing to be intimidated by his aggression. She knew Fox had gone too far, but she wasn't displeased with the outcome. 'No more questions. But I would like to speak to Danny. Is he around?'

When the bell of flat 2, number 12 Marston Street rang at 10.45 a.m., Anne Johnson had only just dressed. She had always – or at least as far back as she could remember – been an owl rather than a lark, so the opportunity for lying in that three weeks of compassionate leave offered was one she had seized at eagerly. Her hair was still wet from the shower, and as she moved toward the front door she hastily tightened the towel which she had twisted turban-style around her head.

'Oh,' she said as she pulled back the door, 'it's you.'

Detective Constable Wilson felt the disappointment in her voice, but ignored it.

'Good morning, Ms Johnson,' he said with his most winning smile. 'I hope this isn't inconvenient for you. It's just that I was in the area and I was wondering if—'

He never completed his sentence because a snort of words erupted from the mouth of Anne Johnson. 'In the area! In the area?' It was strange, she thought, how much less cute he looked this morning. 'Did they teach you that chat-up line at police school?' she continued scornfully. Wilson's poise collapsed like a sandcastle swamped by an unexpectedly large wave. He had been looking forward to interviewing Anne Johnson – she had a sense of fun and spirit that had impressed him on his earlier meeting – but he realized now that he had misread her badly.

'Don't they teach you manners in the police kindergarten, then? Or at least the importance of making an appointment rather than just turning up unannounced on someone's doorstep. Because if you had rung, at least I could have got my hair dry before you arrived with your notebook in your hand.'

'I am so sorry,' Wilson said, floundering in the torrent of her onslaught. 'If you want, I can go away and come back another time when it's—'

His words faded into silence as she turned back into the flat. But instead of slamming the door in his face, she gestured him inside. When he paused, she snapped angrily. 'Oh, for goodness sake, let's just get this over and done with.' She stood in the corridor, by the side of the door, leaving just enough room for him to enter. He did so by turning side on as he approached her, thus ensuring he could pass inside without risking brushing against her. His strategy had been to call on her unexpectedly in order to gain some element of surprise, but he knew that it was she who had outsmarted him.

He made his way along the short corridor into the living room. As if drawn by some magnetic force field, he found himself walking over to and sitting down in exactly the same armchair where Fox had sat a few days earlier. He gestured towards the sofa opposite. 'Would you like to—?'

'No!' she said brutally. 'I'd rather stand.' Wilson squirmed. 'This won't take long, will it?' she asked, and again adjusted the towel round her hair, as if to say that in the scheme of things drying and caring for her hair came somewhat higher up the pecking order than humouring young coppers on the make.

'No,' he replied. 'But I do need to check a few things out.' He paused, expecting some sharp response, but she said nothing. He looked up at her. She had placed her right hand on her hip, and she was examining the nails of the left one without obvious interest – a picture of boredom. 'Well?' she snapped.

Wilson swallowed. 'I just wanted to check where you were on the morning of your sister's death.'

'What a curious question!' she said, with a somewhat forced laugh.

'Not really,' Wilson replied, determined to wrest back some control. 'You are her closest relation, and we are trying to establish the precise circumstances of her death.'

'I was at work,' she said firmly. 'I'm a teacher at St Gregory's in Reading.'

'Can you be more precise please?'

'Precise!? What do you mean? I was in the middle of a lesson when you lot rang the school to tell me my sister was dead. Is that precise enough or do you need to know what subject I was teaching, which class I was teaching, which outfit I was wearing, what I'd had for breakfast—'

'No!' said Wilson, firmly, alarmed by the hysteria in her voice. Then he made a mistake 'It's just that Dr Ratcliffe told me—'

'Dr Ratcliffe!' she snorted. 'What has Dr bloody Ratcliffe been saying?'

'Well,' said Wilson, trying not to be distracted. 'He said you were in late that morning. That you had trouble starting the car.'

'It's not a crime to be late for work is it?'

'Who did you call?' Wilson spoke casually, but he kept his eyes firmly on her face, anxious to see her reaction. 'The AA? The RAC? Because they'll have a record of the time and place.'

'Neither.' She said the word without emotion.

'Someone else then?'

Anne Johnson let out a sigh and smiled at Wilson. 'I fibbed.'

Wilson tried to hold a sudden surge of excitement in check. 'I think you'll have to explain. Please!'

The smile had faded from her face, to be replaced by a look that Wilson hoped indicated anxiety, though he had a sense that Anne Johnson was still playing him. His unease was increased as she moved round the sofa behind which she had been standing, and sat down opposite him. She leant forward, and spoke quietly as if about to share a confidence with a best friend. 'Actually I overslept. So I rang up the school and said I'd couldn't get the car started. Just a little white lie.'

Wilson in turn leant forward, refusing to be intimidated. 'Why not say you overslept? Surely it happens occasionally. After all, it's hardly a sackable offence.'

She laughed softly. 'I think Dr Ratcliffe preferred my white lie. Anyway, he was hardly going to argue. Not when he'd been round at my house the evening before. Fucking me. In fact he can confirm precisely where I was between

7.00 p.m. and 10.00 pm. But not, of course, after that, because then he went back to his lovely wife and children to play happy families.'

'I see,' Wilson said.

'I doubt it,' she replied bitterly.

'Maybe he's done a runner!' Fox volunteered as they swung right into the Iffley Road. Holden said nothing. She briefly shut her eyes, not because she was tired, but because she wanted to try and focus her thoughts. She wanted Fox to shut up, but she couldn't quite bring herself to say so. She felt the car brake, and heard Fox curse a cyclist who had apparently had the temerity to swerve out in front of him. She kept her eyes firmly shut, but focusing was proving elusive. She wanted to concentrate on Blunt, but it was Alan from church who she kept remembering. What was it he had said? 'Jake said something very odd.' The car accelerated, pushing her back gently into the seat. 'He said, maybe she didn't jump.'

Now, why did Jake say that? Why?

'There he is!' For a moment Holden didn't know who Fox was talking about. Then the moment passed, and her eyes snapped open.

'On the left!' Fox said, his voice betraying sudden excitement.

'Steady,' Holden said firmly. 'We don't want to alarm him. We don't want him running off.'

Danny Flynn didn't look in the least bit like he was going to run off. In fact, in the time it took for Fox to pull the car over to the right-hand side of the road and bring it to a gentle halt opposite him, he didn't seem to move a muscle. He was looking up, across the road, above them, one hand shading his eyes. Holden got carefully out of the car, looked left and right, and walked steadily across the road. Danny's eyes flicked down, taking in her arrival, but then returned to their previous position.

'There's someone in there.'

She looked up too, following his intent gaze.

'Look, they've turned the light on,' he said, and the hand that had been shielding his eyes now pointed at the window at the top of the house opposite. Danny's flat.

'Maybe you left the light on, Danny, when you left this morning.'

'I didn't.' His hand lowered back towards his eyes. 'Someone's in my room.'

'Do you want me to take a look?' Fox had followed Holden across the road, and was standing just behind her.

Danny's eyes flicked again, this time across at Fox, but again only momentarily before returning to their aerial vigil. They squinted, trying to access the shadows beyond the windows. Danny moved his head, first left and then right, tilting it as he did, trying to get a different angle that might somehow reveal the unseen intruder. Finally, he turned and looked again at Fox. 'At your own risk,' he said. Then he put his right hand into his back pocket, pulled out a jangle of keys, and thrust them at the big detective. 'It's the purple one,' he added.

As Fox walked across the road, Danny lifted his head up again to resume his search for intruders.

'Danny,' Holden said quietly, standing at his shoulder, and looking up at the window too. 'I need to ask you some questions.' She paused. Danny said nothing. 'About Sarah. And about Jake. It's very important.'

'Shouldn't you have called for back-up?' Danny asked, his mind still anchored in the present. 'Suppose he gets hurt.'

'I'm the back-up,' she said firmly. 'But Detective Fox can look after himself, don't you worry.'

'I don't want blood on the carpet,' he said. 'I'll never get it clean.'

'Do you remember where you were last Thursday night, Danny?' She said it casually, as if the answer mattered not a jot. Danny, to her surprise answered immediately.

'Of course. I was in my flat. All evening.'

'You're sure?'

'Of course I'm sure. That was when Jake died wasn't it. I remember working out that I must have been watching Morse when he was killed.'

'Morse?' Holden echoed.

'I've got the whole set on DVD. It was *The Dead of Jericho*, about this woman that Morse meets at a party and then she goes and gets hanged and there are two brothers and—' Suddenly he paused, and then he lifted his right hand and wagged his index finger. 'Ah! Mustn't tell you anymore. You might not have watched it? Do policemen watch Morse?'

'Did anyone watch Morse with you, Danny?'

'No,' he said. Then he smiled at her, and again he waved his finger as if lecturing her. 'That means I've no alibi, which is bad for me, but it makes it more interesting for you. But I didn't kill him, so I've got nothing to worry about.'

Holden decided to change tack. 'Why do you think Sarah jumped from the car park?'

The question had a dramatic effect on Danny. He twisted his body towards her and looked at her with a face which had crumpled into sudden grief. He opened his mouth, but only three strangled words came out. 'I failed her!' he said. 'I failed her!'

From their left came the sound of sirens. Automatically Holden turned, as two fire engines appeared from over Magdalen Bridge. She watched as they negotiated the roundabout, then accelerated towards her, sirens still blaring. Then they were passed, and across the road she saw the figure of Fox appearing through the front door. He was smiling and gave a thumbs up. 'It's OK Danny. There's no one there.'

It was 2.35 that afternoon that Wilson got called through to DI Holden's office. He hastily locked his computer – on which he had again been trawling through the photos taken by Bicknell – and strode along the corridor. The door was ajar, but he knocked before he pushed it open.

'Wilson, good of you to join us.' The words, and even more the tone of voice in which they were expressed, flashed a warning across Wilson's brain, but he ignored it.

'Not at all, Guv. I mean, I was busy with something but—'

'Fox tells me that you've been holding out on us,' she said sharply.

Wilson blinked, blushed and looked across to Fox, who was sitting casually in the chair to the right of Holden's desk.

'I'm not sure what you mean, Guv,' he said, turning back to Holden. But her face was hard and uncompromising, as were her words. 'We are a team, Wilson. You, me and Detective Sergeant Fox here, we are a team. We may be three separate individuals, each with our own strengths, weaknesses and idiosyncrasies, but we are first and foremost a team. We work together. We share. As far as an investigation is concerned, we share everything. Right, Wilson.'

'Yes, Ma'am,' he said quickly.

'So, Wilson, when your colleague asks you about an idea you have had, you bloody well tell him.'

'Yes, Ma'am,' Wilson said again.

'I prefer "Yes Guv", Wilson, if it's alright by you. But that's beside the point. The point is that you will now share with both of us the idea that you refused to share with DS Fox this morning.'

Wilson was now a picture of abject embarrassment, face flushed, hands twisting uncomfortably at his tie. 'Sorry Guv,' he mumbled. Then, more firmly, and looking across at Fox. 'Sorry Sergeant. It's just that … ' He paused, trying to find the right words, 'the fact is it may be a pretty stupid idea and—'

'Spit it out, Wilson,' Holden interrupted, though in a tone less sharp than previously.

'Well,' he said, 'I was wondering if the woman in Bicknell's pictures really was Sarah. I mean the two sisters are very alike, aren't they, and I just wondered if maybe the woman in the photo was Anne.' He stopped, and waited to see Holden's response.

Fox leaning further back in his chair gave a low whistle. Holden leant forward, her attention fully gained.

'Can you fill in the detail a bit, Wilson? What makes you think Anne was even in Oxford? Doesn't she work in Reading.'

'At St Gregory's,' Wilson confirmed. 'But she was in late that day. Missed her first lesson. Rang in and said she couldn't get her car started.'

'You don't believe her?'

'When I questioned her about it, and asked her if she had used the AA or RAC, she admitted she had lied to the head master. That's Dr Adrian Ratcliffe, with whom she also has some sort of sexual relationship. She says she merely over-slept. She said Ratcliffe had come round the previous evening and, erm ... and fucked her. That was what she said.'

'What time did she get to school then?'

'She was definitely in by 11.30, when she took a lesson, but there's no written record of when she arrived. I suppose if we asked around the staff we might be able to tie it down.'

'But the key thing,' Holden said, 'if I understand it correctly, is that Anne could have been in Oxford at the time of Sarah's death.'

'Yes.'

For a moment the three of them were silent. Fox, still leaning back in his chair as if in one of his beloved multiplex cinemas, began to hum the first few bars of a half-forgotten song from his childhood, then suddenly stopped. 'Sorry to be the wet blanket here, but the fact that Anne lied to her school doesn't mean anything unless we've some evidence that she was in Oxford. Or have you something else you're not telling us, Wilson?'

The sharpness of his comment caused Holden to swivel in her chair and direct a glare hard at Fox, but she said nothing. Instead she turned back towards Wilson: 'Well, Wilson? The sergeant may not have been to charm school, but he is essentially right.'

Wilson swallowed. 'No hard evidence, Guv,' he admitted, 'but I just got the feeling that Anne Johnson was lying. She was evasive, if you know what I mean.'

'That's not enough, Wilson,' Holden said, leaning forward to make her point. 'You need evidence which puts her in Oxford that morning. Let's assume that she was in Oxford and let's assume that she drove over and had some sort of row with her sister. Where did she park her car? Not much room in the street if she arrived early in the morning, or even the night before. More likely she used the car park. Have you checked the CCTV? There's one on the entrance to the car park.'

'No Guv, I haven't,' Wilson admitted.

'Ideas are good, but evidence is better, Wilson. And then there's motive. Plenty of motives between family members. Have you contacted Sarah's solicitor about the will.'

'No, Guv.'

'Not to worry. I'll deal with that. You concentrate on the CCTV. And Fox,' she said swivelling again towards him, 'maybe you'd go and visit the local shops with the photos Bicknell took, and see if they recall seeing her call in for a paper or anything that morning. In fact, give the *Mail* a ring and get a list of anyone they interviewed in connection with the suicide. Maybe one of them will remember something.'

She paused, and Wilson started to get up to go. 'Why were you suspicious of the photo?' she cut in. 'You never said.'

Wilson pursed his lips. 'It's the coat she was wearing, Guv. A long fawn mackintosh. I just thought it was a bit odd. I checked the weather. There hadn't been any rain, and there wasn't any rain later. It was a warm night too. So why was she wearing it? And why had she buttoned and belted it up. Then I got thinking that if it was Anne pretending to be Sarah, a long coat was just what she needed to hide the fact that she was wearing different clothes underneath from what Sarah was wearing.'

Holden leant back in her chair and surveyed Wilson coolly. Her right hand began to drum a pattern of notes on

107

the desktop. 'Hmm!' she said finally, her eyes still fixed on her young constable. 'You really have been holding out on us, Wilson. But in the circumstances, we'll put it down to inexperience. Now, I suggest you chase up that CCTV.'

CHAPTER 8

William Basham of Basham and Smith, Solicitors, stood up as DI Holden came into his office. 'Good afternoon, Inspector,' he said. 'And welcome.' He gestured gently towards the leather chair which faced his desk. 'Please!'

'Thank you,' Holden replied, and surprisingly she meant it. Old-fashioned courtesy was not something she came across too often in her working day, nor did she expect or want it. But somehow here, from this rather old-fashioned man, it seemed appropriate. The building in which Basham and Smith had set up business was a rather ugly 1970s construction, but inside Basham's office it was all tasteful, almost genteel elegance and comfort, as if in defiance of the area in which it was based. William Basham's clothes were also defiantly unmodern. The dark-grey pin-striped suit which hung loosely from his slight frame was discreet and, Holden judged, hand-made. She half expected to look round and see a bowler hat sitting on the side, waiting for his departure home, home not being, she was fairly sure, anywhere too close to Cowley.

'Would you like a cup of tea, Inspector?' Basham continued, the exchange of courtesies not yet apparently complete.

'Thank you, but no,' Holden replied. 'This should only take a few minutes, I hope.'

'Of course, I am sure you are busy, Inspector, but in my experience sometimes one should force oneself to make ones day a little less busy, to take a breather, as it were, from the relentless pace of ones work.'

'I'm sure you are right, Mr Basham,' Holden said, nodding her head as if in deference, 'and I acknowledge your greater experience, but the sooner I get this over with, the sooner I can finish work for the day. So I would prefer to skip the tea and move to the point of my visit. If you don't mind.'

'Ah, a woman of character, I can see,' he said cheerfully. 'Bravo. And to cut to the business, then, you said over the telephone that you were interested in my deceased client, Sarah Johnson, of Marston Street, Oxford.'

'Yes, as part of our investigation, I need to clarify the terms of her will.'

'I suspected as much,' William Basham said, opening a folder on his desk. 'After you telephoned, I took the precaution of reading through her testament again to remind myself of its terms.' He slowly turned the pages of the document within it, as if a single re-reading was not sufficient. Finally, he closed the folder and looked up.

'It's all very straight forward,' he said. 'She left everything to her sister, Anne.'

'When did she make her will?'

'Three years ago.'

'And she has made no changes to the will since first drawing it up?'

Basham frowned briefly. 'No, but—' He didn't finish his sentence, instead opening the folder again.

'But what?' Holden said, irritation with the ponderousness of William Basham beginning to show in her tone of voice.

'She was due to come and see me on Thursday.'

'Oh!' said Holden, her interest suddenly raised. 'And why was that?'

'She wanted to make some changes to her will.'

'Really?' Holden said, fighting to keep her sudden excitement at this development under control. 'I wonder if you could tell me what these changes were?'

'I'm afraid not,' he said, with a slight shake of the head. 'You see, that's what we were going to discuss on Thursday.'

'Didn't she give any clue when she rang up? I mean, do you think it is possible that she going to cut her sister out of the will?'

Basher leant back and smiled, enjoying his position of strength. 'Who knows? Maybe she just wanted to leave fifty pounds to the local cat sanctuary. But as one reflects on it, one can't help but find it a bit odd.'

For a brief but brilliant moment, Holden wanted to grab the self-satisfied ass sitting opposite her by the lapels and shake him as she had once seen a Jack Russell terrier shake a rat till its neck was well and truly broken. Not that she wanted to damage him, merely to shake the mannered pomposity out of him. But instead she counted silently to five, and then said in muted tones: 'Tell, me, Mr Basham. What precisely do you find odd.'

Basham leant forward, the smile still fixed to his face. 'Well, the fact that a person might kill herself days before she was about to make a new will. Somehow, it doesn't make a great deal of sense.' His smile widened even further. 'Does it, Inspector?'

Tracking down someone who had seen Sarah, or her sister pretending to be Sarah, shortly before she had plunged to her death proved, in the event, a straightforward task. But first Fox decided to try and recreate for himself the route she would have taken from her flat in Marston Street to the car park. Along Marston Street she would have walked, then left at the corner as far as the pedestrian crossing, then across the Cowley Road and left again for fifty metres, and then there was the car park. The obvious option for a pedestrian, Fox told himself, was to walk along the front of the car park, past where the student Bicknell had set up his senseless experiment that morning, and then use the stairwell in that far corner of the building. However, suppose, just bloody suppose, that Wilson was right. That the person in Bicknell's photos was not Sarah en route to her death, but Anne? Suppose, Fox thought, that they had both originally gone to the car together. And suppose Anne had wanted them to avoid Bicknell and his camera, then she could have turned right down the side of the car park as soon as they reached it, and led her sister in by the door near the entrance for cars. When they got to the car, parked on the top level, Anne could then have made an excuse – say, she'd forgotten her car keys – and asked her sister to stay with her bag at the car while she returned to get it from the flat. Only she didn't go to the flat, but merely came back down to the street before returning to Sarah. Only this time, she took care to use the more obvious entrance, walking past the student and looking at his plaque for long enough to make sure he would remember her (or, even better, photograph her). So what were the complications in all of this? There was the coat. How the hell did she get that coat onto her sister after she had gone back up to the car? It was this detail that was bothering Fox as he stood at the top of the car park looking down. Whose coat was it in the first place, he suddenly wondered. Sarah's? In which case Anne could just have borrowed it that morning to walk to the car. Or was it Anne's? Did she offer her sister to try it on, or even give it to her as a parting gift? And then what? They look over the car park wall together. Maybe Anne says: 'Look at that student artist down there. You won't believe what he is doing!' Sarah leans over further to get a better look, and then a quick push and she is screaming and falling to her death.

Fucking hell, Fox thought as he made his way down, Wilson really could be right. He really could. But the problem was they had no evidence. They needed a witness.

Yousef Mohammed owned the little general stores shop on the corner of Marston Street and Cowley Road. Did he recognize the woman in the picture, Fox enquired. Of course he did. It was the poor woman who jumped from the car park. So sad. 'She was a regular customer,' Yousef continued proudly. 'Miss Johnson was always popping in for this or that. I think she must have shopped for most things at Tesco's, but like many people if it's just a pack of eggs or a pint of milk you need, then it's easier to call in on your local shop. I may be a bit more pricey,' he grinned, 'but I provide the personal touch, and I am very convenient. And, of course, she always bought her newspaper here.'

'Always?' Fox interrupted. 'Did she have an order with you then?'

'Oh, no,' he said, still smiling. 'She just called in most days and bought one.'

'Do you remember if she bought one the morning of her death?'

For several seconds, Yousef was silent, as he tried hard to remember. Then his face suddenly lit up again. 'No,' he said triumphantly, 'she didn't. I know because I saw her at the door. She hovered outside for a few moments, and I thought to myself, here comes Miss Johnson for her *Daily Mail*. But she didn't come in, she just walked on.'

'What was she wearing? Do you remember?'

'But of course! She was wearing that long coat she is wearing in the picture. I liked it. I like it when women cover themselves up. It shows they have respect for themselves. I remember thinking it was a shame she didn't come in and buy her *Daily Mail*, because then I could have told her how nice she looked.'

'Thank you, sir,' Fox said. 'You've been very helpful. But there is one more thing I'd like to ask you. Do you remember what time it was you saw her?'

Again the grin gave way to a frown, but only for a second of two. 'Not exactly. But of course it can't have been very long before the poor woman's death. Maybe 10 minutes, maybe 15. It is very hard to be sure. You see, it's a very busy time of the morning for me. No time to watch the time, if you know what I mean!' And he laughed at his own joke.

Wilson placed the DVD into his PC and waited as it hummed into life. Technology, he would have been the first to admit, is a wonderful thing, but technology only takes you so far. As he deftly wielded his mouse and started the DVD playing, he was conscious he still had a substantial task in front of him. It hadn't been difficult to get hold of CCTV coverage from the cameras installed at the car park, one covering the entrance and one the exit. But he still had to trawl through the footage and try to identify Anne Johnson's car. It was a yellow Mini, and its number was OU12 AHG. And, of course, it might not be on the film at all, for she may not have come to Oxford at all. Or she might have come to Oxford, but parked somewhere discreetly out of the way of prying security cameras. In which case, Wilson might sit up late into the evening, and yet find absolutely nothing to support his theory.

He had decided to check the exit gate footage first. If Anne had driven to Oxford and had parked in the car park, and had left the car park shortly after the death of her sister, then all he had to do was search between 9.00 a.m. and 9.15 a.m. and it ought in theory to be easy to spot her car departing and thereby prove that she had been lying. Wilson quickly located 8.59 a.m. on the film, and then sat to wait for the Mini to appear. The precise time of Sarah's death was clear: a passing pedestrian had phoned the emergency services from a mobile at 9.08 a.m. Allowing for a minute or two of panic, this fixed Sarah's fall to about 9.06 or 9.07, Wilson reckoned. That was the key period of time. Wilson watched in fascination as the time at the bottom of the screen progressed. Not surprisingly, very few cars left the car park at that time of the morning. First there was a red Fiat Uno at 9.01, then a rather battered blue Montego estate at 9.02. Then nothing. 9.06 came, 9.07, then suddenly a Mini, only it was a black one, with the wrong number plate. Then again a gap. A couple of minutes more passed before a white van followed, then nothing for three, four, five more minutes. At last, another car, this time a dark-green Ford Galaxy, but then again nothing, until Wilson had to admit that it was past 9.15 and no yellow Mini (with or without a number of OU12 AHG) had left the car park. Wilson leant back in his chair and looked up at the ceiling. He was not yet ready to give up. She could have left earlier. Maybe the woman in Bicknell's photos was Sarah, walking to her suicide, but Anne had lied about her car breaking down. Why? Because she had overslept? Wilson shook his head. 'Hardly!' he said out loud, though there was no one in the office to hear him.

Quickly his right hand took hold of the mouse again and rewound the film to 8.00. a.m. This time he played it forward at speed, stopping whenever a car left the car park. There was a spate of three between 8.03 and 8.04 a.m., people who had no doubt parked overnight and were now off to work. Then nothing, a long gap until 8.30 when … Wilson almost gave a whoop of excitement. There it was. Her car. Her yellow Mini. The black windows hid the face of the driver, but the number plate was undeniable. OU12 AHG.

Triumphantly, Wilson printed off several still shots of the Mini, then switched DVDs and began to scroll through the film of cars entering. At 6.30 a white van arrived. The same one as he had seen leaving, Wilson wondered, and made a note of the registration number. Ten minutes later another vehicle arrived. The yellow Mini. Anne Johnson's Mini. 'Jackpot!' Wilson shouted to no one. 'I've hit the bloody jackpot!'

Mace stood outside the shed on his allotment and shone his torch onto his watch. 8.25 p.m. Five minutes early. He looked around, peering into the darkness. He could see no one, hear no one, feel no one.

The phone call had come at 3.30 p.m. He had been in his kitchen, stirring his mug of tea. He had let the mobile ring three times. Only then had he grabbed it off the kitchen worktop, flipped it open, and begun to panic. Even as he had raised it to his ear, the vein down the left-hand side of his neck had started to throb violently.

'Hello?' He had tried to speak calmly, but the simple word was distorted by anxiety.

There had been a brief pause, then a voice. The voice.

'Have you got the money?'

'Yes!'

'All of it?'

'Yes.'

'Take it to your allotment tonight. 8.30 p.m. And take your mobile.'

That was all.

And now here he was at his allotment. Another minute passed, and another, and then a phone rang. Only it wasn't his mobile. He swung his torch round so that it pierced the dark like a searchlight, but it found no one. Only his shed. The shed. The sound of a ringing phone was coming from inside his shed. He trained the torch on the door of the shed, and moved cautiously towards it. The lock, he suddenly realized, was missing. Someone had ripped it right off the door. Nervously, he leant forward and grasped the door handle with his free hand. It opened easily, squeaking slightly. He must oil the hinges again, he thought to himself. He moved forward, playing the beam of the torch around the interior of the shed. No one there. Only – on the floor – a mobile phone, the source of the ringing noise. He leant down and picked it up. Carefully he raised it to his ear. 'Hello!'

'Hello!' came the answer, only it didn't come from the mobile. It came from behind him, from a figure that lurked, almost invisible, in the darkness. A split second later, a heavy blunt instrument smashed into the back of his head, causing him to collapse into oblivion on the floor of the shed.

CHAPTER 9

'Good morning, Ma'am.'

DI Holden's mind was elsewhere, indeed so far distant from the present moment that she completely failed to register the greeting of the young WPC at her shoulder. She locked her car door and turned obliviously towards the station.

'Ma'am!' This time the woman's voice was louder and firmer, and it produced the desired effect of causing the Detective Inspector to turn and appraise its source.

'Good morning, Constable!' she replied, but without enthusiasm, and she turned her face back towards the station, pressing forward up the slight incline that would lead her ultimately to the peace of her office.'

'Your label is sticking out, Ma'am.'

This time Holden stopped fully, and turned to face her interlocutor full on. 'Sorry!' she snapped. 'Did you say something?'

The younger woman flushed, taken aback by the sharpness of her tone. But she was not a person to melt away. 'With respect, I merely wanted to tell you your label was sticking out. If you'll allow me—' And without waiting for a reply, she moved forward round the side of her superior and stretched her hand out towards the nape of her neck. 'Just one moment, Ma'am,' she said softly, and with the gentlest of touches she folded the offending white label out of sight. 'There!' she finished, and then stepped a pace backwards.

'Oh!' Holden said, as enlightenment finally dawned. She paused, embarrassed by her own ill temper. 'Thank you, um, Constable.'

'Lawson. WPC Jan Lawson,' the constable responded. Lawson had no intention of letting this opportunity slip by. She had heard only good things of Holden from the other women in the station in the three weeks since her transfer from Northampton. 'If you don't mind me asking, how is the case going, Ma'am?'

Holden frowned. 'I do mind, Constable, as it happens.'

Lawson cursed herself silently. 'Sorry, Ma'am. I didn't mean to be nosey. It's just that—' She paused, genuinely lost for words. She knew what she wanted to say, but how to say it, how to take this one chance that might not come again? 'It's just that I imagine there must be a lot to do, and well, one day I'd like to be doing what you're doing, so I just wanted to say that if you needed any more personnel, then maybe you would keep in mind that I'm here. I know I'm inexperienced, but I'll do anything.'

Lawson fell silent, and waited as Holden continued to survey her. For a moment or three, she looked back into Holden's eyes, and then submissively dropped her gaze to the ground.

Holden gave a half smile. 'I'll keep that in mind, Constable Lawson,' she said, before walking purposefully on towards the station again.

DI Holden's stock-taking session started at 8.30 a.m. Tuesday morning, and – for reasons beyond her control – lasted barely ten minutes. It was, however, time enough to draw conclusions of some validity. Wilson arrived at his boss's office about ten seconds after Fox, and entered the room whistling the theme tune of his favourite soap Neighbours (not that he got to watch it too often these days).

'OK, Wilson,' Holden said briskly, as the detective constable shut the door, 'let's be hearing from you. You look like the cat that got the cream, so share with us whatever it is you found out!'

'Morning, Guv!' answered Wilson cheerfully, enjoying his moment, and pulling a chair forward.

'Cut the niceties, Wilson!' she warned.

'Sorry, Guv!'

'And don't bloody apologize, either. Just speak.'

'Sorry!' he said, and immediately realized his mistake. Fox laughed loudly. Holden raised her eyebrows in an exaggerated fashion, and looked ostentatiously at her watch. 'She lied!' Wilson said firmly. Fox's laughter died. 'Anne Johnson lied,' Wilson continued. 'She came to Oxford the morning of her sister's death. We have it on camera. We have her driving her car into the multi-storey car park at 6.40 in the morning, and leaving at 8.30.'

'You're sure?' Holden said.

'Yes, it was a yellow Mini and the registration number—'

'Not the car, Wilson!' Holden said sharply. 'Her. Can you be sure she was driving it. Can you see her face clearly?'

Wilson paused before answering. 'The windows and windscreen are that dark, reflective glass. You can see out, but not in.'

'So it could have been someone else driving?'

'Well, yes, I suppose so, but why—'

'Anything else you found out, Wilson?' Holden spoke curtly, so that Wilson looked down at his knees, anxious to avoid her gaze. 'No, Guv,' he said quietly.

'Right, Fox,' she said, swinging her attention to the Detective Sergeant. 'What can you add?'

Fox, who was used to Holden, gave a rueful smile. 'Not a lot. Yousef Mohammed, who runs the corner shop where Marston Street meets the Cowley Road, remembers seeing Sarah – assuming it was Sarah – about ten minutes before her death. She hung around the front of his shop briefly, looking in the window or something. I think Yousef fancied her a bit. He commented on her long mack.'

'Is that it, Fox?' she said in a tone which suggested great disappointment with his efforts.

'I think it may be significant that Sarah didn't come in the shop, didn't even come into the shop to buy her usual newspaper—'

Holden cut in viciously. 'Fox! Would you be interested in buying a bloody newspaper if you were on your way to jump from the top of a multi-storey car park?'

Even Fox was temporarily thrown. One charitable, though very male, part of his brain assumed in that instant that it must be her time of the month. But he pressed on nevertheless. 'But surely she might have wanted to at least exchange words with someone, with anyone, especially with someone who she knew liked her. Yousef smiles a lot. Even when I was questioning him about Sarah, he couldn't think of her without smiling.'

'But if Sarah was depressed,' Holden replied, 'the last thing she might have wanted to do was talk to anyone, especially to someone who is pathologically cheerful.'

'Maybe,' said Fox carefully. 'But remember she then went across the road and looked at Bicknell's blue plaque. Remember we've got a picture of her where she seems to be talking to two other people.' He paused, wondering how his observations were going down with his boss.

Holden frowned, then fixed him with a stare. 'So what exactly, Fox, is your point?'

Fox looked down, happy to give ground to his superior. 'Only that if, by any chance, Wilson's theory is correct, and that the woman in the mack was Anne, then of course Anne wouldn't want to risk getting into conversation with Yousef when she didn't know him, but realized her sister probably did. She didn't want to risk giving herself away.'

'In that case, why hover round the front of the shop at all?' Holden said.

Fox smiled: 'To be seen, I guess.'

Holden stood up and for a moment Fox was concerned he had misread her, and that he was about to receive a broadside of premenstrual venom. But when she spoke she was calm and complimentary.

'Good teamwork. Good thinking. Both of you. You, Wilson, have firmly placed Anne Johnson in the area shortly before the death of her sister, when she claimed to be at home oversleeping after an overdose of sex with her head teacher. And you, Fox, have raised at the very least doubt about the identity of the woman in the long mackintosh.' Holden stopped talking and walked over to the board from which the picture of Sarah Johnson stared out. 'As for me, team, I have had a little chat with William Basham of Basham and Smith Solicitors. And Mr William Basham has confirmed to me that Anne is the sole beneficiary of Sarah's will. Not exactly world shattering news, I know. However—' Holden paused, and raised her right-hand index finger in the air, as if to ensure that she had their fullest attention. She had meant it when she praised them, and yet she was human enough to need both their attention and approval. Both men watched her intently, wondering what rabbit she was going to pull out of her hat. 'However, Mr William Basham did also let slip another interesting fact, namely that Sarah Johnson was about to change her will.'

'Change it?' Fox gasped. Holden almost purred in appreciation of his reaction.

'Indeed, they had a meeting arranged for later this week,' said Holden triumphantly. 'He didn't know for sure what changes she wanted to make, but in my book this all adds up to a very substantial motive. If Sarah had told Anne that she was going to cut her out of her will altogether and bequeath all her worldly belongings – and that includes a flat that I reckon is worth at least £250,000 – to the day centre or a cat's home or maybe even to Jake Arnold, then Anne suddenly has a very pressing reason to drive over to Oxford and, when she couldn't persuade her sister to change her mind, well, to take matters into her own hands. So I suggest the next thing to do is go and pick her up for questioning.'

'Why do you say Jake Arnold?' Wilson asked. 'Is there a particular reason for suggesting him?'

'No,' admitted Holden. 'But frankly if she was changing her will to another individual, then on the basis of what we know so far, Jake would be the most likely suspect. We know they had quite a strong relationship. It may not have been sexual, but from Sarah's point of view at least, it was a very important relationship. Who was it she tried to ring the morning of her death? Jake.'

She stopped and waited. Her theory provoked only silence, as each man tried to work out an appropriate response. This only irritated her.

'Come on, gentlemen,' she said sarcastically. 'I've thrown a hunch up into the air, now is the time for you to shoot it down.'

'So you're suggesting Anne may have murdered both her sister and Jake?' Fox said cautiously.

'Ah, I can see you are not convinced, Fox. But why not? She could have killed her sister because of the imminent will change. And Jake because he must have known about the imminent will change and might otherwise have told us police about it. Or maybe she just thought he was a creep. If you can kill one person, why not a second one?' Again she stopped, and waited for a reply. It came from Wilson, gingerly taking his turn.

'But there is a problem, isn't there, Guv, with the time Anne's car left Oxford. We have it on CCTV leaving the car park at 8.30. That is some three-quarters of an hour before Sarah's death. It's one thing to suggest Anne's visit caused Sarah to commit suicide, but it would be very hard to argue without other evidence that she pushed her sister off the top of the car park.'

Holden smiled, but her response to Wilson was uncompromising. 'That's the key, Wilson. More evidence. I mean, imagine you are Anne Johnson wanting to establish an alibi. What do you do? She knows there are CCTV cameras at the car park, so she drives out at 8.30, and goes and parks it somewhere else. She then lures her sister up to the top of the car park, and pushes her over the edge. Then she leaves by the stairs, and walks to her car. But now, of course, she's got to get to Reading. It's a good hour's drive at the best of time, and probably more at that time of morning, so she has to cry off her first lesson. But that isn't a problem because Dr Adrian Ratcliffe, her amorous headmaster, is hardly going to make a fuss, now is he?'

'No, Guv,' Wilson agreed. 'No, he isn't.' But he wasn't entirely convinced.

It was at this point that Holden's stock-taking session came to an abrupt end. There was a knock on the door, which opened immediately. The face of Sergeant Tolman appeared, his hand raised as if in apology, or perhaps to ask permission to speak. 'Sorry to interrupt, Ma'am, but I thought you'd like to know. They've just found a dead body. Down at the allotments in Meadow Lane. A garden shed went up in flames last night apparently, and some old boy discovered a charred body in it this morning. It's a bit of a mess, apparently, so ID may take a time, but the allotment belongs to a lorry driver. Name of Martin Mace.'

Holden resisted the temptation to drive straight over to the Meadow Lane allotments. There was little to be gained, she reckoned, from rushing round there at breakneck speed. Uniform would be looking after the site, and Dr Pointer had already been summoned. Better to give them a bit of space and time first. Besides, there was still the death of Sarah Johnson to be followed through. First with a phone call to St Gregory's, Reading.

'Dr Adrian Ratcliffe, please?' Holden said to the woman who answered the phone.

'He's rather busy,' came the automatic response of the head teacher's personal Rottweiler. 'Can I take a message.'

'No, you cannot take a message,' snapped Holden, who was still in no mood to take prisoners. 'This is Detective Inspector Holden of the Oxford police, and I need to speak to Dr Adrian Ratcliffe now.'

'One moment,' came the flustered response of a guard dog whose bark was clearly worse than her bite. Several seconds of silence, then a crackle and a man's voice spoke.

'Dr Adrian Ratcliffe here. How can I help you?'

The soft, polished tone of his voice served only to goad, not soothe. 'You can help, Dr Ratcliffe, by getting into your car and driving over here to the Cowley Police Station in Oxford.'

'I'm sorry, what do you mean?' came the blustering reply. 'I have a school to run and—'

'You've a choice,' Holden snarled back. 'Either you can get yourself to this police station by 10.30 a.m. or I'll arrange for a marked police car to drive into your school to collect you. And I'll ask them to arrive with blue lights flashing. Do I make myself clear?'

Having dealt with one problem, Holden addressed the issue of Anne Johnson. 'Right, Wilson. I want you to go round and pick up Anne Johnson. Take WPC Lawson with you. I want someone to be with her at all times. She's not under arrest yet, but I don't want her making phone calls we aren't aware of. Once you're back, you can express surprise that I've had to pop out. I want her to sit and sweat a bit. All right?'

'Yes, Guv.'

'And if, Wilson, you happen to let slip to her the information that we are also pulling Ratcliffe in for questioning, then that won't matter to me. Understood?'

'Absolutely, Guv.'

It was almost 9.30 a.m. when Holden and Fox arrived at the allotments and the first thing Holden noticed was the smell. A smell of badly burnt meat that still drifted through the air along with the flecks of ash being disturbed by the freshening morning breeze. The blackened remains of Martin Mace's shed and the immediate area around it had been surrounded by a makeshift barrier of garden cane and police tape. Four uniformed police, two men, two women, stood uneasily at its four corners, eyes firmly fixed on the crowd of rubbernecking locals and press who had been drawn by the news of unexpected excitement. Cameras clicked as Holden and Fox pushed passed them. They both fought a temptation to scowl, wishing they could get on with their job without interference, yet knowing only too well that violent death both alarms and compels.

'Is it Martin Mace, Inspector?' one of the reporters called out. Holden recognized the rather high-pitched male voice as belonging to Don Alexander, a reporter at the *Oxford Mail*. 'It's his shed, you know.'

Holden turned. 'We will be giving a press conference in due course, Don. I'm sure you don't want me to speculate and give you misleading information. Now, if you don't mind all moving off, we'll try and concentrate on investigating this death.'

Holden waited and watched as the onlookers began to retreat reluctantly from the scene.

'Hey!' she said suddenly to Fox. 'Over there, on the left, in the black jacket. Isn't that—?'

'Danny Flynn!' Fox said, completing her sentence. 'It certainly bloody is.'

'Well!' she added. 'Curiouser and curiouser.'

'Not so odd, if you ask me Guv.'

Reluctantly, Holden pulled her eyes away from the now fast-retreating Flynn, turned and resumed her walk towards the tape barrier.

'Good morning, Dr Pointer!'

It was several seconds before one of the two figures in white protective suits stood up and turned towards the two detectives.

'Not a good morning for this chap.'

'Do you have an ID?'

'Martin Mace is his name. Probably. I understand this is, or rather was, his shed. The fire has done a lot of damage, but the contents of his wallet have survived pretty well. So I think we can say with some considerable expectation of accuracy that either this body is that of a pickpocket, or that he is, indeed was, Martin Mace.' Pointer smiled. 'And the next question?'

'Without wishing to commit you to one hundred per cent at this stage, Doctor,' Holden said, 'can you tell us how Martin died.'

'Well, I think I can say with some certainty that he was alive when the fire started, so I guess we can safely say he burnt to death. His hands had been tied behind him with wire. So had his feet. There are traces of a plastic covering which has burnt off it, so I imagine the killer used garden wire. Plenty of it here,' she said gesturing towards the immaculately cared for plants and canes. 'Also, there was tape round his mouth.'

'To stop him shouting? So he was conscious as well as alive?'

Dr Pointer frowned, then pulled something out of the pocket of her overall. 'I guess so. But the tape had another purpose too. To keep something in his mouth.' She lifted the plastic bag in her hand up high. 'Look! It's amazing how well it has been preserved. But then his mouth was firmly shut.'

'Money?' Holden said in surprise.

'Do you fancy a few new clothes, inspector,' Pointer said with a laugh. 'Maybe we could go fifty-fifty. There's plenty of it.'

'How much?' Holden asked, but without even a hint of humour.

Pointer shrugged. 'I need to keep it for tests, obviously, but it's all twenty pound notes. We reckon £500.'

'This is more like it!' WPC Jan Lawson said as Wilson manoeuvred the car carefully out of the cramped car park at the back of the Cowley Police Station. 'A proper murder case!'

Wilson said nothing. He was trying to concentrate on avoiding the riot van parked immediately to his right.

'Is this your first?' she continued, but he again made no reply beyond an indeterminate grunt as he swung cautiously left past the Chief Superintendent's BMW.

The smile on Lawson's face hardened into a pout. Normally she had little difficulty in getting a man's attention, so Wilson's indifference irritated her. It wasn't that he was that dishy, but when she set her sights, however temporarily, on a man, she expected him to show an interest. She decided to try a different tack.

'I bet you're a virgin.'

The different tack worked: the car lurched suddenly forward then rocked to a halt as Wilson's attention was well and truly grabbed.

She laughed. 'Oops! Steady, Constable. Not the best way to impress Dectective Inspector Susan. Crashing in the car park on the way to arrest a murder suspect! You'll be back on bike duty if you're not careful.'

'We're bringing her in for questioning, not arresting her,' Wilson said pedantically.

'Whatever!' she said, before lapsing into silence. Wilson, who was having trouble finding a gap in the traffic on the Oxford Road, was relieved about that, but no sooner had he slipped out in front of a Morris Traveller than WPC Lawson resumed.

'Anyway, by virgin, I was merely thinking in terms of murder. Your first time investigating one. Nothing else. All right?'

'All right,' Wilson replied, who had hoped that this particular line of conversation had already ended.

'Mind, you,' she continued cheerfully, 'there's nothing wrong with a man being a virgin in my book. Nothing wrong at all.'

Wilson tried to concentrate on the road.

'Not at your age, anyway.'

Wilson felt himself going red, and hoped against hope that she would stop.

'So,' she said, with an effortless change, 'did she do it? This Anne Johnson. Did she kill her sister, do you think?' She didn't wait for an answer. 'I do hope so. It would be so much more interesting than a suicide.'

'Bloody tractor!' Dr Adrian Ratcliffe was last in a queue of ten vehicles – eight cars of various colours and two white vans, to be precise – moving at twenty miles per hour behind the object of his fury. 'Why can't it get off the main road?' he demanded of the empty passenger seat of his Saab. It had not been a very good trip; there were too many lorries on the road for that, not to mention roadworks at Shillingford which had delayed him for a full ten minutes. Even in a good mood Ratcliffe was an aggressive driver, always anxious to get there sooner (wherever 'there' might be). Today, though, he had a genuine reason for such anxiety: if he didn't get to the Cowley police station by 10.30, then that bloody DI woman would be on the phone to school asking where he was or, even worse, sending round a pair of clodhopping coppers to cause maximum embarrassment.

'Get on with it!' he shouted, as the car at the front of the column pulled out and then passed the tractor. 'And you!' he urged as the next car edged slowly to the right, only to lurch back again as a BMW, having just escaped the 30 m.p.h. zone in Nuneham Courtenay, accelerated towards them. 'Damn!' he snarled.

In truth, Dr Ratcliffe still had some thirty minutes to get to his destination, which ought to have been more than enough given that the rush hour had passed, but he was finding it difficult to think rationally. For the fact is that he was worried. Very worried indeed. What if this went to court? What if his relationship with Anne Johnson came up. What if, God forbid, she used him as an alibi in open court? His imagination went into overdrive.

'Miss Johnson, did you visit you sister the night before her death?'

'No, My Lord, I was in bed.'

'Can anyone vouch for that.'

'My headmaster can.'

'Really, and how is that Miss Johnson.'

'Well, my Lord, we were fucking.'

'Between what times?'

'About 7.30 till maybe 11.00.'

'Really. He must have a remarkable stamina!!'

'Actually, it only took three minutes, but that's men for you!'

The whole jury titters, while in the gallery the press hacks rub their hands in delight.

He tried to shake free of his imaginings, but cold reality was no better. If this came out, Alice would never forgive him. That would be it. Finished. Caput. End of story. Hell hath no fury like a woman scorned. It was a cliché, but one which summed up Alice to a tee.

'So, who do you want to be?'

Wilson, who had just pulled up in Marston Street, looked across at his companion with puzzlement writ large across his face. 'Sorry?'

'Good cop, or bad cop?' WPC Lawson said flatly.

Puzzlement was replaced by alarm. 'What on earth are you talking about? We are only going to bring her in for questioning, not force a confession out of her.'

Lawson grinned. 'Hey, Constable, lighten up.'

Wilson tried to smile back, but somehow his face wouldn't cooperate. He tried to think of some appropriate response, but his brain wouldn't cooperate with that either. In the end he just nodded, before getting out of the car.

'Is that it?' Lawson said, indicating a red door immediately opposite them across the road.

'Yes,' Wilson replied.

'Right,' she said, marching towards it. 'I'll be the bad cop, then.'

Wilson locked the car and strode anxiously after her. What the heck was she going to do?

Lawson got to the door first and pressed the bell, once, twice and then again. 'You can lead,' she said, as Wilson caught up with her.

Anne Johnson opened the door. This time, there was no towel swathed round her head, but her welcome was just as hostile. 'Not you again!'

'Good morning, Miss Johnson,' he said. 'I'm afraid we need to ask you a few more questions.'

'Questions?' she exclaimed.

'Down at the station.'

'What the hell do you mean?'

'Do you mind if we come in for a moment?' Wilson pressed on patiently.

'Yes, I blooming do,' she said firmly.

'I really do need to use your toilet,' WPC Lawson said, stepping forward from behind her much taller colleague. 'You know what it's like.' Anne Johnson opened her mouth to object, but Lawson wasn't waiting for an answer. 'Coming through,' she said, and pushed her way past the astonished woman.

'Really!' Anne Johnson huffed, but she knew she had lost the skirmish.

'And who might you be?' Lawson said, as she entered the living area. A tousled figure in crumpled white T-shirt and jeans was just getting up from the sofa. The man said nothing, but Wilson, following his colleague, recognized him instantly.

'Bicknell!' he exclaimed.

By the time Holden and Fox had returned to Cowley Police Station, both interviewees were ready and waiting for them. Ratcliffe was in Room B, on his own, while Anne Johnson was in Room C, with WPC Lawson standing discreetly in attendance. Holden, however, was in no mood to rush. She spent some ten minutes in the ladies toilets, took another five minutes to make herself a mug of coffee, and then strolled casually along the corridor to Wilson's office. The detective constable was bent over the printer next to his desk.

'Any problems, Wilson?'

'The printer's jammed,' he said, without looking up.

'I meant with Anne Johnson.'

'Oh,' he said, looking up with a sheepish look on his face. 'Sorry. No, no problems.'

'Good.'

'But there was one interesting development.'

'Oh?'

'Ed Bicknell was there.'

'Bicknell!' she exclaimed. 'How very interesting. What was he doing there?'

'Can't say they volunteered any information. He just said he had to be off. In the circumstances, I thought it might be best for you to pursue that line of enquiry.'

There was a coughing sound from the corridor. Holden turned, to see Fox entering the open door. 'I hope I haven't been delaying you Guv?'

'No,' she said, and turned back to Wilson. 'While we interview Ratcliffe, can you do me a timeline of everything we know about Sarah Johnson's last hours, starting from 7.00 p.m. when Dr Ratcliffe visited Anne Johnson's house in Reading. Sightings of her Mini. Phone calls, et cetera.'

'Yes, Guv.'

'It's Sam.'

'All right?'

'Yeah.'

'I'm busy.'

'Have you heard from Martin?'

'No.'

'He's not answering his mobile.'

'Oh!'

'Got your ticket?'

'Yeah. Look I've got to go.'

'Okay.'

'See ya!'

'I do hope this is important. I spoke to someone over the phone – name like a carpet, Constable Wilton or Shagpile or something – and I can't for the life of me see what else there is to say.' Dr Adrian Ratcliffe spoke aggressively. He was damned if he was going to be pushed around, and in the circumstances attack seemed the best form of defence. Take charge, throw the enemy off balance, cover his tracks.

'Would you like a coffee?' the woman asked. Trying to lull him into a sense of security, was she? What sort of idiot did she take him for?

'No!'

'Tea?'

'No!'

'Water?'

'Does it come with whisky?'

The woman looked down at the papers in front of her, turned the top sheet over, and frowned. She looked up. 'Why did you lie to Constable Wilson?'

'I didn't.' He said it without blinking, looking straight into her face.

'You said Anne Johnson's car had broken down.'

'That's what she told me.'

'When?'

'When she rang me, that morning.'

'Oh,' the woman said. 'I thought maybe this was an excuse that you'd arranged the night before, while you smoked your post-coital cigarette.'

Ratcliffe's eyes opened wider for a second. He wasn't surprised that Anne had talked about their relationship, but he was disappointed. However, 'I don't smoke,' was all he said.

'That evening, did Anne Johnson intimate that she might be late the next day?'

'No,' he said. 'Definitely not.'

'When did you leave her house that night?'

'What the hell has this got to do with anything?' He displayed anger now.

'Please answer the question,' she insisted.

'I don't know. About ten o'clock probably.'

'Probably!' She frowned again, and rubbed briefly at her chin. 'I suppose … I suppose your wife can confirm what time you got home, and then we can knock off the time for travelling and—'

'Do you take pleasure in wrecking lives?' This time the anger was genuine, fuelled by fear. 'My affair with Anne

132

Johnson has absolutely nothing to do with the death of her sister. Sarah killed herself the following morning. Just after 9.00 o'clock, wasn't it? You have no right to destroy my marriage, the lives of my two children, by bringing this to court, or revealing this to my wife.'

DI Holden leant back in her chair, and brought her hands up together in front of her mouth. If she had been sitting in a church pew, the observer would have concluded that she was praying, but in the context of a police interview, deep thought was more likely. She remained in this pose for several seconds, before abruptly standing up.

'Interview terminated,' she said.

'Are you ready, Guv?' Fox was standing cautiously at the doorway of DI Holden's room. Wilson was half a pace behind him, also unsure whether to enter or not. 'We've kept her waiting quite a long time now.'

'He's a slimy creep, that Ratcliffe,' she snarled. 'Hell, I'd like to hang his balls out to dry!'

'Being a creep isn't a crime,' Fox said patiently.

'Well it bloody well ought to be,' she said defiantly, but the snarl was gone.

Fox stepped forward, apparently satisfied that it was safe to do so. 'Wilson here has got a list of all the phone calls to and from Sarah's mobile.'

Holden looked past Fox at her detective constable and beckoned him. 'Let's be seeing it then, Wilson.'

He moved forward, placed it on her desk, and stepped back. For a full half a minute Holden studied it. Then her finger stabbed down at one particular entry. 'What about this one, Wilson?'

He moved forward again, bending down to get a clear view. 'That's a phone box, Guv. In Iffley Road. Opposite the Cricketers. That's on the corner—'

'Thank you Wilson,' she said firmly. 'I do know where the Cricketers is, as it happens.'

'Sorry!' he replied, stepping back again as his did.

Holden looked up from the list of phone numbers. 'Don't apologize all the time, Wilson, unless you've got something proper to apologize for. You've done a good job'

'Yes, Guv.'

'Now, whatever happened to Sarah Johnson, we know we've got two other murders to solve, so I want you to turn your attention to them. In fact, to Martin Mace. I want you to follow up the money that was stuffed into Mace's mouth.'

'What money?' said Wilson, who had yet to be updated on the allotment details.

'There was a wodge of money,' Holden replied, 'probably £500, stuffed in the dead man's mouth. Assuming, as we are, that the dead man is Mace, I want to know if the money was his or his killer's. Ring Pointer. She's got the wallet that Mace was carrying. Presumably, there'll be a debit card in it. Go to the bank. Check his withdrawals over the last few days. Five hundred pounds is too much to withdraw at a slot machine, so if he withdrew it, he'll have done it in person. We need any clues we can. OK?'

'Yes, Guv. Thank you Guv.'

'For God's sake, Wilson, don't thank me either,' she said wearily. 'Unless I've done you a real favour.'

Wilson opened his mouth to apologize, but shut it again just in time.

'Sorry to have kept you for so long,' Holden said, as she and Fox sat down at the table opposite Anne Johnson.

'Oh, I assumed it was all part of the softening-up process.' Anne Johnson said this without emotion, a bleak smile across her face.

'Would you like a tea or coffee?' Holden said pleasantly.

'No!' The reply was definite.

Holden looked down and opened the folder of paper she had placed on the table. She spent several seconds frowning over the first page. Then she closed the folder and looked up. 'You've been lying to us, Miss Johnson?'

'Have I?' she replied, steadily holding the Detective Inspector's gaze.

'In fact, you seem to make quite an art of not telling the truth.'

Anne Johnson shrugged, but said nothing.

Holden flicked a glance towards Fox, who immediately opened a folder in front of him, and drew from it a photograph which he pushed across the table in front of him.

'Is that your car?' he asked.

'It looks like it,' she said grudgingly.

'The number plate is quite clear,' Fox said evenly. 'For the sake of the tape recording, can you please confirm yes or no if this is your car.'

'You obviously know it is,' she said belligerently.

'This photograph of a car which you have agreed belongs to you was taken at the entrance to the multi-storey car park at the Magdalen Bridge end of the Cowley Road. As you can see from the timestamp at the bottom, it was taken at 6.40 a.m. the morning of your sister's death. Were you driving the car?'

'I suppose I must have been.'

Holden leant forward. 'In your original statement to DS Fox, you told him you hadn't seen her for some weeks prior to her death.'

'Did I?' she said, as if she was genuinely surprised.

'In fact, Miss Johnson,' Fox said, 'you told me you hadn't even spoken on the phone?'

'Look, what does it matter? My sister had jumped from the top of a car park. I was still very distressed. I might have said anything.'

'We are trying to establish the precise circumstances of your sister's death,' Fox continued doggedly. 'If you lie, it is a very serious matter. Now the fact is that we have photographic evidence of you arriving in Oxford and parking very near to your sister's home less than two and a half hours before she died. We also know from Miss Sarah Johnson's mobile phone records that she rang you up the previous night.'

Anne Johnson laughed. 'Haven't you been a busy boy! A gold star for you.'

Holden leant forward and took up the baton. 'Why did she ring you?'

'Why do you think? She was depressed.'

'More so than usual?'

'Well, I guess so,' Anne Johnson said, her voice heavy with sarcasm, 'given that she then committed suicide. It's not the thing you do if you're feeling on top of the world.'

'But that's something we are trying to establish. If she did indeed commit suicide, and if so, why. Because the evidence so far is circumstantial.'

Anne Johnson's attitude of bored intolerance disappeared. 'What the hell do you mean? Of course she committed—'

'There's no of course in my book,' Holden snapped, 'merely evidence – good, bad or circumstantial. And so far it doesn't add up to anything conclusive. There's nothing that says she must have jumped rather than she was pushed by person or persons unknown.'

'So,' Fox cut in, 'perhaps you can tell us in more precise terms what she said when she rang you up.'

Anne Johnson dropped her gaze, so that when she replied, she addressed her words towards the table.

'She was very distressed. She said how she was feeling very low. How she hated herself. That she wasn't sure she could carry on.'

'What was making her feel that?' Holden said.

Anne looked at her questioner as if she couldn't quite believe that she had heard her correctly. 'She was a manic depressive. Up sometimes, down sometimes. There didn't have to be a reason to be down. Sometimes she just was.'

'What did she tell you about her will?'

Anne looked at Holden sharply. She started to open her mouth, as if to speak, then closed it. She gave a shrug that Holden thought rather theatrical, the sort of gesture she remembered from a largely forgotten school production of *Grease*. 'I really don't know what you're talking about,' she said firmly. 'Are you saying she was making a will?'

Holden hoped her face wasn't giving anything away. She had hoped she would catch her adversary out with this question – cause her at the least to admit to knowledge of the will – but like Muhammmad Ali in his prime Anne Johnson had swayed out of the way of the intended left hook with contemptuous ease, leaving Holden feeling stupidly clumsy. Holden, almost desperately, tried a right hook: 'I gather you and Bicknell are very good friends? Rather strange that, to get so chummy with the man whose lunatic art project may have inspired your sister to kill herself.'

'Ah!' said Anne Johnson, 'I wondered when you'd bring him up.'

'How long have you had a sexual relationship with him?' Fox said, trying to bring relief to his boss.

'Sexual relationship?'

'How long have you known him?' Holden came in.

'In the biblical or non-biblical sense?' she replied with a smile. She waited for a response from Holden, but none came. Eventually, she gave another of her theatrical shrugs. 'A few days. That's all.'

'You expect us to believe that?' It was Fox again.

'What exactly are you implying?' Anne Johnson snapped.

'Let me give you a scenario,' Holden said calmly. 'You are at home. Dr Ratcliffe has just left and you get a phone call. From your sister. She is, as you say, maybe distraught, maybe depressed. But that is not what grabs your attention. It is what she tells you. That she is going to change her will. A will which until that time left everything to you. She is not a poor woman. She owns her own flat. You find it difficult to sleep, wondering what the hell to do. So early next morning you drive to Oxford. You park in the multi-storey, and go and see her. What goes on between the two of you only you know. But let's suppose that you try – but fail – to persuade her not to change her will. You leave, and you drive your car out of the car park at about half past eight. But my question would be: what did you do then? Because half an hour later your sister plunges off the top of that same car park. Now, can you fill in the gaps for us?'

Anne Johnson had been watching Holden very carefully right the way through this exposition. When Holden stopped talking, she puffed out her cheeks. 'Wow!' she said. 'You've obviously missed your vocation. As a writer of fiction.'

'Not much fiction there,' Holden said with a smile, and she turned briefly towards Fox.

'We know,' he said, 'from Sarah's phone records that she rang you that night at about 10.10. Fact. We have your car arriving on CCTV. Fact. We have your car leaving on CCTV. Fact. At 8.30 a.m. Yet you only get to school in time to teach the third lesson, which commences at 11.30. Again, fact. We have spoken to Sarah Johnson's solicitor, who has confirmed that she had arranged a meeting to change her will. Fact. And, of course, your sister's death is a fact. Only its cause remains uncertain.'

'Another point of fact,' Holden said, leaning forward again, 'is that much of the fiction has been coming from you, Miss Johnson. For example, you lied to your school about your car breaking down. You lied to DS Fox when you told him you hadn't seen or even spoken to your sister recently. So why should we believe you when you claim to have no knowledge of Sarah's will. And why should we believe you when you say you have only very recently met Ed Bicknell. It doesn't take much imagination to suppose that he was part of your plot, conveniently standing there at the bottom of the car park with his suicide plaque, and even more conveniently photographing her looking at the plaque.' Holden paused, pondered and then decided to take the plunge. 'Only who is to say that it was her, standing there in her long mackintosh. Who is to say it wasn't you? That you were making sure that Bicknell got some photos of you pretending to be your sister, contemplating her suicide, before you made your way to the top of the car park, and there pushed your waiting sister over the edge.'

She stopped then and silence descended on the room. Holden and Fox sat unmoving, their eyes on their suspect, wondering, hoping against hope, almost (in Holden's case) praying for the woman opposite to break down and confess. Eventually Anne Johnson leant back in her chair and let out a deep sigh. 'Are you,' she said coldly, 'accusing me of murder?'

Holden pursed her lips together, knowing she had not won. 'At this point, I am merely trying to point out the possibilities.'

'In that case,' her interviewee said, 'I've changed my mind.'

'In what sense,' Holden responded instantly.

'In the sense that, if there are any more questions, I'd like to have a solicitor present.'

CHAPTER 10

A four-minute phone call was all it took for Wilson to ascertain Martin Mace's bank. And much of that four minutes was taken up with waiting while Dr Pointer checked the contents of Mace's wallet. There then followed a short exchange.

'There's a debit card for the National Exchange bank, but no credit card,' Pointer began briskly. 'The account name is Martin N. Mace. The account number isn't entirely clear. The edge of the card is a bit scorched, but the first six digits are two, one, five, four, two and I think that's a six. But I expect that is enough to be going on with?'

'Thank you, yes, Dr Pointer,' Wilson replied gratefully, and remembering his previous meeting with the pathologist. 'I am sure that will be fine.'

'The nearest branch is in Headington, by the way,' she continued.

'Thank you,' Wilson said again.

'I bank there myself.'

'Right. Well, thank you for your help.'

'Is that what DI Holden expects?' Pointer said.

The question, not surprisingly, threw Wilson. A pause was followed by an 'Um, er', and only after another brief silence did Wilson come up with a coherent response. 'I'm not sure I know what you mean, Dr Pointer.'

At the other end of the phone line, a laugh rang out. 'Does she expect you to say thank you all the time? Because you've said it three times to me already!' And she laughed again.

A wave of embarrassment swept over Wilson. He felt himself flush, and ridiculously had the thought that Dr Pointer could detect this even down a phone line. Desperately, he tried to think of something to say in defence of his own boss, but he could think of nothing. In the end, all he was able to utter was the rather feeble 'DI Holden treats me very well', which in turn provoked another distant burst of savage laughter. Wilson felt very small and inadequate, and was glad that this conversation was all happening over the phone.

'You're beginning to sound like her lapdog,' Pointer concluded viciously. And with that parting shot, she hung up.

'Are you all right?' It was ten minutes later, and it was Lawson who was speaking. By this time they were already halfway to Headington, travelling smoothly along the Slade after a slow, stop-start procession along Holloway. Lawson had been notably silent so far, and Wilson, after the sharpness of Pointer's tongue, would have preferred anything – even her joking about his virginity, in fact especially her joking about his virginity – to silence.

'Yes,' he said automatically. The car in front pulled to a halt as a mother and pram waited to cross at the pedestrian crossing. 'Actually, what I mean is, no! Dr Pointer gave me a bit of an earful.'

'Ah!' Lawson said. Wilson waited in vain for her to say something more. The car in front moved forward again, and he in turn followed.

'I'm not sure she likes the Guv,' Wilson said.

Lawson, as Pointer had at the other end of the phone line, laughed, but it was a harmless, tinkling laugh. 'Haven't you heard the rumours?'

'Rumours?'

'You've not heard, have you?' Lawson continued with delight.

'No,' admitted Wilson.

'Well, the story is,' she said with another giggle of pleasure, 'the story is that Pointer hit on Holden the first time they met, and Holden freaked out and—'

'I don't think we should be gossiping about the Guv,' Wilson said prissily.

'OK,' Lawson replied casually, but ignored his admonishment nonetheless. 'I'll gossip. You stay quiet. Anyway, the story is that Pointer put her hand on the Guv's arse, and Holden slapped her round the face.' She laughed again. 'I wish I'd been there to see it. Imagine!'

Wilson, despite his best intentions, smiled. He looked across at the profile of WPC Lawson, who was now looking forward. He noticed that the right-hand corner of her mouth was twitching, in response no doubt to her imaginings. He turned his eyes back to the road in front, and frowned as the sun suddenly emerged from behind the clouds and forced him to squint against the intense change of light. But inside, his smile remained.

'You going to do the talking?' Lawson said as they approached the door of the National Exchange bank.

'I could do,' Wilson said uncertainly.

'I'll act the dumb blonde,' running her hand through the back of her neat bleached hair.

'Is that a threat or a promise?' he replied.

It is amazing what a police uniform can do. Even before Wilson had displayed his ID card, the sight of Lawson brought immediate attention from behind the glass security panels. They were ushered through to a small office, where the manager, a Mr Ronald Knight, greeted them, rising anxiously from his seat.

'How can I help you?' he said, holding his hands up in a feebly melodramatic gesture. 'I hope you haven't come to arrest me!' he joked.

Wilson ignored the opportunity to respond in kind. 'We want to check out a withdrawal by one of your customers. A Martin Mace. We believe he may have withdrawn £500 in cash in the last few days.'

'Can I ask why?' Knight said. 'We do have rules of confidentiality.'

'He's dead,' Wilson said firmly. 'So he's not going to object. And we wouldn't have trailed up here unless it was important for our investigations.'

'Of course,' Knight replied. 'It may take a few minutes. Please sit down.'

'Thank you,' Lawson said for both of them, and flashing one of her brightest smiles at Knight. 'That's very kind of you. And if Mr Mace came and collected his money in person, perhaps we could talk to whoever it was gave him the money?'

'Of course,' Knight said again.

'And coffee for three?'

'Yes, sorry, I should have offered you some.'

'Bless you,' Lawson smiled again.

'Bless you!' Wilson said after Knight had scurried out of the room. 'I don't remember that in my training course.'

'I learnt in from my Dad,' she grinned. 'It's very effective.'

'Is he a vicar?'

'Now, that would be telling,' she teased.

Ronald Knight returned a couple of minutes later with a tray of coffee in his hands and a young, nervous-looking woman at his back. She was dressed in black trousers and white blouse, with a fine gold chain round her neck, and a tiny gold stud through her left-hand nostril.

'This is Sunita,' he said. 'It was she who served Mr Mace with the £500.'

'Thank you, Mr Knight!' Wilson said warmly, rising from his chair. 'Please sit down, Sunita,' he continued, gesturing to a chair and at the same time so positioning himself that Knight knew that his own presence was not needed. 'We'll give you a shout, Mr Knight, when we are finished.'

'How do you like your coffee, Sunita,' Lawson was saying as Wilson shut the door. 'Milk? Sugar?'

'Just milk,' she said. Her hands were clasped tightly in front of her, Lawson noted as she poured some milk into each of their cups. She realized that she didn't know if Wilson took milk, but frankly now wasn't the time to ask him. He'd have to like it or lump it.

'I like the stud,' said Lawson.

'Thank you,' came the reply.

'I really do. I wish I could wear one, but my boss would never approve.'

'Oh!' Sunita said, and glanced across at Wilson, who was doing his best to be the proverbial fly on the wall.

'Oh, not him!' Lawson giggled. 'He's just my driver!'

Sunita giggled in return, while Wilson stiffened slightly, feeling that WPC Lawson was overdoing it.

'Can I be very personal?' Lawson said, leaning forward conspiratorially. 'You've got a really lovely complexion. What do you use?' The conversation continued like this for some time. Wilson was reminded of his sister and her friend Mandy's after-school discussions. As he sipped his coffee, he allowed his memory to float to times gone by, to sitting in front of the TV while the two girls chattered on and rubbed apricot-smelling moisturiser into each other's faces, while he pretended not to listen.

'So,' Lawson was saying with great reluctance, 'I suppose we'd better talk about the £500. Otherwise your Mr Knight is going to wonder why it's all taking so long.'

'He's probably counting the minutes on his watch,' Sunita said with a grin. 'He's very strict on our coffee breaks, you know. Fifteen minutes maximum.'

'In that case, we'd better get down to it,' Lawson replied. 'First of all, when did Mr Mace take out the money?'

'Yesterday afternoon. Round about 2.15, 2.30.'

'So, you remember serving him?' Lawson asked off-handedly.

'Oh, yes! He comes in quite often. Usually to pay money in. He's got his own business. Drives a lorry, I think he said once.'

'And do you remember how he was?'

'Oh yes!' she said again. 'He was in a foul mood. Really foul. I knew that as soon as he opened his mouth. Normally he's very cheerful. "Hello darling!" he'd say. Or "Hello duck," sometimes. I remember the first time he said it, I said to him what did he mean, because I was no duck, and I didn't take kindly to being called one. And he was very apologetic, and he said calling someone duck was, like, friendly. His mum was always calling people duck, and he had just picked up the habit. And then he had winked at me, and asked me what was wrong with being called duck because he always thought ducks were the nicest of all birds. And I said well in that case I didn't really mind. Anyway, he didn't call me duck this time, and he didn't call me darling or anything. He just handed over his chequebook with a cheque made out for £500 and said he needed cash. "Going off on holiday, are you?" I said, or something like that, but he just said "Get on with it". So I did.'

She paused, looking up at Lawson as if for approval. Lawson nodded encouragingly. 'So he was quite aggressive then?'

Sunita pursed her lips – rather attractively Wilson thought – as she considered this. 'I'm not sure aggressive is quite right. Anxious perhaps. Very anxious. Edgy.'

'That's very helpful,' Lawson said. 'Thank you.'

They lapsed into amiable silence. Sunita, holding her mug in both of her delicate hands, was temporarily oblivious of the situation. Like Wilson only a few minutes earlier, she had slipped back into childhood: she was a little girl again, savouring the slightly naughty thrill of a few minutes out of class. A wistful smile spread imperceptibly over her face. Finally, Wilson leant forward.

'Sunita,' he asked quietly, as if unwilling to break into her reverie, 'was he on his own?'

She turned towards the previously silent detective. Her brow furrowed slightly as she tried to recall. 'I think so,' she said eventually. 'I mean there wasn't anyone standing with him when I gave him the money. But there were several people behind him. It's a small foyer, so maybe one of them had come in with him. I don't know.' Sunita gave a sudden shout – 'Oh!' – which she strangled as soon as she made it. Her hand came up, as if trying to attract the attention of the teacher in class. 'He got a phone call!' she squeaked excitedly. 'While he was queuing. I'd just finished with one customer and I looked up to beckon him forward, and his mobile rang. I thought he'd turn it off, but he answered it straight away.'

'Could you hear what he said?' Wilson asked eagerly, a young hound scenting a fresh trail.

'Oh, yes!' Sunita said, excited by her own remembering. 'He said something like, "I thought you were someone else," and then he said something rather odd. Only, I didn't think it was odd at the time, but of course it was.' She paused, as if to get her breath back, and then turned towards Lawson, as if she was happier confiding in someone of her own sex. 'The person who rang him must have asked him what he was doing, because he said he was paying money into his bank. But then of course, he came up to me and asked to withdraw some money. Now that's pretty odd, isn't it?'

'You need someone to talk to, you know.' Jane Holden dropped her pearl of wisdom casually as she placed a cup of black coffee in front of her daughter, and sat down opposite, with her own half-filled cup.

'Since when have you been a fan of therapists?' Susan said incredulously.

'Therapists?' came the wide-eyed, innocent's response. 'Whoever said anything about therapists? When I say someone to talk to, I just mean a friend. You know, someone you can pour out your day to – good, bad, or indifferent. Though of course it's most important when you've had a bad day.'

'I'll keep it in mind,' Susan said uneasily, suspicious of the way the conversation was heading.

'A nice man, for example,' Jane added.

'Mother!' Even though she was half expecting it, Susan Holden couldn't help screeching her response.

'Or a nice girl friend,' Jane Holden continued calmly. She paused. Then recommenced even more casually. 'If, that is, men are off the agenda for now!'

'Stop!' Susan held her left hand up to emphasize the word. 'Stop right there!'

Her mother shrugged, said nothing, and took a sip from her coffee. The two women sat in a distinctly non-cosy silence for perhaps a minute, though to Jane it seemed a lot longer. Susan was glad of the peace, but her mother, then as so often, was uncomfortable with silence.

'Well,' she said abruptly, 'What sort of day have you had? Because to judge from your mood, I assume it's not been a good one?'

Her daughter shrugged.

'For goodness sake,' her mother said, exasperation evident in every syllable. 'Why don't you tell me about it? You obviously need to talk to someone, and right now the only person available is me. Pretend I'm not your mother. Pretend I'm Robin Williams, or Freud, or whoever you'd rather I was. Only don't just sit there bottling it all up.'

Susan Holden exhaled an exaggerated sigh, and gave her mother her long, hard look. 'Didn't you see today's *Oxford Mail*?' she asked irritably.

'No,' her mother said defensively, before continuing untruthfully: 'I have to economize somewhere.'

'Did you watch the local news?'

'No!'

'Or listen to the Radio Oxford news?'

'Did I miss something?'

'A man called Martin Mace was murdered. He had been tied up and burnt to death in his allotment shed.'

Jane Holden gulped. 'How horrible!' she said. But her horror would not have registered high on any Richter Scale for such things. And indeed it was quickly engulfed by curiosity. 'Is it connected to the other deaths?'

'They knew each other. Mace was a lorry driver, but he had been attending anger management sessions at the day centre. Arnold was one of the facilitators.'

'Gosh!' Jane Holden said, as she tried to weigh up all this new information. 'And I take it from your less than ecstatic mood that you haven't arrested anyone yet?'

Susan responded by getting up from her armchair and walking over to the window where she looked out into the fading light. Grandpont Grange had been built with a deferential nod to the quadrangles beloved by Oxford colleges. Her mother's flat was on the first floor of the southern side, near the eastern corner, and as she stood there looking diagonally across to the opposite corner, she pretended briefly that she was a student in college. Two old men were walking uncertainly towards her along the path that diagonally traversed the grass square, like two senior dons stumbling back towards their rooms after a large dinner and several glasses of port from the cellar.

'No prime suspect even?' Like her daughter, Jane Holden was not someone who gave up a line of questioning until she had exhausted it.

Her daughter turned and faced her, but stayed silhouetted against the window as she began to answer the question obliquely. She made no mention of the fruitless interviews with Ratcliffe and Anne Johnson, preferring instead to talk about what had happened since, for it was these more recent events that were dominating her thought processes as she struggled to derive some clear sense of direction out of them.

'We went to visit Martin Mace's house. In Bedford Street. A rather nice three-bedroomed terraced house. Well, that's how an estate agent would describe it, though the third bedroom was very small and had been turned into an office-cum-shrine.'

'A shrine?' her mother said.

'To Oxford United. Photos of players all over the walls. And scarves and football shirts displayed as if they were pieces of art. Or at least they had been. Only someone had been in and ripped a lot of it down from the walls, and the drawers of the desk had been tipped upside down, and paper was scattered everywhere. Whoever it was had been round the whole house. Clothes were all over the bedroom floor, and the living-room was a right mess.'

'Do you know what the intruder was looking for?'

Susan Holden uttered a sound that was somewhere between a screech and a laugh. 'For God's sake, Mother, if I knew that then the chances are that I would know who the killer was and I'd have arrested him – or her – and I bloody well wouldn't be prowling round here like a cat on a hot tin roof.'

Jane Holden, untypically, went silent, stunned by the ferocity of her daughter's onslaught. Susan, perhaps embarrassed by her own tirade, turned away and again looked out of the window.

'Stupid question,' her mother said apologetically. 'Stupid, stupid question.'

'Anyway,' Susan said emphatically, now in control again, 'after that we went round to Jake Arnold's flat. I guess we should have done that before, but there always seemed to be more pressing matters to attend to, and of course it too had been turned over. Only the kitchen had survived largely unscathed, but elsewhere the floors were covered with clothes, papers and God knows what. So, as you can see, it's been a pretty bloody day.'

Mrs Holden smiled in sympathy at her daughter, and racked her brain for something positive and practical she could say. 'Well,' she said cautiously, 'I suppose that does at least prove one thing.'

Her daughter looked at her sharply. 'What do you mean?'

'The two men's homes have been searched. That as good as proves that their deaths are connected, in fact that they were killed by the same person.'

'Or persons,' Susan corrected.

'Quite,' she replied meekly, and waited for her daughter to say something else.

Susan turned back to the window and pulled the curtains across. 'I need a whisky,' she said, and began to walk over to the kitchen without waiting for permission.

It was only when they were both settled down to their drinks – Susan had poured herself a double on the rocks, while for her mother she had poured a bare single and then drowned it with soda – that Susan returned to the subject that was preoccupying all their thoughts.

'The intruder, the killer in fact, must have been concerned that Mace and Arnold might have had something in their possession that would have linked them to him or her.'

'You mean like a diary, or an appointments calendar?'

'Yes.'

'But you didn't find one?'

'No, but we're pretty damn sure that there had been a calendar in Jake Arnold's kitchen. There's a nail there with nothing hanging on it.'

'Let me guess!' her mother said eagerly. 'There was a square of lighter paint, and around it the wall was darker, from dust.'

'Hey, you've missed you vocation!' Susan said, genuinely impressed.

'Well, I'm not a moron, you know,' she replied firmly. 'I've done enough cleaning in my time to know that!'

'Of course you have,' Susan replied, somewhat chastened. 'But there was no such patch on any of Mace's walls?'

'No.'

'Maybe he had a diary?'

'Almost certainly, I'd say,' her daughter agreed. 'He was a self-employed lorry-driver, so he must have kept some record of what jobs he had when, but there was no sign of one so we are assuming it was found and taken by the intruder.'

'Unless he kept it in his lorry?'

'Unfortunately not. We found his lorry, parked in its usual place just off Meadow Lane, but there was no sign of a diary there. And there was no sign of one in his charred pockets either. So it looks like the killer found it.'

The two women relapsed into silence. The older woman sipped daintily at her still three-quarters-full glass. 'Maybe everything will be clearer in the morning,' she said optimistically. 'I bloody well hope so!' the younger woman said vehemently. And with that she drained the rest of her whisky and got up to leave.

'They're playing tonight.' Detective Constable Wilson and WPC Lawson were about to drive out of the Cowley Police Station car park again, only this time Wilson was signalling right. 'I think I might go.'

Lawson yawned theatrically, and pumped her hand in front of her mouth like a five-year-old auditioning for the role of Native American Indian in a multi-ethnic, non-nativity, Christmas show.

'More of a rugby girl are you?' Wilson continued cheerfully, his mood lifted by the prospect of visiting the Kassam Stadium in work time.

'I prefer tennis actually,' Lawson replied tartly. 'And, in case you hadn't noticed, I am a woman, not a girl!'

'Sorry!' said Wilson, the apology rising instantly to his lips.

An awkward silence fell. Wilson pretended it hadn't by concentrating extra hard on the traffic lights in front of him. Nevertheless, he was relieved when Lawson broke it.

'The thing I most like about tennis is serving.' She paused. 'You get a pair of balls that you can squeeze and bounce as much as you like, and then you get to whack them over the net as hard as possible. I find that very satisfying.'

Wilson looked across, expecting to see a grin on her face, but she was facing forward, apparently oblivious of him, her mouth and eyes (or at least the one eye he could see) expressionless. Not for the first time in his acquaintanceship with

Lawson, he found himself at a loss to know what the hell to think.

Silence descended again, and this time Wilson was happy that it had. It continued while he drove up the Watlington Road, then swung right along the Grenoble Road, which separates Greater Lees from a countryside whose most obvious features are a proliferation of power lines and the stench of the sewage works. At the fourth roundabout he took the second exit, which led into the car park that served the complex constructed by Firoz Kassam. To the left stood the barely complete Bowlplex and Ozone Cinema, and to the right the three-sided Kassam Stadium, home of Oxford United, a team who had once in the heady days of Robert Maxwell and Jim Smith risen to the very top league, but which now languished in the bottom one. For a few seconds, as he drove round to the front of the stadium and parked his car, Wilson was no longer a policeman, but only a wide-eyed boy at one with his football team.

'Well, let's get on with it!' WPC Lawson was outside the car looking in, waiting for Wilson to emerge from his dream. 'You're the blooming football expert, not me.'

Wilson smiled and clambered out. 'I bet you know much more than you're letting on. I can see you mixing it with the boys in the playground, sliding in with two-footed tackles just to show them who was boss.'

She grinned back. 'Maybe you're smarter than you look, Wilson.'

'I guess that wouldn't be difficult,' he replied.

'Hi there, I'm Alan Wright.' The greeting came from a man who had appeared from a door to the left of the ticket office windows. He was short, wore glasses and was dressed in jogging bottoms and a bright yellow open-neck shirt which said more about his football allegiance than his sense of sartorial style. They exchanged introductions, and then he took them inside.

'Coffee?'

'No thanks. We just need some information. As I mentioned on the phone, we need to get a handle on the habits of two men. We know they are both fans. We want to know if they had a habit of sitting together. One is Jake Arnold and the other Martin Mace.'

'Well, if they booked by phone, or used a card to pay, we'll have a record. What sort of time frame are we looking at?'

'Last season and this,' Wilson replied.

Wright's fingers flew confidently across the computer keyboard on his desk. 'Yes!' he said triumphantly. 'Here we are. Jake Arnold. Been to a couple of home games this season. Rochdale and Rushden. Sat in the South Stand Upper the first time, and the South Stand Lower the second time. Do you want me to print the details?'

'Yes,' Wilson said. 'But what about last season?'

Again the fingers got to work. 'Hm! Interesting. Only four games. The first was in January, against Wrexham, then one in February, none in March, and two in April.'

'How many tickets did he buy?' Lawson said, her first words since they had entered the building.

'Just one in the first two games, then two in the next two.'

'Really?' Wilson said.

'And always in the South Stand,' Wright added. 'Though not in the same place. He obviously didn't have a favourite seat.'

Lawson had moved over to the printer and was scrutinizing the sheet of paper she had picked up from it. 'He bought two tickets for the Rochdale and Rushden games too.'

'So the question is: who was the other person?'

Wright looked up. 'Sorry, who was the other person you were interested in?'

'Martin Mace.'

Again the fingers tapped into the keyboard. 'Sorry. No sign of him. Not this season or last.'

'Are you sure?' Wilson said in surprise.

'Of course I'm sure. Maybe he paid by cash. Turned up on the day.'

Lawson produced a photograph and placed it next to the keyboard. 'Ring any bells?'

Wright looked briefly at the picture and looked up with a grin. 'Oh him. Oh yes, I know him. He nearly always cycles here, usually late in the afternoon, and pays cash. He nearly always buys three tickets. And always for the Oxford Mail Stand. Always on his bike no matter what the weather. I asked him about it once and he told me he needed the exercise. Well he sits in a lorry most of the day, so I guess he didn't want to put on too much weight.' Wright paused, and then laughed. 'Not that he was entirely successful. He obviously liked his beer.'

'Can I ask a stupid question?' Lawson said, flashing her dumb-blonde smile at Alan Wright.

Inevitably the approach worked. Wright smiled eagerly back, a puppy dog eager to please. 'Of course!'

'We're just talking home games aren't we? What about away games?'

'Yes, home games. Away games is different. Often people just buy them at the gate on the day. Unless it's a local derby and they make it all ticket. Then they have to buy them here in advance.'

The dumb-blonde smile flashed again, followed by a look of puzzlement. 'And when they are away, can they sit anywhere they like?'

'No,' he explained benevolently, 'all the away fans are put in one place. To avoid trouble. You're police. You must know that?'

Lawson smiled again her smile. 'I suppose I must. But I am only a woman.'

Wright looked at her suspiciously, suddenly aware that perhaps she wasn't being straight with him. 'Is that all?' he said tersely.

Lawson appeared not to be aware of this change of attitude. 'You've been so kind,' she purred, her smile even wider. 'Some men' – and as she said this she glanced point-edly across towards Wilson – 'some men just don't want to talk about football to women. They behave as if we can't possibly understand it. But anyway, we'll leave you to it. But if anything occurs to you, perhaps you could give me a ring?'

She looked across at Wilson, and he nodded and they turned as one to go. They had hardly taken two steps, how-ever, before Wilson stopped and spun round. 'One more thing!' he said, in a tone of such abruptness that both Lawson and Wright looked at him like horses startled by a backfiring car. 'Did he buy tickets for tonight's game?'

Wright dragged his hand through his hair as he tried to recall. 'I think so,' he said uncertainly. 'I seem to remember his coming over Thursday or Friday.'

'You wouldn't know which seats?' Wilson said.

Wright shrugged. 'Sorry. If he paid cash—' His voice trailed away. Wilson stood there unmoving, reluctant to bring the meeting to an end. 'Still,' said Wright, 'I guess you'll recognize him now, if you want to arrest him.'

'He won't be coming tonight' Wilson said brutally. 'Didn't we mention it? He's dead. Burnt to a cinder. It's his friends we are interested in.'

'Oh!' Wright said. 'Well, if we can be of any help—'

'You've already been a great help,' Lawson said, inter-vening. Wilson's boorish aggression was beginning to irritate her. Couldn't he bloody see that a bit of flattery and thanks was going to work a lot better with Wright than his we're-in-bloody-charge approach? 'But I was wondering if there wasn't another area in which you could help us even more? I know you must be very busy, but—'

'Just ask' he said, anxious again to please the really rather attractive WPC.

Lawson smile again. She could almost see his tail wag-ging like a windmill. 'Well, I was thinking about how we might identify these friends of Martin Mace, and then it sud-denly occurred to me that you must have got closed circuit

TV. So if you could help us locate Mace from a previous game, we should be able to identify his friends.'

'I'd be delighted,' Wright said.

*

It took Fox three prolonged rings on the bell before he and Holden were rewarded by the sound of something falling, and then by the appearance of a figure at the back of the gallery. As Les Whiting walked towards them and then fiddled at the locks and bolts which secured Bare Canvas from the outer world, Holden looked again at her watch. 'How does he make any money if he's not open at this hour?'

'How does he make any money at all,' Fox responded sourly. 'Who the hell wants to pay hard earned cash for rubbish like this,' and his hand gestured towards the stark primary-coloured canvases which hung on his walls.

The door opened. 'Not come to buy something to cheer your living spaces up, have you?' If Les Whiting had heard Fox's comments, he wasn't showing it. Holden briefly thanked God that she didn't have to be perpetually cheerful in order to do her job.

'I'm afraid not,' she replied. 'But perhaps another time.'

'Police business then,' Whiting said, holding the door open so that they could enter. 'Is it OK with you if I open up?' he asked. 'I'm not expecting a flood of visitors, but a single buyer is all one needs sometimes.'

'Best not,' said Holden firmly. 'Sorry, but this is serious police business, and if all goes well it'll only take a few minutes.'

Whiting locked and bolted the door. 'Well in that case,' he said rather petulantly, 'I won't risk delaying you by offering you a coffee.'

'Good,' Fox said uncompromisingly, 'because all we are interested in are some straight answers to some questions. Then, as the Inspector said, if we are satisfied with the answers we'll go.'

'And if you're not?'

'Where were you on Monday night?'

Whiting frowned. 'Why do you ask?'

'Would you rather we did this down at the police station?' Fox asked belligerently. 'Because if you don't bloody well answer our questions, that's where you'll be going, and your precious gallery will be staying shut for a lot longer.'

Whiting looked across at Holden, but if he hoped to gain comfort there he was disappointed. The woman's face was hard, stripped bare of emotion, and her eyes met his unflinchingly. He turned back towards Fox. 'I was here,' he said. 'We had a private showing, to open this exhibition. It started at 6.00, though I had been here most of the day getting ready for it with Kim. Kim Carpenter. The exhibitionist.' He gestured towards the walls. 'It finished about 8.00 p.m.'

'Did you leave immediately?' Fox pressed.

'Not immediately. I had to clear up, but I probably left about 8.30.'

'Can anyone verify this?'

'Well Kim offered to stay behind, but her son and daughter had come up from London, so I told her to go and I finished off on my own.'

'We'll need to get her to verify this.'

'Look, what exactly is all this about?'

'Don't you know?' Fox asked.

'Well, of course I don't. I mean, you come here and start asking—'

'Mr Whiting!' Holden spat the words out like an archetypal sergeant major bringing a new recruit to order. Whiting stopped, and for three or four seconds silence fell. When Holden continued, her voice was quieter, but equally as firm. 'Tell us about your break-up with Jake. If I recall correctly, you said he had an affair with another man, but I don't think you told us who this man was.'

'I think you recall incorrectly,' Whiting replied. 'I am certain I told you he had a one night stand with someone.

And the reason I never told you his name was because I never knew what it was.'

Holden chewed at her lip, while her brain apparently lost itself in puzzled thought.

'So how did you find out about this, this er … one night stand. Did Jake confess it over his cornflakes the next morning?'

'What the hell does it matter?'

'It matters,' Holden said, reverting to her sergeant major tones, 'because I want to find Jake Arnold's killer.' Even as she said this, Holden was undecided as to what to say next – if anything. Whiting, she was sure, had not been entirely truthful about the end of his relationship with Jake, but that merely made it all the more important to choose her line of attack with care. There seemed to be two possible approaches: one softly, softly, probing with questions gently, remorselessly; or there was the opposite approach.

'You must have hated Martin.' Holden said this in a matter-of-fact, doesn't-really-matter tone. She tried to look as if she was uninterested in the answer, merely going through the motions for the sake of it, but she was watching intently for Whiting's reaction, conscious that it was that first second of time, that first unguarded expression to flick across his face, maybe – if she was lucky – his first utterance that would tell her that her suspicions were well founded. Or not.

Whiting opened his mouth as if to speak, but then shut it again. He smiled, and then opened his mouth again, this time to speak. 'Martin? Martin who?'

'I think you know.'

He scratched his head theatrically. 'Hm!' he continued. 'I think I know at least three Martins, and then of course there's also Mr Martin who runs the corner shop. I find him perfectly pleasant.'

Holden changed tack abruptly, switching back to her original line of enquiry.

'You haven't yet told me how you found out about Jake Arnold's one night stand.'

'Haven't I? Is that a crime.'

'Christ!' Fox broke in angrily. 'Let's just take him down to the station. If he wants to play silly buggers with us, then we'll fucking well do it properly. We could start by sticking him in a cell for a few hours while we search his flat, and then we could question him for half the night, and then maybe he'll stop pissing us about.' Fox stepped forward as he stopped talking, causing Whiting to step back. Then, pleased with the effect of his outburst, he produced a pair of handcuffs from his pocket. 'Do you want to tell him his rights, or shall I?'

'I saw a text message on his mobile,' Whiting blurted out. He was unsure whether the hulking great sergeant was serious or not, but he found him frightening nevertheless, and suddenly his own appetite for playing games was gone.

'What message?' Holden asked quickly.

'A suspicious one.'

'That's not good enough,' Fox said bluntly.

'You want chapter and verse? Word for word? Well, let me think. "When can we do it again?" I think that was pretty much it.'

'Did you often check his mobile messages?' Holden said flatly.

Whiting shrugged. 'No. But the fact is he had been behaving pretty suspiciously, so I took my opportunity.'

'So you asked him about the message?'

'Yes.'

'And?'

'And he admitted it. That he'd met this guy.'

'What was this guy's name?'

Whiting gave another shrug. 'Don't know.'

'You're lying,' Fox snarled.

Holden held up her hand, gesturing Fox to silence. 'Let me just run over the scene. You ask Jake about the message. He admits to meeting someone else. He says it was just a one-off. You don't ask who he was. You don't ask where he met him, or when he met him or anything. You just say: "That's

OK, Jake, let's pretend it never happened and why don't we crack open a bottle of champagne to demonstrate how grown up we've been about it all." Now, are you seriously expecting me to swallow that story? Because if you are I'll stop right now and start following Sergeant Fox's advice.'

Whiting shut his eyes and lifted his hands to his face. Slowly he sucked in a deep breath and then nosily released it. He opened his eyes and looked with an air of resignation across at Holden 'MM. That's what his initials were. They were stored on his mobile. But he wouldn't tell me any more about him. I swear. Not his full name or where he met him, or the colour of his underwear or anything. He was very protective of him. Maybe he was worried I'd storm round to where he lived and cause a scene.'

'Did you?'

'No I didn't. I don't know where he lives. How could I?'

Holden suddenly stood up. Fox followed suit. Whiting nervously did the same. 'Is that all?'

'No,' said Holden. 'We're taking you down to the station.'

'Why?' Whiting replied in obvious alarm. 'I've answered all your questions, and I've got a gallery to open up.'

'Because,' she said, 'I need a formal statement. Martin Mace was brutally murdered on Monday night, and the way things are at the moment, your name is pretty much top of our list of suspects. And, of course, if my memory serves me right, you didn't have an alibi for Jake Arnold's death either.'

*

Dr Karen Pointer was in her office, seated at her desk, her fingers moving deftly over her laptop keyboard.

'Come in!' she called in response to the knock on her door, but she continued typing, her eyes refusing to look up as DI Holden entered the room, though whether it was because it was Holden (she had seen her get out of the car that pulled up outside her window), or whether she was genuinely preoccupied with her report, only she herself knew. 'Sit down,' she said, but still her eyes and fingers remained committed to their computer task. Holden sat down silently, and waited. Eventually, Dr Pointer's hands slowed down. Her right thumb and forefinger briefly moved to the bridge of her nose, alighting there for several seconds, before they moved to the screen of the laptop and firmly closed it down. Only then did she look up. When she spoke, it was with brisk efficiency.

'I need to check a couple of things out, but otherwise my report on Mace is pretty much finished. I'll get it over to you this afternoon.'

'Thank you. I would appreciate that.'

The two women eyed each other. 'Good,' Pointer replied, wondering why Holden had come over, and had come on her own this time. It was, she suddenly realized, the first time she had been alone with her since, well, since the incident.

'I don't mean to hassle you,' Holden said apologetically, 'but I need to know about the time of death. I don't know how accurate you can be with a burning.'

'8.45 p.m. Or thereabouts.'

'Wow!' she said, taken by surprise.

'Actually, it's not particularly clever,' she said with a thin smile. 'His watch stopped. Presuming it was the fire that did it, then I reckon that ties it down pretty tight. Certainly it is in accordance with the forensic evidence.'

Holden made no reply. Silence hung between them, but – perhaps surprisingly – it wasn't an oppressive one.

'Does it clarify things?' Pointer asked.

Holden wasn't sure that it did. She had been trying to weigh up the possibility of Whiting getting from his gallery to the allotment in time to commit murder, and all in all she reckoned he could have, albeit without much time to spare. But in any case Pointer's question only lightly registered on her consciousness, for something else was oppressing her. This was an opportunity – with no one else here to witness it – that she ought to take. She cleared her throat noisily. 'I'd like to apologize.'

'Apologize?' Pointer was puzzled.

'For slapping you.'

'Hell!' she replied, and her eyes now locked with Holden's. Then, curiously, she smiled. 'I probably deserved it.'

'Yes,' Holden said, rather too firmly for Pointer's liking. 'Nevertheless,' Holden continued after a brief pause, 'I'm not sure I needed to do it with quite so much force.'

Pointer smiled again. Her hand moved up to her left-hand cheek and stroked gently across the skin. 'I can still feel it,' she said.

'Sorry!' Holden said, and stood up to go.

'It's taken, love.'

The woman, dressed in jeans, pink T-shirt and denim jacket, had just sat down. She turned and looked at the large man in the seat next to her. She smiled. 'By me. Seat F28. That's what it says on my ticket.'

She was a looker, no question, maybe 22 or 23 to his 35, but the man felt uncomfortable. She was on all counts out of his league. Women like her just didn't open conversations with him, eye him up, flirt. He felt himself getting flushed, and that made him aggressive. 'It's my mate's seat!' he insisted loudly. 'He'll be here any minute.'

The woman smiled again. 'Who's your mate?'

'What's it to you? This is his seat.' The man in the seat beyond him leant forward. Even though he was sitting down, it was obvious to the woman that he was shorter and altogether a less imposing a specimen of male, but he placed his hand lightly on his companion's shoulder as if to calm him down. 'He doesn't mean no harm, dear, only we always sit together – him, me and Martin. So why don't you just show us your ticket and we'll sort out where you're meant to be sitting. All right?'

'All right,' the woman said with a shrug. She unbuttoned the breast-pocket of her jacket, pulled something out of it, and then discreetly displayed it for the two men. 'If it's all right by you, my governor would like a word.'

'Fuck!' they said, in perfect unison.

*

'So what's this all about?' Al Smith demanded fiercely. 'The game starts in ten minutes, and I'm not missing it, not for you and not for anybody!'

'I'm not asking you to,' the dark-haired woman said. 'Just answer my questions, and you can get back to your seats.'

'Is Martin all right?' Sam Sexton asked. His eyes flicked around the room, alighting nervously on the face of each of the four inquisitors, only to move on to the next almost immediately – but if he was seeking reassurances, he sought it in vain. The blonde who had flirted with them in the Oxford Mail end was now standing by the door, all cheer wiped off her face. A young man – a detective constable presumably, though hell he hardly looked old enough – was standing in the corner on the opposite site of the room. His face, too, was swept clean of emotion, and his arms hung loosely by his sides. Immediately opposite Sexton and Smith – across a wood-effect table – sat the woman who had introduced herself as Detective Inspector Holden and a sour-faced man whom she had introduced as Detective Sergeant Fox. He was a big man, imposing even when seated, and Sexton felt himself shudder involuntarily. He moved his attention onto Holden, glad it was her who was calling the shots.

'Why do you ask that?' Holden replied.

'He's never bloody late for a game,' Smith butted in. 'And here you are asking bloody questions. So the fact is we reckon something must have happened to him. It stands to reason, don't it.'

'I'm sorry to have to tell you that Martin Mace is dead.'

'I knew it!' said Sexton, his voice shrill with hysteria. 'I bloody knew it!' Holden's eyes, though, were fixed not on

Sexton, but on Smith. But whatever emotions Smith was feeling at the moment, he wasn't showing them. His face was not so much blank as bored. He looked at his watch ostentatiously, then looked up at Holden. 'So are you going to tell us what happened? Because if so, perhaps you can get on with it.'

Holden twitched her head. Fox leant down to his right, thrusting his hand into a bag, from which he drew out a newspaper. He placed it carefully in the middle of the table, so that the two men opposite could see its front page.

'Didn't you see Monday's *Oxford Mail*?'

'Only the back pages,' Smith said casually, but his eyes were anything but casual. For several seconds there was silence, as Smith and Sexton took in the somewhat arch headline ('The Allotment of Death'), the gloomy photo of the charred remains of the garden shed, and the first few lines of the article which accompanied them.

'So, you've not arrested anyone yet then?' Smith said, with a sneer in his voice. He was looking at Holden now, apparently having read and seen enough.

'Where were you on Monday night,' Holden asked.

'Oh, we're suspects are we?' Smith replied aggressively. 'Just because we're his best bloody mates, you think we killed him?'

'I don't think anything,' Holden said, her own voice louder in response. 'But we need to know where you were at the time of Martin Mace's death. So just tell us where you were on Monday from, let's say, 6.00 o'clock onwards.'

'I was working, wasn't I, till about 7.00. On a house in Cornwallis Road. Doing an extension out the back for them. With Sam. Then I went home, had a shower, had a pizza out the freezer, then went to the Wellington in Between Towns Road. Sam was there.'

'When did you arrive at the Wellington?'

'About nine o'clock I'd say.'

'Yes,' Sexton said. 'That's right; I had only been there a couple of minutes when he arrived.'

'And where had you been before that, Mr Sexton?'

'I was with Al in Cornwallis Road till about five o'clock, but I left him to finish off cos I had another job to price up. I got home about six – my wife will confirm that, but she went out about seven; she works nights at the hospital Monday to Thursday – and I watched the telly and did the ironing.'

'So between seven and roughly 8.45, you were at home, but no one else was there? Is that right?'

Sexton, who appeared to have been starting to relax, suddenly lifted his right hand to his forehead and dragged it through his hair with such violence that he wrenched his head back. 'Are you accusing me?' He squealed the words. 'I was his mate. A good mate. Why should I want to kill him? Why should anyone want to kill him?'

'That's what we want to know,' Holden said firmly. 'But the fact is that someone wanted to kill him, and did so. If we can find out why, then the chances are we'll find out who.'

It is impossible to know who had the idea first. And later, when discussing it in the pub after the case had been closed, both Wilson and Lawson acknowledged the part the other had played in the genesis of the idea. But one fact is as certain as can be: that the idea came very shortly after the final whistle. After Holden and Fox had finished questioning Smith and Sexton, the four of them had had a short debriefing before Holden signalled that their working day was over. Fox offered to drop his boss off at her flat, but Wilson said he thought he'd stay and watch the game. Lawson, rather to his surprise, had said that she'd keep him company. But it was, unfortunately, a distinctly uninspiring game. Oxford scored a minute after half-time, and then conceded a goal two minutes later. And that, in terms of goals and excitement, was pretty much that.

'If that doesn't put you off football, then nothing will,' Wilson said to his companion gloomily. The two of them were still sitting in their seats, as they waited for the other spectators to disperse. Wilson opened his programme and began to read through the manager's notes again.

'Do you always buy a programme?' Lawson asked.

Wilson, engrossed, appeared not to have taken in the question. Over the tannoy, a disembodied voice reminded fans that there was another home game the forthcoming Saturday. As silence returned to the echoing roof of the stand, Wilson looked up and turned his head towards Lawson. 'Why do you ask?' he said warily.

Lawson was equally cautious in her reply. 'I was just thinking,' she said.

Wilson looked down at his programme, folded it carefully shut, and looked at her again.

'About programmes?'

'Yes.' The thought, or maybe two identical thoughts, had now entered or been created within their separate brains.

'Mace had loads of programmes in that room of his,' Wilson said quietly, as if afraid that saying it loudly might somehow reveal a fatal flaw in his thinking.

'So did Arnold,' said Lawson. 'On the bookshelves in his bedroom.'

They looked at each other for several seconds in silence. The stand in front of them was now almost totally deserted except for a couple of stewards at the bottom of the steps.

'What about Sarah Johnson?' Lawson asked.

Wilson tried to think back to the search he and Fox had made after Fox had interviewed Anne Johnson. The problem was they hadn't been looking for anything like football programmes. Drugs and signs of depression and that diary that they had found, but football programmes? 'I just can't recall noticing,' Wilson admitted. 'And besides, there's no real reason to believe she didn't just commit suicide and—'

'It would be a connection, wouldn't it,' Lawson said assertively. 'Another connection besides the day centre. Suppose they always sat together—'

Wilson, aware that Lawson was half a step in front of him, cut in angrily: 'A programme won't tell you that!'

Lawson pursed her lips, while she considered her next sentence. A look of innocence emerged from her features, and from her mouth there came an equally innocent tone of voice. 'When I was a kid and went to watch something – a pantomime, or an outdoor Shakespeare play, or once I went to Wimbledon – I always kept my programme and my ticket. Didn't you?'

CHAPTER 11

He was eating breakfast when the call came, and he swore involuntarily. He was not a morning person. He would have admitted as much if he had been asked, though he would have expressed it differently given that he was a call-a-spade-a-bloody-shovel type of person. He slurped at his still-hot black coffee and grimaced. Only then did he flick open his mobile to see who the hell was calling him. A number flashed up on screen, a number which neither his mobile nor he recognized. His first impulse was to ignore it, but his curiosity was aroused, and instead he leant forward and picked it up.

'Yes?' he demanded.

'It's me!'

'What the fuck are you doing?'

'I'm ringing you up.' The familiar voice spoke calmly. 'I'd have thought it was obvious.'

'We agreed, didn't we. No bloody phone calls. If they were ever to check my mobile—'

'I'm ringing from a phone box. I'm not an idiot.'

'Where from?' His voice was raised now and angry.

But the caller ignored his question. 'Can't we meet?'

'You must be fucking mad! We agreed. In six months' time, maybe.'

'I didn't mean Oxford, stupid. But London or Bristol. Or Paris even. Where's the risk in that.'

'I'm not taking any risks for you,' he said coldly. Then he pressed the red button on his mobile and swore again.

Meanwhile, not so far away across the streets of Oxford, Detective Inspector Holden had just slumped down at her desk in the Cowley Police Station. On automatic pilot, she powered up her PC, and waited as it struggled into some semblance of life. She had slept badly, waking at 2.30 and again at 4.15, and then sleeping through the alarm. So she'd got to the station later than she'd wanted and tired. The log in screen had just appeared in front of her when the phone rang. She picked the receiver up, placed it against her left ear and spoke. 'DI Holden here.'

'Good morning,' came the reply. She recognized the high-pitched voice, and immediately wished she had let her voicemail handle the call. It was Don Alexander, from the *Oxford Mail*.

'So what do you want this morning?' she asked tartly. 'Short of copy are you?'

He laughed. 'Just want to keep the public informed. That's all, Inspector.' Then the laughter had disappeared from his voice. 'Look, people are worried. Hell, I'm worried. Even my cat is worried. So the question we need an answer to is, when are you going to arrest someone?'

'How long is a piece of bloody string?' was her instant response, and immediately regretted it.

'Is there a prime suspect?' he pressed.

'No comment,' she replied. 'And don't quote me about pieces of string.'

'What leads are you working on, Inspector?'

'I can't comment on that either.'

He paused. Then continued more caustically: 'Inspector, just for the record, how many more deaths have to occur before you do comment?'

Holden had to choke back the impulse to scream into the phone. When she did speak – and this was very much to her credit – it was in an only slightly heightened tone. 'Look, Don, I really do have a lot of work to do, so if it's OK with you, or even if it isn't, I'm going to put the phone down now. Good bye.'

It took Wilson and Lawson most of Thursday morning to search again the accommodation of Martin Mace and Jake Arnold and Sarah Johnson. Mace's was the quickest since his small third bedroom had been devoted to his sacred team. Football programmes, home and away, were carefully organized in date order on the shelves that lined the walls. Labels on each shelf indicated the season. They placed the programmes for the current season and all of the previous season into two cardboard boxes. Tracking the actual tickets Mace had bought and used proved no more difficult. A shoebox on the top shelf contained envelopes. Each was marked – '2001-2002 season' for example – and inside each were two wodges of tickets, each with an elastic band around it. As a brief glance revealed, one consisted of tickets for home games, and one for away.

'Talk about making things easy for us,' Wilson grinned.

But Lawson said nothing, for she was already walking back down the stairs, a box under each arm, and a small but as yet untested idea in her head.

At much the same time, Danny Flynn stood in the middle of his room and looked critically around. He lived in a bed-sitter on the top floor of a four-storey house on the south-eastern side of the Iffley Road. It was a large room, taking in the full depth of the building, though the eaves of the roof had the effect of making the room seem somewhat smaller than its official dimensions. Danny walked across to the front window, which afforded a view across the Iffley Road towards the university running track, the very one on which Roger Bannister had been the first man to break the four-minute barrier for the mile all those years ago. But this feat was not at all on Flynn's mind. As he peered out of the window, it wasn't across the road that he was looking, but rather down at the road, and in particular at the pavements on either side. He stood there for several minutes, hardly moving, but assessing the individuals, couples and groups who were walking up and down them. A grey-haired woman and small child – grandmother and granddaughter presumably – made their way very slowly from right to left as he looked, hand in hand. Two men in dark suits strode past them in the other direction, walking together but not, as far as Flynn could see, talking together. Next into Flynn's view came a group of five students. Dressed in T-shirts, shorts, and trainers, they rapidly overtook the woman and child, before turning right down the private road, bound perhaps for the running track and Bannister's footprints.

None of these moving people held Flynn's attention for any length of time. What did, however, was first a car, and then a woman. The car was pulled up on the far side of the road, facing the city centre but ignoring all the parking restrictions clearly indicated by the double yellow lines running along that side of the road. A man was sitting in the driving seat and he was talking into a mobile phone. This carried on for over a minute – Flynn kept checking his watch every ten seconds or so – before the car moved jerkily off, the mobile phone still clasped to the man's right ear. Instantly, Flynn's attention was transferred to a woman leaning against the railings. For Flynn realized with a start that he hadn't noticed her before. He hadn't seen her stop. He hadn't seen her walking along the street. It was as if she had materialized on that paving slab. Anxiety surged around his body, and his hands, hanging down in front of him started to move from side to side, as if controlled, like those of a marionette, by strings. How long had she been there? She was in the shade created by the overhanging branches of the large beech tree that stood on the far side of the railings. She might have been there ages. Watching. Watching his window? Watching out for him? But her face, the position of her head, told another story, and as he realized this the anxiety began to slowly seep from his body. She was not looking up. She was looking down the road now, to the left as Flynn saw it, and every movement of her body suggested that she, too, was anxious. She looked nervously at her watch, she pulled abstractedly at a lock of hair, she looked back up the street, and then back down the street again. She was waiting for someone, and he – or she – was late. Flynn watched her intently. His hands had stopped moving, and his breathing now eased. She hadn't looked up towards him even once. So, maybe she wasn't a spy. Maybe she wasn't one of them after all. Then, all of a sudden, the woman took another final glance at her watch, before turning and starting to walk back towards the city centre, first slowly, even reluctantly, and soon more purposefully, her legs striding out as if she was determined to leave this embarrassing place behind. She had been stood up. Flynn grinned in relief. But as he watched her disappear from view, he found himself feeling sorry for her, and even angry on her behalf. How dare he stand her up? For a he it must have been, Flynn decided. What had she done to deserve that? Bastard! Flynn watched where she had disappeared for several seconds, in case by some chance she should turn around and retrace her steps. But when she didn't, he let out a deep breath and sighed. There was no one watching, of that he was certain – well almost certain. He was safe. Flynn stepped back from his window, turned round, and reviewed the state of his room again.

The first thing that would have struck a visitor was the neatness of the room. Apart from the slightly faded pattern of the duvet cover, the bed might have been part of a window display: the two pillows were plumped, the duvet was rumple free, and a towel lay folded into a square at its foot. On the small chest of drawers next to the bed there stood a lamp with a pale-green lampshade and a small black alarm clock. Nothing else. A three-door wardrobe dominated the wall to the right of the bed (as Flynn looked at it), and the long mirror on the central door showed not a single mark (Flynn had cleaned it just before going to sleep the night before.)

Next to it was a doorway that led to the shower room and toilet, as well as to the front door of the bedsit. And next to that were bookshelves that covered the wall right up to the front of the room. Flynn frowned, and moved forward. He peered at two wooden figures, Norwegian trolls, which stood in the centre of the shelving as if they were guardians of all the books and magazines that were stacked above, below and to either side of them. They were squat figures, with cheerful faces and bulbous noses, but Flynn was not satisfied. He grunted, and then moved the male figure a few millimetres backwards. He stepped back a pace, grunted again, stepped forward, and this time moved the female figure slightly to the right. He stepped back again, surveyed the figures, and this time nodded in satisfaction. He continued then with his 360-degree sweep of the room, looking for anything that had got out of place. Eventually he nodded again, before advancing towards to the side of the wardrobe closest to the doorway. He removed a ring with three attached keys from a hook screwed into the wood and thrust them deep into his right-hand pocket. There was a second hook. On this there hung a Swiss Army knife. Flynn ran the thumb and first finger of his left hand down its red casing. When Fox had visited, he had noticed it hanging there; in truth Flynn rarely removed it from its place. But on this particular morning Flynn picked it gently off its hook and examined it closely. Then without a sound he put it into his left-hand pocket, before flicking the two light switches upwards and opening his door to leave.

*

Jake Arnold's flat was a mess. Even before the intruder had been in and tossed things around it had been a mess, and no one had been allowed to put anything back. Although it was smaller than Mace's house – a double bedroom, a small guest bedroom, a very snug bathroom, and a large open space that served as a sitting and dining area, with galley kitchen off to the side – finding football programmes and other memorabilia proved a much more exacting task for Wilson and Lawson. He had bookshelves, built in either side of the fireplace, but most of the contents of them were on the floor.

'Maybe you could sift through these,' Wilson suggested, with a wave of his hand, 'while I go through his drawers.'

'Of course,' Lawson said mildly, but with a flash in her eyes. 'Whatever turns you on.'

The drawers did not, however, prove in any sense exciting. They had already been half ransacked, and it didn't take Wilson long to discover that Jake Arnold hadn't stashed his football programmes under his pants or his pullovers. A box at the bottom of the wardrobe briefly offered hope, but it turned out to contain a collection of gay magazines much too explicit for the rather prudish detective constable. Wilson found himself wishing he'd chosen the shelves.

'Nothing here,' Lawson called through.

'Nor here!' he shouted back, and shut the wardrobe door firmly. He walked back through to the living room where he found Lawson standing with hands on her hips and a frown on her face. 'Do you think he threw his programmes away?' she asked.

'It's possible, I suppose,' Wilson replied with a shrug.

'Maybe he didn't bother buying them. Maybe he just borrowed someone else's,' Lawson suggested, and then added dryly. 'In my experience, men can be very tight with their money.'

'And in my experience,' Wilson said, trying not to rise, 'men who go to football like to buy a programme. They like to make a note of who played and who came on as a substitute, and who scored. And then they keep those programmes. For a while, at least.'

'So where are Jake Arnold's?' Lawson demanded.

Wilson shrugged. 'Well, unless there's a roof space that I haven't spotted, there's the kitchen and the bathroom.'

'I'll take the bathroom,' Lawson said hastily, conscious that she had drunk too much coffee that morning. 'If that is OK with you, that is?' she added.

Wilson made no comment. He moved slowly towards the doorway of the small kitchen and looked in. His attention was immediately drawn to a row of several books in the corner behind the kettle. The name of Delia Smith on a spine of the nearest confirmed the obvious – that they were recipe books. He picked up each one in turn, flicking through each methodically in the hope, futile he knew, that Jake Arnold had kept his programmes tucked inside for some obscure reason. Well, Delia was famously a supporter of Norwich City FC. But no. Nothing. He then started to go through the drawers and cupboards. Cutlery, crockery, glasses, tinned food, dry food, saucepans, a wok, another kettle, still in its box.

'Alleluia!' Wilson turned, surprised by the sudden and high-pitched shout of his colleague. She was standing just behind him in the doorway, and her right hand brandished her discovery. 'Six programmes, all from last season.'

'They were in the bathroom?' Wilson felt a little cheated that it had not be he who found them.

'Four home games and two away. They were on the chest of drawers by the loo. Under the leaflets on depression, self-harm and hearing voices. A choice of reading for the happy crapper!'

Wilson grinned despite his unreasonable irritation. 'Two down and one to go then.'

When DI Holden's phone rang only ten minutes after her brief conversation with Don Alexander, her first reaction was to ignore it, but she knew she couldn't. On the third ring she picked it up and immediately heard an all too familiar voice. She immediately began to count silently to ten. 'Sorry darling,' her mother gushed. 'You know how I don't like to bother you at work but, well, I've had an idea.'

Her daughter, who had now reached ten, continued her silent count on towards twenty.

'Hello?' her mother had said. 'Can you hear me Susan?'

Fifteen … sixteen … 'Yes Mother, I can hear you.'

'Well do you want to hear my idea? It's about your case!'

Nineteen … twenty. 'Yes Mother,' she fibbed, 'I'd like to hear your idea. But,' she added, still in untruth mode, 'I do have a meeting very shortly.'

'Well, assert you authority,' she barked. 'Make them wait. They'll respect you more for it. Anyway, this is my idea. Only, I bet you'll think it's a silly one.'

Susan recognized the game. 'Tell me mother, just tell me.'

'After all, who am I but a silly old woman who knows nothing of the world of real crime and—'

'Cut the self-pity, Mother, and just tell me your idea.' Again, there was silence – at both ends of the phone conversation. Susan took in a deep breath of air through her nose, held it, and then expelled it through her mouth. 'Please!' she added firmly.

'All right,' came the grudging reply. 'If you're sure.' But this time there was no further dramatic pause. 'I woke up in the middle of the night, three o'clock it was, and so I got up and made a cup of tea. There I was, sitting at the kitchen table nibbling on a ginger nut, when it came to me. You see, there are three deaths. The first one may or not have been suicide, but the second and third ones were murder. And they were both killed by the same person. We can be certain of that because the murderer then went and searched both their homes. Now, all three dead persons were connected by the day centre but one was a worker, another attended the day centre as a patient or client or whatever you call it, and the third one went along to the anger management group. They weren't all three best buddies or anything. Sarah had a dependent relationship with Jake. Jake had a fling with Martin.'

'Mother!' Susan Holden butted in. She was impressed and appalled at the detailed grasp of the whole business that her mother seemed to have gained from their chats over coffee and down the phone. 'We talked all about this last night. Now I know you're keen to help, but I have got a lot of things to do, so if you could just get to your point!'

'My point, darling, is that the key to this is the relationship between Sarah and Martin. Jake was the middle link if you want, but if you can find out what incident or common interest or emotional bond links those two, well, then your murder's solved.'

'Yes,' said her daughter, conscious that she had to respond somehow. 'Maybe.'

'There's no maybe about it. You mark my words. Anyway, I must go and get ready. I'm meeting Doris in ten minutes.'

'Going shopping?' Susan asked, anxious to grasp any opportunity to steer the conversation away from her mother's big idea.

'No!' came the scornful reply. 'She's my prayer partner. Didn't I tell you? We meet once a week to pray for and with each other. Anyway, don't you worry dear. You're top of our list.' And with that, Mrs Holden terminated the phone call.

Les Whiting took the decision not to go into the gallery as he was standing on its doorsteps. He had walked there, as he did every morning. It had taken not much more than ten minutes of vigorous activity, and that had included a couple of enforced stops while he waited for the lights to change, first at the junction just beyond Folly Bridge, and then at the bottom of St Aldate's where one of the buses coming up from London had swung just a little bit too wide and caused him to nervously hop back a step. It was as he strained a bit harder up the slope to Carfax that his emotions began to pulse as hard as his body. Jake. It had all started so well. He had been attracted to Jake from the moment he had stumbled, wet and bedraggled, into his gallery. They had hit it off immediately, and very quickly their relationship became more than just friendship. For the first time in his life, Les had felt really at one with someone. He didn't believe in fate or there only being one guy out there in the world for him, or any rubbish like that, but Jake had been special, one in ten thousand if not a million. It had been magic, a real genuinely loving relationship, and Les had begun to dare that this would be the longed-for life partnership that had seemed so elusive.

It was then that there had been the incident at the day centre. Jake had come home from work late. It was almost seven o'clock when he turned up; typically he would be home long before that. And he had promised that he would cook that night, and yet when he came in he was reeking of alcohol and refused to answer any questions. Only later, after leaving half the supper that Les had prepared, and drinking most of the two bottles of wine he had opened, did he tell him about Jim Blunt. Jim bloody Blunt.

Somehow things had changed after that. Les couldn't put his finger on why. He had listened for hours that night as Jake had told it and retold it, but the next evening, when Les had tried to discuss it again, Jake had blanked him and told him never to mention it again. After that, things between them had been …. What had they been? Different, certainly. Unease had slipped surreptitiously into Les's head. And close behind had followed suspicion. Les had found himself watching Jake, checking his post, and even sneaking a look at his text messages, and it was during one of these snoops that his suspicions had been justified. Jake was seeing someone else.

Les stood at the doorway. The set of keys for the gallery were in his right hand, but he made no attempt to use them. He looked at his watch. Ruth would be in shortly. Finally back at work after her two weeks in Portugal with that tedious boyfriend of hers. She could hold the fort for a while. Why not? He put the keys back in his right-hand pocket, pulled the mobile out of the left-hand one, and fired off a curt message. 'Will be late. Take charge. LW' Then he was headed off down the High Street, though at a slower pace than before. He knew he had to confront Blunt – for the sake of his own peace if nothing else – but he was in no rush to do so. It was odd to be wanting so earnestly to protect a man with whom he had had such a bitter parting. Perhaps it was the guilt he felt that drove him forward down the slow curve of the High, guilt that he had somehow failed Jake when he had most needed him. It was easy to blame others – Blunt or Mace or Jake himself – but Les knew that the fault was his too. Now, as he crossed Magdalen Bridge, he realized that what he sought was redemption, and by hell if he couldn't obtain it, well it wouldn't be for lack of trying.

For the third time that week, Anne Johnson answered her sister's doorbell and found herself face-to-face with Detective Constable Wilson. His pushy WPC was at his back, but Anne Johnson had no intention of letting her force her way in. She smiled frostily as she stood firmly in the middle of the doorway. 'Not you again!' She spat the words out as if they were the stones of unripened plums.

'We need to have a look round your sister's flat again,' he said, holding her gaze.

'It's not very convenient.'

'We have a warrant,' he replied firmly. 'We'll try not to make a mess.'

'Don't just try!' she said tartly, but she knew she had no choice. Bicknell had departed with his cameras, so at least there wasn't the embarrassment of him hanging around in the background. She turned and retreated back inside.

Lawson and Wilson were in the flat less than five minutes. Three Oxford United programmes were quickly located on the bookshelves in the living room, tucked between a large format *Know your Lucky Stars* book and a coffee table book called, simply, *Paris*. It was Wilson who found them, and he left the flat absurdly pleased by this fact. Not, of course, that he could have admitted as much, but the fact was that he was beginning to feel distinctly threatened by Lawson.

Fox and Holden travelled from the Cowley Police Station to the Evergreen Day Centre in grim silence. Back at the station, they had disagreed strongly, and tension hung thick and heavy in the air between them. Holden leant back in the passenger seat, closed her eyes, and tried to concentrate on the case, but her mind was in non-cooperation mode. It was only a few minutes after she had spoken to her mother that DS Fox had blundered in. 'I need to speak to you, boss.'

'Did you knock?' she had said caustically, but Fox had ignored the question and the other warning signs that a less insensitive man would have identified.

'Maybe you're missing the obvious,' he had stated bluntly.

'The obvious?'

'The obvious suspect.'

'And who would that be?'

'The man who most obviously links all three of our victims together.'

'And this man is?'

'Danny, of course. Danny bloody Flynn.'

'Why Danny?' She had spoken calmly, but in reality she was shaken by the blustering aggression of her sergeant. 'Why not Les Whiting?' she followed up. 'If Jake had an affair with Mace, then he had every reason to kill both of them. Or why not Jim Blunt or indeed one of any number of people at the day centre? Anyone in the anger management group is potentially a suspect, I'd have thought.'

'Danny Flynn was devoted to Sarah. Danny Flynn was jealous of Jake's relationship with her. Hell, he smashed his car when he saw it parked outside her flat.'

'And Mace? What reason did he have for burning Mace to death?'

'He was there, in the crowd of nosy parkers that morning at the allotment when we found Mace's body. Maybe he was checking he'd done the job properly.'

'The fact that he was there does not mean that he was the killer,' Holden said, but she spoke without conviction. Fox, conscious that he had made an impression, waited. Holden's brow crumpled in a frown of concentration. Eventually she looked up again at Fox. 'So what about Sarah?'

'Easy,' Fox said. 'She killed herself. She felt abandoned by Jake. Remember how he refused to answer her calls or ring her back. Danny blamed Jake for not supporting her. So he killed him. And Mace – well, he must have done something or known something that so angered Danny that he killed him too.'

'There's no evidence of that Sergeant,' Holden said, testily pulling rank, 'only a lot of supposition. I can accept that Sarah killed herself and I can accept that Danny might have had reason to kill Jake, but there is nothing that we have found that would explain Danny killing Mace.'

'He's a nutcase,' snorted Fox angrily. 'It doesn't have to be a logical reason. Mace and Jake had a relationship. So once he had killed Jake, Danny wanted to complete the job by killing Mace. Maybe Mace had threatened him.'

'The fact that Danny, as you so delicately put it, is a nutcase does not make him a killer.'

Fox shrugged, but he hadn't quite finished. 'And the fact that he is a grade one nutcase doesn't mean we should back off from applying a bit of pressure. So why don't we just pull him in and search his flat?'

Holden hadn't replied. But now, as Fox steered them with exaggerated care down the Cowley Road, she felt almost sick with anger. Don Alexander, her mother and Fox – each had contributed to this, but above all her anger was born of her frustration with herself, that she had not been able to crack the case. And how much longer would she be given by the press, or indeed the Chief Superintendent? Maybe she should follow Fox's demand, haul in Danny and see what happened. But why Danny? Why not Les Whiting? Didn't he have a stronger motive to kill both Jake Arnold and Martin Mace? The killing of Mace in particular was carefully and brutally carried out, surely more likely to be the work of someone like Les than the paranoid Danny? Or was she underestimating Danny, blinded by his presenting symptoms. She shut her eyes and tried to clear her mind, concentrating instead on the car, noticing each increase and decrease of speed, and the gentle pulling left or right as it changed direction. Eventually there was a much greater pull on her as the car turned sharply left and then after a few more seconds sharply to the right.

The car slowed, and Holden knew that they had arrived. She opened her eyes reluctantly. A figure was coming out of the day centre, in a hurry, head down, and stumbling so violently that he almost fell over. The man grabbed at the back of the bench he was passing, to steady himself. As he straightened himself, his face came fully into Holden's view.

'Speak of the devil!' she said, despite the fact that she had been silent for some minutes now. It was Les Whiting. But it was not the Les Whiting of previous meetings. Not the Les Whiting who offered elegant cappuccinos and politely humoured philistine policemen. The Les Whiting who stared at her as she got out of the car was a man on the very edge. His face was contorted with internal pain, and Holden thought immediately of Edvard Munch's *The Scream*. Whiting stood there, his left hand still attached to the back of the bench.

'Good morning, Mr Whiting,' Holden said, while moving steadily towards him. She wasn't at all sure that he wouldn't bolt past her, but in the circumstances this seemed like an opportunity. 'You haven't hurt yourself have you?'

'Are you after that bastard Blunt? I do fucking hope so!'

'Why should we be after Blunt?' Holden asked calmly.

Whiting looked at her as if he felt she was deranged for asking such a stupid question. 'Because he's a bastard. A complete and utter bastard. And let me tell you, if anyone had a reason to kill Jake, it was him. I told you that when you came round to my flat, but you've obviously ignored it because it didn't fit in with your pet theory. Just because he's the head of a day centre, you think he's a model citizen, caring for the least unfortunate members of society, incapable of harming the proverbial fly. Well that's … that's …' For several seconds Whiting sought the perfect word to express his feelings, but it failed to materialize. 'Look,' he said finally, now speaking in a markedly calmer tone, 'I'm going to tell you what Blunt did to Jake, and then you can decide for yourself what he is and isn't capable of. But in my book, he's capable of murder. I can't prove he killed Jake, but I reckon he did'

Holden nodded encouragingly. 'I'm listening.'

'I bet you always say that,' he snapped back, reverting to a theatricality that Holden recognized from her first encounter. But he got no response from her, and indeed seemed to expect none, for he plunged on without delay. 'Blunt never liked Jake. And vice versa. I remember his first day at the day centre. He came home full of it. He reckoned he had found his niche. The work, the members, the other staff – they were all great. Except for Blunt. He wasn't sure about Blunt even then. "Not a man to cross," he told me that night, and there was something in his voice when he said this that made me worry. Jake wasn't a tough nut. He was nice and most people liked him, but he lacked confidence in himself, and when push came to shove, he was the one to be shoved over. Hell, even I could push him around, so God knows it must have been easy for Blunt because he's a tough bastard.' Whiting paused, and looked around at Holden and Fox, as if to check that his audience was with him.

'Have you got any hard information for us?' Fox broke in. 'Because we're not here for a gossip. This is a murder investigation.' Holden looked across at her sergeant with alarm in her eyes. The last thing she wanted was for Whiting to shut up. But she underestimated Whiting's determination to tell his story.

'This is hard information, Sergeant' he snapped back. 'I'm providing you with motive, why Blunt might have killed Jake. And if you're not interested, then maybe you should go back to rounding up cycle thieves. But I'm going to tell you anyway. And hopefully your superior is prepared to listen even if you aren't.' He pointedly turned away from Fox towards Holden. 'Blunt gave Jake supervision every three weeks or so. That's one-to-one, alone in a room after the day centre has closed. For about three months, there were no major problems. Jake passed his probationary period. But soon after that it all changed. There was an incident in the centre. Blunt threw someone out. Jake criticized him in front of the rest of the staff team. Blunt didn't like that. Not one little bit. So he started to bully him.'

He paused again. This time Holden broke in, but carefully.

'Lots of people are bullied. Can you be more precise?'

'Imagine it. The two of them in a room. No witnesses. Blunt starts to give him the verbals. Calls him all sorts of names. Threatens him. Says he won't stop until he hands in his notice and leaves. Jake tries to stand up to him. Tries to ignore him. For a while it works, but then one day Jake needs to go to the loo in the middle of supervision. He makes his apologies to Blunt, but he walks over to the door, locks it and removes the key. "Not till we've finished" he says with a smirk smeared from one side of his face to the other – that's how Jake described it. So Jake tried to hold on, but Blunt drags the whole thing out. Supervision was usually forty-five minutes, or an hour maximum, but this one went on and on, and eventually Jake wets himself. And still Blunt carries on for another five minutes before unlocking the door. Then he just stands there, holding the door open, waiting for Jake to leave. Only as Jake reaches the door, he leans forward all confidentially and says: "You're waddling, Jake. You're waddling." '

Whiting stopped talking. His eyes were moist, and for a moment Holden thought he was going to cry. But she was wrong. For relating Jake's humiliation had released not only grief, but also an even more powerful anger.

'That's why I came here today,' he said, his voice now raised to the level of a shout. 'To confront the bastard. To force him to admit what he had done. For Christ's sake, can you believe it? I wanted Jim bloody Blunt to confess. I wanted to see him ask me for forgiveness. I must be stark staring mad. And of course, what he actually did was laugh at me.' And then, quite suddenly, Whiting started to laugh himself. A high-pitched see-sawing laughter that made Holden flinch and move back a pace. The noise continued for fifteen to twenty seconds, and then died as abruptly as it had taken life. But then Holden became conscious of another noise, or rather another set of noises. They were coming from inside the day centre, and so intense were they that all three persons standing there outside – Holden, Whiting and Fox – turned their heads as one towards the source of the noise. 'Don't go, Mr Whiting', Holden said, as she began to stride forward at speed towards the front doors of the Evergreen Day Centre. She pushed hard at the left hand door, and it swung back, admitting her to the main social area. The last time she had been there, it had been teeming with people, but this time she was confronted by a cameo of just three. In the foreground stood the two main protagonists, facing each other like wrestlers at the beginning of a bout, each sizing up his opponent and looking for a point of attack. To the right was Danny Flynn, crouched and swaying from side to side. To the left was Blunt. He stood more erect, but tensed and alert. Behind them, the sole spectator, was a woman Holden recognized as another day centre worker, Rachel Laing. The noise that had drawn Holden into the centre had stopped, and as the door banged shut behind her, both men turned to see who was interrupting them. 'Wait there Inspector,' Blunt ordered firmly, before turning to face Flynn again.

'You called the Police!' Flynn screamed. 'You called the bloody Police!'

'Don't interfere, Inspector,' Blunt demanded again. 'This is between Danny and me. It's a private matter.'

'Yeah, stay out of it!' Flynn was still shouting in a high-pitched, squealing voice. 'Or it'll be the worse for you.' His hands were circling and floating in the air, up and down, side to side, and Holden suddenly realized that Flynn was holding something in his right hand. A knife. The blade was only short – a pen knife or small kitchen knife she reckoned – but even a small sharp knife could slice through an artery or puncture an eyeball in an instant.

'Put the knife down, Danny,' Holden said firmly.

'Let me handle this, Inspector!' Blunt snapped at her, but his eyes remained fixed on Flynn. 'Now Danny, I know you're upset, but this has got to stop. If the police get involved, then it'll be out of my hands. So give me the knife and then we'll talk about this man to man, and that'll be the end of the matter.' And as he said this, he moved forward one step and held out his left hand, palm up. He was cool, Holden admitted to herself. He was taking a risk, but he certainly had balls. Mind you, maybe he had been watching too many Clint Eastwood movies, because in real life toughing it out sometimes backfired disastrously. Behind her, Holden felt another presence. She turned and caught sight of Fox out of the corner of her eye. She stretched her arm out, palm face down, motioning him to hold back. There was no harm in letting Blunt try and do it his way – at least she hoped so.

'Yeah, I bet you'd like this to be the end of the matter. It would suit you, wouldn't it? I put the knife down. You get me sectioned. No one asks any questions. Case closed, job done. And three cheers for Jim bloody Blunt. Yahoo!' As he shouted this last word, he lunged forward, swinging his knife in an arc through the air. Blunt swayed his head and upper body backwards, but his feet stayed fixed to their position, and his eyes remained locked on to Danny's eyes. Army training. Blunt had been in the army, Holden remembered. He could look after himself. But she knew she couldn't just wait and watch. It was time she intervened.

'Danny,' she said firmly. 'I've come here to try and find out about Jake's death. If you put the knife down, then you'll be free to go. Otherwise, I'll have to arrest you.' She advanced a step forward. 'So put it down.'

'Why should I believe you? You all tell lies when it suits you. Anything to shut Danny up. Lie, lie, lie!' His hand was waving erratically in front of him, and his eyes were swinging left and right too, for as soon as Holden took a pace forward Fox had himself started to move, circling round the other way. 'Stand still!' Danny screamed, realizing that the situation was slipping out of control. 'Or else!'

It was at that very moment that Blunt, adrenalin pulsating through his veins, pushed forward off his left foot. One, two paces, and he was within touching distance of Flynn. He made a sudden lunge towards his right wrist, but Flynn

186

reacted faster, twisting away and then bringing the knife flashing down with such force that it cut deep into his own left wrist. A diagonal line of red sprayed through the air and across Blunt's white T-shirt.

'Damn it!' Blunt swore, though whether in horror at the spoiling of his clothes or disgust at his own failure to stop Flynn, Holden never knew. Not that she was thinking about that just then.

'Drop it, Danny!' she demanded. Like Blunt she had closed in on Flynn. With her left hand she grabbed his right wrist and twisted hard. There was no resistance. The knife slipped with a clatter onto the floor, and Flynn himself followed, falling limply onto his knees and emitting a terrible despairing howl. Then he fell silent and collapsed forward onto the floor.

'I'll call for an ambulance,' Fox said quietly.

CHAPTER 12

Receiving a text message from a dead person is, one might reasonably suppose, an unnerving experience. Even Al Smith, a man who prided himself on being frightened of nothing and no one – and had the scars to prove it – felt a sudden rush of emotion that others would have described as fear. But it lasted only a few seconds. He shook himself, much as a dog does after it has been doused in water, and then another more familiar emotion – anger – took hold. For anyone close enough to hear (and there was just one such person), the evidence was obvious and incontrovertible: a string of swear words emitted at a volume and tone that told its own story.

Smith looked at his mobile. There it was at the top of his messages inbox. That four-letter word. Jake. There was no mistaking it. A message from the dead. Only, dead men don't send text messages. Which meant? Smith didn't wait to ponder what it might mean. He pressed his thumb hard on the central button on his mobile and swore again as his eyes and brain took in the three words that were displayed. 'You are next'.

'Is everything all right?' Sam Sexton was standing in the doorway of the kitchen extension, a screwdriver in his hand. He was anxious about the speed of progress on the job and the last thing he wanted was a disgruntled Smith not pulling his weight. They were being paid a fixed fee to fit out the kitchen, not by the hour, and the sooner they could get it finished, the sooner they could get on with the next and bigger job he had lined up, in Kineton Road.

'Why shouldn't it be?' Smith snapped, staring aggressively at Sexton.

Sexton looked down at his feet. 'Well, when you've finished, I need your help in here.' And he withdrew into the shelter of the four walls.

Smith looked again at the message, then turned the mobile off and thrust it into his back pocket. The last thing he wanted was Sexton to know about this. He'd be straight off to the police, and then they'd be up to their eyes in shit. But he wasn't going to let that bastard killer call the shots. He was going to get him – not for bloody Jake, but for Martin. If there was one thing that Martin deserved, it was justice. Just let him get his hands on the killer and he'd show him. He'd be fucking next. Oh yes, he'd be bloody next. And once he was dead, there'd be nothing to worry about.

'Hey, what's going on here?' Wilson was concentrating on reversing the car into a narrow space in the car park at the back of the police station. He pulled on the handbrake, turned off the ignition and looked to see what had prompted Lawson to say what she said. 'It's Fox and the Guv,' she continued, 'and they've got someone with them.'

'Blunt,' Wilson said, feeling somewhat smug. 'Jim Blunt, head of the Evergreen Day Centre.'

'Have they arrested him?' Lawson said with a hint of alarm in her voice. The last thing she wanted was to miss out on the climax of the investigation.

Wilson shared her unspoken alarm. 'Well, he's not cuffed.'

Holden, who had seen the two of them arrive, gestured Fox to take Blunt inside, and began walking briskly over towards them.

'We've brought Blunt in for questioning,' she said, anticipating their thoughts. 'We've had an incident down at the day centre.' She proceeded to bring them up to date, about both Flynn and Blunt, and also the conversation she had had with Les Whiting. 'Danny was very distressed, and in view of what he said, we need to talk to him. He may just be paranoid, but he spoke as if he really did know something about Blunt. Whether it's relevant to the case, I don't know, but I want you both to visit the hospital and find out what you can. Wilson, I want you to concentrate on the staff, chat up the nurses, see what you can learn from them. But you stay away from Flynn. Lawson, you're female, and I want you to get Flynn talking. Be his friend, be his mother, be whatever. Just get him to talk about Blunt.'

'Yes, Guv,' Lawson said brightly, her face revealing all too well her delight at being given this task.

Wilson said nothing, and turned abruptly back towards the car.

'Are you all right with that, Wilson?' Holden spoke sharply, irritated by his all too obvious change of mood.

He stopped and turned back towards her, though his eyes avoided hers. 'Yes, Guv, you're the boss.'

'You're spot on there, Constable, and just you remember it. Because if you can't take orders, you're no use to me.'

Wilson felt a tremor of humiliation running up his back. Memories of being bawled out by the PE master at school jumped into the forefront of his mind. He tried, but failed, to look her full in the face. 'I always try to follow orders, Guv,' he said defensively.

'Well that's good, then, Constable. We'll get along fine. But try one thing for me. Try not to sulk. That's the sort of behaviour I'd expect from a teenager.'

'Sorry, Guv,' he said, this time almost looking her in the eye.

'One more order before you go. Drive the scenic route to the hospital.'

'Scenic route?' Both Wilson and Lawson stared at her, faces blank with incomprehension.

'The scenic route via wherever it is that Lawson lives. Then, Wilson, you can give her no more than ten minutes to get out of that bloody uniform and into something more casual. The last thing we want is Danny knowing she's a cop as soon as she walks into the room. Or indeed thinking she's a shrink. So no white blouse, and no knee-length black skirt. The sloppier and more low key, the better. Right?'

'Right!' they replied in unison.

'I'm curious.' Detective Inspector Holden, supported by Detective Sergeant Fox on her right, was sitting opposite Jim Blunt in Interview Room 2. She was leaning forward, both elbows on the table, resting her chin on her linked hands and looking directly at the man before her. He was leaning back in his chair, as if to maintain a distance between himself and his questioner, and he had adopted an air of studied casualness, his hands cupped behind his neck.

'Curious?' Blunt uttered the word as if he was tasting wine, swilling it around in his mouth while he analyse its blend of flavours. 'You say curious,' he said preparing to spit the mouthful out, 'others might call it nosey.'

Holden ignored the remark. 'I'm curious as to what technique you use to cause someone like Whiting to hate you so much.'

'I hardly know him.'

'In that case, I'm even more impressed!'

Blunt looked at Holden hard, assessing which way to play it. 'Is that why you've dragged me here. Because of Whiting's hyperactive rantings.'

Holden shrugged, and changed tack. 'Jake Arnold's death is very convenient for you, isn't it?'

'Convenient? What the hell do you mean by that?'

'If his allegations that you had bullied him had been upheld, you'd have been out of a job.'

'It was his word against mine. The complaint was going nowhere.'

'In fact, your whole career would have been at risk.'

'Bollocks. There was absolutely no proof. Just a load of hysterical whining.'

'Les Whiting didn't think it was hysterical whining. You've got a bit of a reputation, haven't you? A hard taskmaster. You took against Jake Arnold by all accounts. Decided he wasn't right for the job. So you decided to force him out. Hard to prove, I agree. But easy enough lay the seeds of doubt. One or two more complaints, maybe an article in the local rag, and who knows, suddenly it might have been you that management decided to get rid of.'

If Blunt was worried by this line of questioning, he didn't show it. 'Are you telling me,' he said with a grin across his face, 'that you think I killed Jake Arnold because I was worried about my job?' He began to laugh then, shaking his head as he did so.

'You don't have an alibi,' Holden said firmly. 'As I recall, you claim to have been in your flat, on your own, watching a DVD. Not exactly the most original story.'

'Are you accusing me? Or merely speculating out loud? Because if it's the former, I think it's about time you got me a solicitor.'

'Tell me about Danny,' she replied, conscious that she had gone as far as she could down that particular avenue.

The grin returned to Blunt's face. 'I don't discuss clients. It's a question of confidentiality.' He leant back and crossed his arms. 'Sorry!' he concluded, without, of course, meaning it.

'Why did he come to the day centre and start waving a knife around?'

'Maybe you should ask him.'

'When you were trying to calm him down, you promised that if he put the knife down, you'd discuss it man to man. What exactly was it you were going to discuss?'

The grin, though becoming increasingly synthetic, was still plastered across his features. 'When a man is threatening

192

you with a knife,' he said evenly, 'you'll say anything to calm him down.'

'And why was Danny so uncalm?' she pressed.

The smile finally faded. 'Either you let me go, or you get me a solicitor.'

Holden hesitated, but only briefly. She stood up, picked up the pile of papers, and moved towards the door. 'Sergeant Fox will show you out,' she said without looking back.

Al Smith watched as Sam Sexton's van disappeared up the street. Sam had left his sandwiches at home, so even if he came straight back he'd be gone for twenty minutes at least. So he had plenty of time. He pulled his mobile out of his pocket, unlocked it, and flicked to his messages. He read again the one from Jake's phone. 'You are next.' He muttered something inaudible to himself, rang the number and waited. If he hoped or expected someone to answer, he was disappointed. It went straight to the answering service, in fact to Jake's own voice, eerily telling him that right now he was busy, but that if he were to leave a message he would ring back as soon as possible.

'It's Smith here. Al Smith.' As if it would be anyone else. He spoke calmly, though he wanted to shout and swear. He wanted to scream at the bastard at the top of his lungs, but he knew he had to keep calm. 'It's me you want. Just me. I was the driver. It was my fault. So let's meet. Anywhere you want. Then we can sort it all out, one way or another.' He paused, but only briefly because he had planned what he was going to say. He needed to provoke the guy into a meeting, and he could think of only one way of doing that. 'And just so that you know, I'm not scared of you.' He pressed the red button on his mobile and let out a sigh. God, he hoped that would do it. He wanted just one chance to get revenge for Martin. He had to keep Sam out of it. The bastard was after him anyway, and what were his options? To go to the cops? And admit what he'd done last May? Or try to get the bastard out into the open? Because if there was one thing he could do, he could handle himself in a fight.

It took Whiting over an hour to walk from the day centre to his gallery. This was not because of some physical restriction. He had banged himself on the right thigh when he had stumbled against the bench in full view of the detectives, but it was nothing more than a bruise. Much more painful, however, had been the emotional assault he had received from Jim Blunt. So rather than go straight back to the gallery, he entered a trendy little café which stood on the right-hand side of Cowley Road just short of the Plain roundabout. Once inside, he selected a peppermint tea, a piece of carrot cake generously topped with buttercream icing, and a copy of that day's *Guardian* which the establishment provided gratis for its customers. Armed with these, he had sat in the corner, away from the window, and shut out the world.

Only a text, some half an hour later, from Ruth at the gallery asking when he would be back, woke him from his cocoon. He poured out the last few drops from his teapot, drained them, and reluctantly stood up. It was time to get on with his life.

When he got back to his gallery, Ruth met him at the door. 'Where the hell have you been?' she hissed. 'This guy's been waiting for ages. He says he had an appointment.'

One might have expected – and Ruth almost certainly did – that Whiting would have told his employee how brown she looked and asked if she had a fabulous holiday. But in fact Whiting pushed past Ruth without so much as a greeting, and instead gave half a wave and all of his attention to the man standing on the far side of the room. 'Sorry, Bicknell,' he said. 'I got held up. Just couldn't get away.'

Bicknell looked at him with a face that told both Whiting and Ruth that he was not impressed: 'I hope you're not pissing me about, Whiting, because let me tell you that you're not the only fish in the sea.'

'Come, come!' Whiting replied, as if he was soothing a small child. 'The last thing I wanted to do was keep you waiting. Heaven forbid. Now, why don't we go and discuss things over a drink. There's a new wine bar just opened up the road.'

'Hello Danny.'

Danny Flynn was sitting on a red, moulded plastic chair, looking absent-mindedly out of the window. The voice, a female one, seemed to come from somewhere away to his left. He didn't recognize it, so he knew it must be real. His own voices were, with one exception, always male, and nearly always harsh, demanding and insistent. This new voice matched none of these descriptions. For several seconds he continued to look out of the window while his mind – which seemed to have been operating in slow motion ever since he arrived here (wherever here was, he couldn't quite be sure) – processed his thoughts. Eventually, he turned to see to whom the voice belonged.

He frowned. The woman who stood there was no one he recognized. Her hair was short and blonde, she was wearing a bright pink T-shirt and jeans, and she had a small gold-coloured handbag dangling on a long strap from her shoulder. She looked a bit like the girl who sometimes served behind the bar in the Cricketers, but he was pretty sure it wasn't her. Or maybe she was the girl from the chemist, only she was always heavily made up, whereas the person standing in front of him was anything but. Not even lipstick, and certainly no mascara or whatever else it was that girls put around their eyes.

'Who are you?' he asked.

'I'm Jan,' she said in that same soft voice. And she smiled. He liked that. It was a really friendly smile.

'I don't think I know anyone called Jan.'

'No, we've never met,' she said. She had decided that honesty – though she wasn't sure about total honesty – was the best approach. It was certainly the approach she felt most comfortable with. That was her parent's fault. 'How are you feeling?' she asked, conscious that she needed to steer the conversation. He looked, as she had been, at the white bandage that swathed the wrist and lower part of his left arm. He lifted it up and moved it slowly around while he inspected it. They had done a good job, Lawson concluded silently, not a trace of blood to be seen. Flynn allowed his arm to subside back to a resting position.

'It aches,' he said flatly. Then he leant forward. 'I think,' he said in a conspiratorial whisper, 'they've given me something. You know, drugs or something.'

'Do you mind if I ask you a few questions, Danny?' she said, in that same caressing voice.

'Are you from the social services?' he asked.

'No!' she said.

'So who are you?'

She paused, but only for a millisecond. What the hell? She was her parents' daughter. 'I'm in the police. A constable. Lowest of the low. I'm out of uniform because my boss reckoned you wouldn't talk to the police. But what does she know? She's only been in the force ten years.'

She fell silent and waited. If Danny freaked now, that would be it. Her first day out of uniform would be her last. A life of traffic control and male chauvinism beckoned. And all because she thought she knew better than DI Holden.

'Open your bag,' he said, his voice a little stronger than before.

Lawson bit back the urge to ask why. Instead, she slipped the bag off her shoulder and opened it. Then she stepped forward and gave it to him. 'Take a look,' she said, 'but there's nothing very exciting.'

He took the bag, and very carefully began to take the contents out one by one, inspecting each as he did so: a purse, which he opened and then, after a brief examination of its contents, closed; a pack of paper hankies; a tampon; a small bottle of toilet water; and a biro. It was this last item which interested him most – he clicked it one, two, three times, then ran it across the back of his hand to see if it worked (it did), before finally dismantling it, checking each piece, and then putting it back together. This took at least five minutes, and all this time Lawson remained silent. Finally he passed the bag back to her.

'How do I know you're not lying?' he asked.

'You don't,' she said. 'But maybe this will help.' And she pushed her hand into her back pocket, drew out her identity card, and handed it to him. He looked at it, this time only briefly, before handing it back.

'You remind me of my sister.'

She nodded in acknowledgement. 'What's her name?'

'She's dead,' he said.

'Oh!' Lawson was taken aback by this, and briefly at a loss to know how to continue.

'A car accident,' he said simply.

'I'm sorry!' She was conscious that this was a feeble response, but what else do you say? 'Really sorry.'

But Flynn was already moving on in his head. 'These questions you want to ask – are they on the record?'

'No, definitely not. There's just me and you, no one else to witness anything you say. It's just a chat. OK?' She paused, waiting to see how he reacted, but he sat there unmoving and silent. She frowned, and then she said something that as soon as she heard herself say it, made her flinch in surprise. 'I promise you, on my heart.' Where the heck had that come from? On my heart! What was she saying?

'OK', he said, pursing his lips. 'Ask away.'

'Thank you, Danny,' she said quietly, while her mind desperately sought for the right words. 'I was wondering, my boss was wondering, well in fact we were all wondering why it was that you were so upset with Jim Blunt.'

Flynn didn't answer immediately. Instead, he shut his eyes, screwing them tight while he tried to concentrate on that question. Jealousy? Mistrust? Hatred? Well, the first two of those certainly. But hatred? Did he hate Blunt? Yes, perhaps he did. But was that what she wanted to know, this woman with the nice face? Flynn opened his eyes, and looked across at her.

'They were lovers,' he said.

'Lovers?' Lawson replied, taken by surprise. 'Who were?'

'Blunt and Sarah.'

Lawson did not immediately respond. Whatever it was she was expecting Danny to say, it wasn't this. If he had told her that Blunt was a spy, she would have smiled politely at his paranoia and started to execute a polite exit strategy. But this was much more unexpected to her, and thus more plausible.

'Is that what you said to Blunt, that you knew they were lovers?' she asked.

'Not exactly,' he replied. 'I just told him I knew there was something between them because I'd seen them together two nights before Sarah died. He got really angry.'

'Danny,' Lawson said in a confidential tone. 'I really need you to think very hard about this and to tell me in as much detail as you can about what you saw.'

'So, you believe me?' he asked.

'Yes,' she said without hesitation, 'I do. That's why I want you to tell me all about it.'

'I saw them at his house. He lives in Bedford Street, and I went round there on the Wednesday night before she fell from the top of the car park.'

'Why did you go there, Danny, if you don't mind me asking?'

'Because whenever I went to the day centre, he was watching me. Like he was spying on me. Waiting to catch me unawares. So I thought I'd go round and watch him, you know, to get my own back. That Wednesday was the third night I'd been round. There's a derelict house opposite, which some builders are doing up, so I hid in the front garden behind the hedge and watched. The first night he wasn't in. I stayed a couple of hours, but he didn't come home. The next night he was already home when I got there. I saw him through the windows, but he stayed in all evening. And then the next night, he was in as well, only I realized there was someone else there too, and about ten o'clock they came to the door, and I saw them kissing. Him and Sarah. And then she left and walked off up the hill.'

'Did you follow her Danny?'

'No!' he said. 'I was worried he might see me, so I stayed hidden behind the hedge for maybe ten minutes, and then I went back to my flat.'

'It must have been quite dark, Danny. Are you absolutely sure it was Sarah?'

'His hall light was on. I could see them. Don't you believe me?'

'Yes,' she said quickly, too quickly maybe.

'You don't believe me, I know,' he said in a now much raised voice. 'You think I'm a paranoid nutcase. You're just like all the others!' He shouted these last words, and then began to rock backwards and forwards in his chair, hugging himself as he did so. A nurse, alerted by the noise, appeared like some genie in the doorway. 'It's time you left,' he said firmly.

'So, how did it go?' The four of them, Holden, Fox, Wilson and Lawson, were sitting in a circle around Holden's rectangular desk. It was Holden asking the question. She had called Lawson and Wilson in when she heard their animated voices in the corridor, and had summoned Fox via the phone. 'You start, Lawson,' she ordered. 'Tell us how you got on with Danny.'

'Pretty well, I think.'

Holden made a face. 'Pretty well? What exactly do you mean by that? It's not an expression that fills me with confidence.'

'We got on fine, thank you, Guv,' Lawson replied, trying but not quite succeeding in looking Holden full in the face. 'Though to be honest,' she continued, her eyes now flicking down, 'we didn't end that well. In fact, Danny freaked a bit and the nurse suggested that I leave, but before that—'

Holden lifted both hands in the air, as if surrendering. 'Please, Lawson, why don't you cut out the bad bits and confine yourself to the good news, such as whatever it was that Danny told you about Blunt, because I assume that with all your charm you managed to hold a conversation with him before he, as you so delicately put it, freaked.'

Lawson swallowed. She glanced across at Wilson, but if she was hoping for some moral support, she was out of luck. He was staring fixedly downwards as if pretending that he wasn't there. She shrugged, and looked back at Holden. 'Danny told me that he saw Sarah Johnson at Blunt's house two nights before her death.'

Holden's ears pricked up, metaphorically at least. 'And?'

'I thought that might be significant.'

'Why? They knew each other from the day centre, didn't they? Why should it be significant? Maybe she was feeling desperate and had called round for some support.'

'Danny said he saw them kissing.'

'Did he?' Holden's interest was now fully engaged. 'Well, that is interesting. Assuming, of course, that Danny is to be trusted.'

'Why shouldn't he be?' Lawson said protectively. 'Just because he—'

'He's bloody paranoid.' Fox laughed. 'There's every reason not to trust him.'

Lawson turned towards the sergeant, her face flushing, though whether in anger or embarrassment the still silent Wilson wasn't sure. 'I was there, sir,' she retorted. 'And I do have personal experience of paranoia. And in my opinion he wasn't making this up, or imagining it.'

'Let's assume,' Holden cut in, 'for the sake of argument, that Danny did see Blunt and Sarah Johnson kiss. The question we need to ask is where does that leave us? Wilson,' she said changing tack, 'how did you get on with Danny's nurses?'

'Sorry, Guv,' he said. 'I'm afraid I didn't get anything out of them. I spoke to a chap called Kay, who was about to go off shift, and he told me Danny had barely said a word.'

'Any visitors?'

'No!'

'Phone calls?'

Wilson paused. 'Not that Kay said.'

Holden frowned. 'Next time, make sure you ask? Sometimes you have to work for information.'

Lawson cleared her throat. 'Um, can I ask how you got on when you interviewed Blunt, Guv.'

'Of course,' Holden said with a smile, conscious that Lawson was trying to take the spotlight of criticism off Wilson. She liked the way Lawson operated. She'd definitely got character. Holden turned towards Fox. 'What would you say, Sergeant? Did we get anything useful out of Blunt do you think?'

Fox laughed, though this time it was not a laugh designed to put anyone down. 'I'd say we did about as well as Wilson. Jim bloody Blunt told us nothing. In fact, he basically refused to talk without a lawyer present.'

'But that tells us something, doesn't it?' Lawson said eagerly. 'That he had something to hide. That he was worried about what Danny told him.'

'In that case,' Fox replied, 'maybe we did do a bit better than Wilson.'

Wilson tried not to feel irritated. Instead he joined in. 'Are we saying that Blunt killed Sarah Johnson? And then Jake Arnold? And then Martin Mace?'

For a moment no one answered. Lawson looked at Holden, for guidance and reassurance. Where the hell were they? It all seemed to be getting more complicated, not less. Murkier, not clearer.

Holden sighed. She leant back in her chair and looked up at the ceiling, buying time while she framed her response with care. 'Blunt, I think, is not a man to be messed with. He served in the army for five years. He is, I would suspect, quite capable of killing if he thought it was necessary. But what are we suggesting? That he killed Sarah Johnson because she threatened to tell on him. Well, that's certainly not beyond the bounds of possibility because, let's be clear, having a sexual relationship with a client is a serious disciplinary offence in that field. Just as, of course, would have been his bullying of Jake if that had been proved. But why kill Mace?'

'Maybe he got a taste for it,' Fox suggested.

'Maybe,' Holden said without conviction. 'Maybe not.'

'Should we get a search warrant?' Wilson said eagerly. 'Maybe we'll find something that'll prove it.'

The frown that was already on Holden's brow deepened. 'I think,' she said slowly, 'I think that first we need to think about this a little more.'

'Wittenham Clumps car park. 5.00 tonight. ALONE.'

Smith looked at the message and felt a slight surge of optimism. It was hardly seismic, but he felt it nevertheless. The bastard had taken up the challenge. He had agreed to a meeting. OK, it was risky. The bastard would be waiting for him. He would have all the advantages of surprise. Probably he'd be armed too. But he wouldn't be the only one. And all he needed was a chance. An opportunity for revenge. Just one.

He pressed 'Reply' and keyed in his response. Just two letters and an exclamation mark. 'OK!' A couple of clicks later, and the message was sent. He locked the mobile, pushed it back in his pocket, and felt for his cigarettes. Hell, he needed one.

If anyone had offered Holden a cigarette at that moment, she might well have succumbed to the temptation. She had ended the meeting with Fox, Wilson and Lawson by getting up and saying she needed the toilet, and had spent ten minutes there, first squatting for an unnecessarily long time in her cubicle, then splashing her face repeatedly with water, as if refreshing herself physically might also cause her to be refreshed mentally. It didn't work however, and she returned to her room feeling even more frustrated than she had when she left it. As she slumped heavily into her chair, the phone rang. With a groan, she stretched to pick it up. Just as long as it wasn't that ruddy reporter again.

'Darling!'

It wasn't the reporter.

'Mother!' she replied.

'Is this a bad time?'

'No!' she lied. Three unexplained deaths, two of them unquestionably murder. Several leads, but no clear pattern to them. Junior staff looking to her for inspiration and guidance. Of course, it was a bad time! But, curiously, Holden found herself relieved to hear her mother's voice.

'We've been thinking about you, Doris and I have.'

'Well, that's good of you,' she replied.

'And praying for you, of course.'

'Of course,' her daughter echoed. She didn't believe in prayer – not really – but it was ridiculously comforting to know that these two old women had been spending their time praying for her. After all, what sane person would not like to be prayed for?

'So, any progress, then?' her mother asked eagerly.

'If you mean by that, have we arrested anyone, or are we about to arrest anyone, the answer is no. There's been no spectacular break through.' She spoke firmly, as if she was a parent lecturing a somewhat dippy child. But of course the thoughts of stern parents do not always match their outward demeanour. And tapping away inside her head was a question that was becoming more insistent by the minute. What about Blunt and Sarah Johnson?

'Well, there will be,' came the confident reply. 'We have asked the Lord to show you the truth, and he will not refuse the prayers of those who cry out in faith to him.'

'I am busy, Mother,' her daughter said hastily, suddenly keen to disengage. A born-again Christian mother. God, was that what she had been landed with?

'Remember what I said this morning,' Mrs Holden said, ignoring her daughter's alleged business. She had never been a woman to be swayed from her objective. 'Mace and Sarah Johnson. They are the key to the mystery. I just know they are.'

'Is that what God told you?' her daughter replied waspishly.

From the other end of the phone there came a gasp that was fully audible to the younger woman, and she felt immediate shame at the cheapness of her own remark. There followed only silence, as each waited for the other to make the next move. Eventually it was the older woman who spoke.

'We will continue to pray for you,' she said firmly. 'Goodbye!'

'Guv! We've found a link.'

It was a bare two minutes since Holden *mère* and Holden *fille* had terminated their conversation. The latter looked up at the intruders, irritation and mayonnaise smeared across her face. Her right hand brandished two-thirds of a tuna mayonnaise sandwich, the first third of which was wedged irrevocably inside her mouth. Talking was briefly out of the question, so she waved the two young puppies that stood eagerly in her doorway towards the chairs.

'We could come back in a few minutes,' WPC Lawson said in an only slightly apologetic tone. The cat that got the cream, Holden decided, as the animal analogies came thick and fast. She shook her head, returned the uncommitted part of the sandwich to its plastic triangle, and concentrated several seconds on chewing. Then a sip of coffee, and she looked up again at Lawson and Wilson.

'OK,' she said, 'Tell me about it.'

'As you know, Guv,' Wilson started, 'we've been searching the homes of Sarah Johnson, Martin Mace, and Jake Arnold. Mace was a dyed-in-the-wool supporter. Went to nearly every home and away game. The two guys you interviewed at the Kassam stadium before the game, Sam Sexton and Al Smith, they were his best mates and it looks like they always sat together. In the case of home games, that was always in the Oxford Mail stand. He kept a programme from every game he went to, and the tickets. He missed just four games last season, two in early September – holiday we reckon – and two in early December – more holiday, or maybe he was ill. However, Jake is a very different story. He went to just six games. One in January and one in February, both home games. Then Leyton Orient away in March. Two more home games in April. And lastly the away game at Wrexham on 5 May.'

'And did he sit in the Oxford Mail stand too?' asked Holden.

'No, Guv. The South Stand. The connection isn't with the home games.'

'So they sat together at the away games, then?'

'One moment, Guv,' Wilson said, trying to wrest back control of the story. 'We found just three programmes in Sarah Johnson's flat. For the same two home games in April that Jake Arnold went to, and the away game at Wrexham in May.'

'So Jake and Sarah went to the same games,' Holden summarized. 'So they maybe went together.'

'That seems likely. We know Jake bought two tickets for those April home games, whereas he bought only one ticket for the games he went to in January and February.'

Holden leant back and surveyed Wilson and Lawson. Was this all they had? Was this what they meant when they had said they had found a connection, because she sure as hell needed more than a pattern of Jake and Sarah building up some sort of relationship over football. She needed something, if not concrete, then at least solid.

'That Jake and Sarah had some sort of personal relationship isn't exactly news,' she said quietly.

'We know,' said Lawson, finally breaking her silence. 'But take a look at this. It's a programme from the away game at Wrexham. We found it in Mace's house.' She laid a programme carefully on the table in front of Holden. Then repeated the process with two more. 'This one came from Jake Arnold's loo, and this from the bookshelves in Sarah's flat.'

'What's your point exactly?' Holden said sharply.

Wilson leant forward now and, like a conjuror performing a card trick, very deliberately turned each programme over. As was traditional, the back page showed the two squads of players, Wrexham down the left, and Oxford as the away team down the right. As was also traditional, the fans who bought these programmes had marked the players chosen for the team that day. In biro. In fact in a rather unusual colour of biro. Purple. All three programmes were annotated in purple biro.

'It looks very much like the same biro. We think they must have sat together for the game, Jake and Sarah and Martin Mace,' Wilson said.

Holden peered closely at the programmes. She was no forensic expert, but if that wasn't the same biro then it was one hell of a coincidence. 'It is certainly a connection,' she admitted grudgingly. 'But do you think they travelled to the game together, or just bumped into each other beforehand and so went in together?'

'We think they travelled together,' Lawson said.

'Think!' Holden snorted, turning to face Lawson. 'What do you mean, think? Because thinking isn't enough, Lawson, as I'm sure you know.'

'It's not just guesswork,' Lawson said, while producing another piece of paperwork from her lap. But this was just a single sheet of A4, a police incident report. 'On the evening of 4 May,' Lawson continued, 'Jake's car was vandalized.'

'By Danny Flynn,' Holden replied, stopping Lawson in her tracks. Holden smiled a rather smug smile, pleased to see the surprise on both their faces. 'Danny admitted as much when we saw him the other morning. He burst in when we were interviewing one of the workers, Rachel Laing. But at the time, I don't imagine Jake knew who had done it. Still, I am interrupting you. Do carry on.'

'Well, the fact was Jake had a problem when he saw his car Saturday morning. He and Sarah had tickets but no transport to get to Wrexham. So what do they do? They get a lift. With, to judge from the purple biro, Mace.'

'And,' added Wilson, 'maybe with Al Smith and Sam Sexton too, since they were inseparable from Mace on match days.'

The three of them fell silent. Outside, an irate driver hooted impatiently at another road user. Inside, Lawson and Wilson waited for their boss to pronounce. 'So,' she summarized, 'we have a connection, in point of fact a very strong connection. Five people drive to Wrexham on 5 May in a vehicle. Of these five, three are now dead. Sarah Johnson jumped – or was pushed – to her death, Jake Arnold was slugged over the head and dumped into the river, and Martin Mace lured to his allotment and burnt to death. Al Smith and Sam Sexton are still alive. But I'd bet my life they know something. Sexton was very on edge when we interviewed him. So my question is, what happened on 5 May? That's what we've got to find out.'

'Why don't we go and pick up Sexton and Smith,' Lawson said. 'They must know something.'

'Do we know where they'd be? Still at work presumably.'

'They do building work together often,' chimed in Wilson, who had typed up the notes the morning after the match.

'Which means they could be working anywhere presumably?'

'Sexton has a wife,' Lawson said, anxious not to be out-done by Wilson.

Holden looked at her watch. 'You could waste a lot of time trying to find them. Let's leave it for now, and pick them up once they get home from work. In the meantime, I want you two to do some research. Police records. Press reports. What I want you to look for is something that could have caused someone to want revenge. Anywhere between here and Wrexham, on 5 May.'

'What are you going to do, Guv?' Wilson said.

Holden looked at him sharply. 'Why, Wilson. Are you monitoring me?'

'No, Guv, definitely not, I was just—'

'I'm going to take another look at Sarah Johnson,' she continued in a voice that would have sliced through pack ice. 'If, that is,' she added, 'it is all right by you, Wilson!'

For several seconds, a freezing silence descended on the trio. Holden knew she had gone too far, but had no intention of saying sorry. She sniffed, and when she spoke again, her voice was under control, and almost human.

'Wilson, would you mind getting the file on her, please.'

Wilson needed no further asking. 'I think it's on Fox's desk.' And with that he scuttled out the room.

Holden looked at Lawson, who in turn looked back at her. A woman who had got somewhere, and a woman who wanted to be there. 'You think I'm too hard on him?' Holden asked.

Lawson shrugged, but offered no comment.

'Tell me!' she insisted. 'Woman to woman. Off the record.'

Lawson shrugged again. 'A bit hard, yes. But mind you, he does ask for it.'

'And are you hard on him, Lawson?'

This time there was no shrug. 'Yes. But I look after him too.'

'So do I, Lawson.'

'Damn!' The curse came from the corridor, and both women immediately recognized it as Wilson's. Out of their sight, the flustered constable dropped to his knees to pick up several sheets that had fallen from the file in his arms. Then, back on his feet, he hurried the last couple of paces to the door and pushed into DI Holden's office, head down. 'Here you are,' he said 'that's everything off Fox's desk.' And he set the bundle down in front of Holden, oblivious to the amused smiles that the two women were exchanging.

Holden didn't notice them at first. It was some 20 minutes since Wilson and Lawson had retreated from her room down the corridor to their own, and in that time she hadn't so much as opened the file on Sarah Johnson, let alone reread it. What with visiting the loo again – she really should cut down on the coffee – getting some paracetamol from her car, and then being ambushed on her way back by Linda from personnel, the time had raced unrelentingly forward, leaving all her good intentions in its slipstream. Back in her office, instead of sitting down and opening the file, she stood and gazed out of the dirty office window. Not that her brain registered anything that was happening in the stop-start Oxford Road traffic, for it was focused on violent death and also on her mother. Not that she was wishing one on the other, far from it. But somehow her mother's words refused to go away. 'Martin Mace and Sarah Johnson,' she had insisted. 'They are the key to the mystery.' Who the hell did she think she was? Miss Marple? What the heck did she know about solving crimes? And yet maybe she was right. They were linked by this game of football at Wrexham, of course. But they were linked too by Jake. Jake and Sarah had a strong relationship, and Mace and Jake were or had been lovers. And then there was Blunt, a man Holden neither liked nor trusted. But that, she had to remind herself, did not make Blunt a killer. But he was another link, no question. And Blunt and Jake disliked, maybe even hated, each other.

'Guv! Guv!'

Holden turned round reluctantly, to see Lawson and Wilson in her room again.

'We've found something, Guv!' said Wilson.

'What?' she said pulling herself irritably into the present moment.

'A car crash on the 5th. On a side road just off the A5, about 10 miles south of Wrexham. A VW van went off the road, about eight o'clock at night. Six passengers, all killed.' Wilson paused and glanced at Lawson,

'I rang the locals,' she said, taking over the baton. 'The van was from Oxfordshire. Three of them from Witney, and three from Oxford itself. They were peace campaigners, on the way home from some demo.'

'You have a list of names?'

'Yes, and pictures,' Wilson said, holding out a wodge of paper in his hand.

'One more thing,' Lawson said. 'We think it might be relevant, given the nature of Martin Mace's death. The van caught fire. They reckon the petrol tank burst open on impact. It looks like all the occupants burnt to death.'

'You think it may be relevant, Lawson?' Holden exclaimed. 'That's the understatement of the year. Well, drop everything and for God's sake go and pick them up – Smith and Sexton – before the murderer gets to them too.'

Two minutes later Holden frowned hard at the sheet of paper she was reading, and scratched at her forehead. She had just finished reading the single-page report of Fox and Wilson's visit to Anne Johnson. She leafed quickly through the rest of the file, not reading, but looking. Then she got up, crossed the room to her open door and walked purposefully down the corridor. 'Wilson!' she called, as she turned into the second doorway on the left. The startled constable looked up. He was sitting at his desk, with one hand holding a bag of salted crisps in its palm while the fingers of the other deposited some of its contents into his mouth. He jumped to his feet, almost dropping the bag as he did, wondering what the heck he had done now.

'Just waiting for Lawson. She's in the loo,' he said defensively.

'Where's the diary?' she asked.

'Diary?' Wilson replied, feeling hopelessly lost.

'Sarah Johnson's diary,' Holden snapped. 'When Fox and you visited Sarah Johnson's flat and met Anne Johnson there, you found Sarah's diary. It's in the notes that you wrote up, Wilson. But it's not in the file. So where's it got to?'

Wilson scratched his head. 'I can't recall seeing it recently. But I do remember it. It was a red diary, A5, you know, a desk diary. Maybe it's in one of the drawers.' He moved over to Fox's desk and leant down, tugging at the nearest handle. When it refused to moved, he tried the next drawer, and then the third. 'They're locked, Guv.'

'And presumably Fox has got the key.' She sighed loudly. 'Where is he, anyway?'

'Gone to the dentist again. He thinks he's got an abscess.'

'I see,' Holden said, though she wasn't sure that she did see. What the hell was he doing buggering off to the dentist without telling her first anyway? 'Well, ask around. Someone must hold a spare set of keys for these desks, or a master. Anyway, use your initiative and find the diary, and bring it to my office. And sharpish!' Holden turned and left him to it. What was it her father used to say? Don't keep a dog and bark yourself. One of the few sensible things he did say. So let Wilson get on with it.

Barely three minutes later, Wilson appeared triumphantly at her door, with Lawson at his shoulder and the elusive red book in his hand. 'Bingo!' he said with a grin. 'It was in Fox's bottom drawer. I couldn't find a key so I had to—'

Holden had raised her finger to her lips, like a librarian bringing a noisy reader to heel. Wilson dribbled to a halt.

'Too much information, Wilson. You got the diary and I assume you didn't cause any serious damage doing so. That's enough for me.'

'Yes Guv.'

'So bugger off and find Smith and Sexton.'

Doreen Sexton looked at her watch for the fourth time in ten minutes and swore. Not that anyone would have known for she never cursed out loud. 'It's not lady-like,' her mother had drummed into her throughout her childhood. Not that being lady-like was high in Doreen Sexton's priorities for herself. She was far too practical in her approach to life and too committed to her nursing to give herself airs and graces. But, nevertheless, she – like her mother and her mother before her – left the swearing to the menfolk, and even then insisted that it remain outside the house.

'Where is he?' This time her words were audible, although there was no one else in the house to hear them 'He promised!' she pleaded to herself. Sam Sexton had indeed promised to be back in plenty of time to give her a lift to the hospital. Normally she caught the bus, but she had four bags of bric-a-brac and clothes for Alice's jumble sale. She looked at her watch again. She'd give him a couple more minutes, but then she'd have to go and catch the bus and leave the jumble behind. It wasn't like Sam to let her down. Whatever he was or wasn't, he was a very reliable man. It was one of the things about him that she'd always liked. Once in a while, a bit of romance would have been nice too, but most of the time she was content with reliability. So where was he, and why was his mobile turned off? Surely he hadn't let the battery run flat? Normally he was so careful to keep it charged. Again, she looked at her watch. She couldn't wait any longer. It was time to get her coat and go. 'Sam Sexton,' she said out loud, 'you'd better have a very good excuse!'

And then the front doorbell rang.

At much the same time that Doreen Sexton was opening her front door, Detective Inspector Holden was sitting at her desk staring into space. If the *Oxford Mail* had chosen that moment to ring up and check on progress, or if Linda from Personnel had appeared at the door (as she had threatened) to collect the long overdue appraisal forms, or indeed if the Queen herself had dropped in for a chat, it is doubtful whether any of them would have been able to attract her attention. For her mind was in freefall, and it was spinning wildly as it fell.

After Wilson and Lawson had scuttled off down the corridor, Holden had laid the diary down on her desk and opened it. Flicking through the pages, she had soon come to the month of May. There it was. Down the left-hand side were Monday 30 April, then Tuesday 1 May and Wednesday 2 May. She had run her eyes down the right-hand side of the page looking for Saturday 5 only it wasn't Saturday 5. It was Saturday 12. 'Damn!' She had sworn. And then repeated herself in an increasingly noisy staccato. 'Damn! Damn! Damn!'

Someone had ripped a page out of the diary, the very date they were interested in. Sarah herself, before she died? But why? Or someone else who had got to the diary before Fox and Wilson. Or, someone since, in which case who? Who had access to it? Fox? He must have looked at it in the first place. Or Wilson? Come to think of it, he had located it pretty quickly. Steady, Holden. Don't be bloody paranoid. These are your colleagues you're talking about. She picked up her mug and drained the remains of her coffee. It was cold, but she barely noticed. But Fox. Where was Fox? Where the hell was he? She picked up her mobile, flicked her way through her list of names until she came to 'Fox mob' and rang. It cut straight into an answering message. She terminated the call. The dentist. Maybe he was still there? But which dentist did he go to? If her memory hadn't gone AWOL, she was pretty damn sure it was that one down the road, past the hardware store. Stewart wasn't it? Or Stuart?

'Right,' Holden said out loud to herself, as she pulled the Yellow Pages down from the bookshelves. 'Where are you?' It took her a minute to track down the number, but only seconds to dial it.

'Good afternoon, Mr Stewart's dental practice,' came the almost immediate answer.

'Is Derek Fox there?'

There was a muffled giggle from the dental practice. 'Sorry?'

'Derek Fox. You do know him, don't you? He's one of your patients. I understand he was due in for an appointment and—'

The receptionist cut in aggressively, irritated by the domineering tone of the caller. 'Yes, I know who Derek Fox is, but who are you? We don't give out information to just anyone.'

'I'm sorry,' Holden said in a softer tone, realizing her mistake. 'I should have said. I am Detective Inspector Susan Holden. I am DS Fox's superior officer and I urgently need to contact him.'

'Well, he's not here,' the reply came.

'When did he leave?' Holden pressed.

'Leave? He's not been to see us for a while. Let me see. I'll just bring his records up. That's right. He last came in March for a check-up, and he's due in next month, for his next check-up.'

'You're sure?' Holden knew it was a stupid question as soon as she said it, but she had to make certain.

'Of course I'm sure,' came the hostile reply. 'What do you take me for? A dumb blonde?'

*

'Mrs Sexton, is it?'

Sexton peered uncertainly at the blonde-haired young woman who stood on her doorstep, and then at the man lurking at her shoulder. 'Who are you?' she asked irritably. 'I'm just off to work.'

'I'm WPC Lawson and this is Detective Constable Wilson,' the woman replied, showing her ID as she spoke.

'What do you want?' she demanded, but this time less stridently. Anxiety, too, was evident in her voice.

'Do you mind if we come inside?' came the evasive response.

Doreen Sexton hesitated for moment, as if she was considering saying she did mind, but then she just shrugged, moved to the side and motioned them in with a movement of her head.

'I'll get in trouble if I'm late,' she said, as she shut the door behind them.

'We'll try not to be long,' the man said. 'It's just that we want to speak to your husband.'

'Sam? Why?'

'Do you know where he is?' the man continued, side-stepping her question. 'Or perhaps you could give us his mobile number.'

'Look,' she said firmly, trying to assert herself. 'What is this all about? Has he done something wrong? Because if you want me to cooperate, then I need to know.'

'Perhaps you should sit down, Mrs Sexton,' he said, still failing to address her questions.

'Don't patronize me,' she snarled. 'Just because I'm a woman.' If looks could kill, Wilson's blood would have been smeared across the kitchen wall, but no such thing occurred. Eventually, Doreen Sexton emitted a snort of disgust and turned her body and face towards the female detective.

'Mrs Sexton,' Lawson said, intervening. 'We don't mean to patronize you. But we are concerned for your husband's safety. We really do need to locate him.'

'What do you mean?' She spoke with alarm in her voice. 'His safety? What are you talking about?'

'You are aware of Martin Mace's death?' Lawson continued determinedly. 'We understand he was a good friend of your husband. And we think it is possible that Martin's killer has a grudge against Sam and also Al Smith.'

'God!' she said, breaking the habit of a lifetime. 'Oh, God!' And she grabbed the back of a kitchen chair to steady herself.

'Please, sit down Mrs Sexton,' the blonde woman suggested. This time Sexton obeyed.

'He's not answering his mobile,' she said disconsolately. 'It's turned off. It's not like him, you know. He always keeps it on. Always.'

'When is he due home?' Lawson asked quietly.

'He's late! He promised to be back to give me a lift to the hospital. I've got all these things to carry, you see, too much to take on the bus, and he promised. He normally keeps his promises. Something must have happened to him. He'd be here if he could. Something must have happened to him. Oh my God!'

'Please, try not to worry,' Lawson said, conscious that this was asking the impossible, but conscious too that she had to keep the woman from freaking. She'd had quite enough of that today with Danny. 'Where was he working today? He's a builder, isn't he?'

'He finished early. He rang me, and said he had to go and meet someone about a job, but he wanted me to know that he hadn't forgotten me, you know that he had remembered that I needed a lift.'

'Did he say who this meeting was with, or where it was? Maybe he's just got held up—'

'Some rundown cottage, he said. Off the Garsington Road. It had an odd name. I remember thinking, that's a funny name for a house—' She trailed off, as she tried desperately to recall the name from her memory bank. 'Like in a fairy tale. Not a real life name ... Oh, God, I can't remember. I can't remember!'

'Don't worry Mrs Sexton,' Wilson said soothingly. 'It'll come to you in a minute. That's what my mum always said to my dad when he couldn't remember something. As soon as you stop trying to remember, then it'll pop straight into your head. And it always did. Always!'

An observer could not have divined whether Doreen Sexton took in, or was even aware of, these words of home-spun wisdom, for her head remained tilted slightly to the right, while her eyes were fixed on a distant point beyond and above Lawson's shoulder. The only thing that moved was the expression on her face, from one of intense con-centration to increasing blankness and then, remarkably and suddenly, transfiguration. 'Of course,' she said triumphantly. 'Of course. Dingle Dell. That's what it was! Dingle Dell Cottage.'

At much the same time that Wilson and Lawson were ringing the Sextons' doorbell, DS Holden was ringing the *Oxford Mail*. Given that every time her phone had rung that afternoon she had hoped against hope that it wasn't Don Alexander asking her for news of developments, this was at one level a remarkable turnaround. But although Holden had an in-built suspicion of the media, the bottom line was that she needed his help, and she needed it fast.

'It's Detective Inspector Holden,' she said as soon as he answered the phone.

'What a pleasure, and what an unusual event to be rung up by you, Susan,' he replied suavely.

Holden ignored the familiarity. If he had been ringing her, she would have taken him on, but right now she had no option except to swallow her irritation.

'I need your help,' she said bluntly.

'Well, Susan,' he said, enjoying his position of superi-ority, 'that's a turn-up. But of course I wouldn't be being public-spirited if I didn't give you every possible assistance in your investigations.' He paused, and then noisily cleared his throat, before continuing. 'However,' he said with emphasis, 'of course I do have to answer to my editor for my time and it is only fair to—'

'You'll get first bite at the story!' Holden said sharply. 'Don't you worry!'

'Oh, I'm not worried Susan. I know I can rely on your word. So what is it I can do for you?'

Al Smith was losing his cool. He had arrived early at the Wittenham Clumps car park. Deliberately so. He had wanted to get there in plenty of time to suss out the area. To see if he could gain any sort of edge. There were three cars parked up when he pulled in, and he felt better when he saw them. If the bastard was going to try and kill him, he wouldn't want to do it in front of witnesses. So as long as there were other people there, he was safe. But suppose one of the cars was the killer's. Maybe he too had come early. Maybe he was up there in one of the Clumps, hiding amongst the trees in the undergrowth. The Clumps were aptly named: two clumps of trees which appeared to have been plonked at random on the tops of these two hump-like hills by some higher power. A god with a love of camels and a sense of humour perhaps. But for Smith the place had a sense of something more sinister, a pagan god. Smith had been there only once before, and he remembered seeing a wicker figure in the nearest wood. He must have been eleven or twelve, and he remembered the fear he had felt. Not that he had admitted it to his mum or dad – that would have been sissy. But he remembered how very cold the wood had felt and how glad he had been to reach the far side and emerge into the bright, warming sunshine.

Suddenly he was back in the present, and realized that, ridiculously, he was shivering. He tried to ignore it and scanned the open grassland that surrounded the two hillocks. A woman with two small black-and-white dogs, Jack Russells probably, was walking up towards the left-hand copse, while a man with a light-coloured Labrador was climbing the slope towards the nearest copse. The driver of the third car was nowhere to be seen however. He – or she – could be anywhere: in one of the copses, or the other side and out of sight. A simple visitor enjoying the view and the air. Or the killer.

And so Smith waited, constantly surveying the terrain before him. Occasionally, he looked round behind himself, as a vehicle drove along the lane, but none slowed down to turn into the car park. Where the fuck was he? For the twentieth time he checked his watch. It was 5.15. How much longer should he give it before he … before he did what? Just drive off? Or should he ring Jake's mobile? What the hell was the bastard playing at?

'Good evening!' The woman with the Jack Russells took him completely by surprise. He had noticed her returning down the hill, but he had been so intent on looking out for the killer and so wrapped up in his own thoughts that he had completely overlooked her, and now here she was walking past him so close he could smell her perfume.

'Good evening,' he parroted back. He watched as she opened the rear passenger-side door. The dogs jumped dutifully in, and she slammed the door shut. Suppose the killer was a woman? Why the hell did it have to be a man? Wasn't a woman just as capable of thumping Jake over the head or burning Martin to death in his own allotment shed. In fact, wasn't a woman more likely to have done it than a man. If you thought about the planning and execution of Martin's death (and Al had, like many others, followed every detail avidly in the local media), wasn't that degree of malicious cunning typical of a woman? He watched as the woman, who had made no attempt to murder him, turned right out of the car park and began to accelerate down the hill towards the village. He stood watching until he could hear her engine no more. Then, he jumped. Almost literally.

'Fuck!' he swore, disgusted with his own reactions and feelings. His mobile was ringing. Hastily he dragged it out of his pocket. A quick glance showed it was Jake's phone. He pressed the green button and pushed the mobile against his left ear. 'Where the hell are you?' he said aggressively. 'I've been waiting ages.'

'Tut, tut!' came the mocking voice. 'That's not a very nice greeting!'

Smith was swivelling around, left and right, to see if he could see the killer. Was he waiting there in the wood, or behind the hedge, a rifle in his hands, playing with him before he fired? There was no one visible. The Labrador and his master had disappeared from view. Smith suddenly realized how vulnerable he was, standing there in a lonely car park with no other humans in sight. He must have been stark staring bonkers to imagine that the bastard would just turn up and fight, man to man.

'You said five o'clock!' he said.

'Change of plan. Sorry!'

'What do you mean? You made the arrangement.'

'That's right, I did. And now I'm making a different arrangement. Because I'm calling the shots, arsehole. So I'm telling you to drive to the Bullnose Morris and wait in the car park till I call again.'

'How do I know you're not just taking the piss?'

The man did not answer the question, unless an explosion of laughter can be called an answer. But it died as suddenly as it had started. The phone call was over.

Holden heard the footsteps in the corridor, and looked at her watch. It was barely twenty-five minutes since she had spoken to Don Alexander. She had asked him to bring over every photo he had on file from the inquest and funerals of those six people who had died on 5 May.

'Use a messenger,' Holden had said, 'and we'll pay. Just as long as it's quick.'

'I've got a motorbike,' Alexander had replied with the smugness of a card-sharp who knows he's got an unbeatable hand. 'Saves me loads of time round the city. I'll bring them myself. Then if you need any help with identification, or anything—'

'Fine!' Holden had agreed. Not that she had had any choice. It was as obvious as the dog-shit on the pavements of Oxford that Alexander wanted to be sure that no one got the inside story before he did, and she could hardly blame him for that. But if the photos were to confirm her darkest fears about Fox, if there was just one photo with his face lurking in the background, then she would be faced with the additional problem of stopping Alexander releasing the story before she was ready. 'Bent cop is serial killer' was not a headline she wanted appearing on the front page without the press office being fully briefed in advance. She had not, of course, told Alexander of her suspicions, but he would soon put two and two together, and then, whether she liked it or not, the cat would be out of the bag. She would have to prevail on his good nature. Hell, even journalists must have a good nature hidden somewhere deep down within them. Maybe a bit of flattery, or rather a lot flattery, would do the trick. He was probably vain enough. With this final uncharitable thought in her head, and with the tread of footsteps getting ever closer to the doorway, she stood up, ready to receive him.

'Bloody hell!' she said. Then there was silence. Her jaw dropped as low as any jaw has ever dropped in amazement.

'Sorry, I'm a bit late Guv,' came the reply. 'Is something wrong?'

Holden stared at DS Fox until her jaw regained movement.

'Where in God's name have you been?' she demanded.

'I told Wilson,' he said defensively. 'Didn't he tell you? I went to the dentist.'

Smith pulled up in the car park of the Bullnose Morris in Garsington Road, and turned off the engine. The light was fading fast. He looked around, but there was no one to be seen. Half a dozen cars and, as far as he could see, no one sitting in any of them. Wherever he was, it wasn't here. He flipped open his mobile and rang Jake's number. The voice answered: 'Where are you?'

'At the Bullnose. Where else?'

'Set your milometer to zero.'

'What?'

'Drive one point one miles towards Garsington, then turn left. Drive zero point four miles down that road. You'll see a farm track leading off to the right, and a sign saying "Private – Dingle Dell Cottage". Follow the track till you reach a dilapidated stone cottage. I'll be waiting for you.'

'What if I don't?' Smith asked. But there was no response. Only a dial tone.

'Fuck!' he said. He held the phone to his ear for several more seconds. Then he tried a redial, but it just cut straight into Jake's message and his answering service. 'Fuck!' he said again.

When you're faced by a man whom you suspect has committed three murders, and you are alone in a room with him, every word you utter and every move you make has to be weighed with the greatest of care. DI Holden looked across at her sergeant and smiled. It was, in the circumstances, a pretty convincing smile, and Fox, who wasn't sure what he had walked into, gave a somewhat sheepish grin back.

'What was it?' she asked with apparent concern. 'An abscess?'

'Yeah,' he said with shrug.

'Hmm!' she said neutrally, before she began what she hoped was unobtrusive probing. 'I was beginning to wonder where you'd got to. It's just that you've been out quite a time, and you're with Mr Stewart just down the road, aren't you? And of course,' she added with a thin smile, 'we are in the middle of a murder investigation!'

A helpless grin spread across Fox's face. 'Sorry, Guv. It's a bit embarrassing, really,' he said. And, as if to reinforce his words, Fox gave a pretty good impression of looking embarrassed too. 'I fainted!'

'You fainted?' Holden echoed, trying to spin out the time available to her, only how much was available to her she really didn't know. And Fox, she realized with a start, had pushed the door shut behind him.

'I'm not very good with dentists, especially when they're brandishing needles.' Again he flashed that sheepish grin. 'That's why I changed dentists, from Mr Stewart to Mrs Stephenson.'

'You changed dentists?'

'Yes. It's silly, really. Me being a policeman and yet having a phobia of going to the dentist. I was talking to the pharmacist about it and she suggested that maybe I'd be better with a woman dentist, and she told me about Mrs Stephenson, who she goes to. So I thought I might as well try her out. And to be honest, Mrs Stephenson was very nice and reassuring, but I still fainted, and then she insisted that I sit down and rest up with a cup of tea, but I realize I should have rung in and, well, I'm sorry, Guv.'

As Fox's little speech petered out, Holden allowed herself to sink back down into her chair. She was conscious of tension across her shoulders and the nape of her neck, and a throbbing at the back of her head. It ought to feel better than this, when you suddenly realize you've been an inch away from making a terrible mistake, but it didn't. Perhaps that was because suspicion still lurked, not yet fully under control, at the back of her brain.

'Fox,' she said, 'tell me about Sarah Johnson's diary.'

He frowned. 'I'm not with you Guv. What about it?'

'It wasn't with the file. It was in your desk drawer, locked away,' she said, and then played her final card. 'Someone had ripped out a page. Can you explain that?'

'I'm not sure what you're suggesting, Guv,' he said cautiously. Suspicion was roused and active at the back of his head too. 'That I should leave my desk drawer unlocked? That I should have noticed a page was missing from the diary? Or what? Because to be honest, I never got round to reading it properly. I mean I flicked through it at the beginning, but after that I put it in my drawer because it seemed safer, and besides my desk diary is very like it. And then I forgot all about it.'

'You forgot all about it?' Accusation, doubt and suspicion accompanied these words, but they were more to do with Fox's lack of professionalism than anything else. The idea of Fox as killer had almost completely receded, and she felt deflated and irritated as a consequence.

At which point in their conversation, the door burst open and in walked a figure known to both of them.

'Don!' Holden said brightly, 'Is it good to see you!'

'The pleasure is all mine,' he flashed back, all charm and smarm. He placed a thin bundle of papers on the desk.

'Is that all there is?' Holden said, disappointment apparent in her voice.

'There's this too,' Alexander replied, pulling a CD out of his pocket as a conjuror might pull the missing card. 'We're in the twenty-first century Inspector, where we come from, and photos are mostly digital.' Holden snatched it irritably from his hand and moved round the desk to sit back down at her PC. Fox, a man happier with old fashioned photos and grubby newspaper cuttings, began to leaf deliberately through those on the desk.

'So what is it exactly we are looking for?' he asked eagerly.

'There's no need for you to hang around, Don,' Holden said dismissively. 'We'll take it from here.'

'I can't let these out of my sight, Inspector,' he said pompously. 'I'm doing you a big favour as it is.'

'Well, sit down over there,' she said indicating a red chair in the corner of the room. 'We can't work with you peering over our shoulders.'

'As you wish,' he said, and moved away. He was not unhappy. He was in the room and on the spot. Whatever kicked off, he would know. The story was safe.

Barely a minute had passed before Holden broke the silence. 'Look!' she said.

Fox, who was in the middle of reading a newspaper report, moved round the desk. 'Well, damn me!' He found himself staring at a pair of sombre-looking men standing in front of a large rectangular hole in the ground. One he didn't recognize, but the other, the one of the right-hand side, was all too familiar.

'Can I help?' Alexander asked, standing up as he did so.

'No!' Holden snapped, as she clicked again with the mouse. Another picture came up. There were five people in this one. Holden and Fox stared for three or four seconds before the sergeant spoke:

'Isn't that what's her name?'

'Rachel Laing, you mean?'

'Yes.'

'I think so. And the guy next to her, in the anorak, I've met him in church.'

'Church?'

'He came up and spoke to me. He knew Jake and Sarah, from the day centre.'

'And the others? Do you think they are from the day centre too?'

Alexander had made his way round to the desk and was himself peering at the PC monitor. 'That's from the funeral of Alice Smith. Up at the cemetery in Between Towns Road.'

'What do you know about her?' Holden had given up trying to keep Alexander at a distance.

'She was a benefits adviser, or something like that. She used to go round the various day centres in Oxfordshire, handing out advice.'

'And one of those day centres was the Evergreen one?'

'I guess so.'

'So,' said Fox, 'if these killings are about someone taking revenge for her death, then we've suddenly got a hell of a lot of suspects.'

'Revenge killings?' Alexander said, already writing the next day's headline in his head. 'That's your theory is it? Can I quote you on it?'

'No!' both Fox and Holden said in unison.

It was then that the phone rang. Holden snatched it. 'Holden here.'

It was Wilson, and he was in a state. Fox could hear a frantic buzz of fast-forward chatter from the other end of the line.

'OK, Wilson,' Holden was saying, 'OK. Now just slow down and tell me from the beginning what the situation is.'

Wilson slowed down and explained, but even so he hardly drew breath as he did so. They were with Doreen Sexton, and Sam had not come home, and in fact he was late, and neither Sam nor Al Smith were answering their phones, but Doreen had spoken to Sam earlier and he had said he was going to meet a client at a place called Dingle Dell Cottage which was somewhere out of town on the way towards Stadhampton they thought, only Doreen was very worried because Sam had promised not to be late and normally he was very reliable. 'Just a minute!' Holden cut in noisily, and wondering why the hell Lawson couldn't have made the call. 'Wait while we check.' And thanks to the wonders of the Internet, it took less than a minute to track down Dingle Dell Cottage. 'Right,' she said, 'we'll meet you on the Garsington Road. Wait by the Bullnose. Don't go after them on your own. I'm bringing armed back-up.'

Smith pulled out of the Bullnose Morris car park and headed south. He drove slowly along the thirty mile limit, much more slowly than usual. At the roundabout, he was used to turning right, along Grenoble Road towards the football stadium, but this time he went straight on. He was out of the restricted zone now, but he drove barely forty-five miles an hour. He watched carefully as the milometer progressed: point eight, point nine, one mile. There it was. A left turn. He carefully swung the car round, and peered ahead. It was less than three miles from where he lived, but he couldn't remember ever having driven along this road. He glanced down at the dashboard. One point two miles. Not far now. One point three. One point four. There it was, on the right, a rough farm track, and a sign. Dingle Dell Cottage. He swung right, slowing his car as it bumped uncomfortably over the rugged surface. He changed down another gear and twisted hard right and then left as he tried to avoid – unsuccessfully – a deep rut. Lurching around, he nevertheless gently pressed down on the accelerator, anxious to get to the rendezvous. He kept his eyes fixed ahead, but with his hand he felt across the passenger seat, searching with his fingers until the found the reassuring presence of the baseball bat. He found it an easy weapon to handle: whether with a full swing of the arm or a short stabbing movement into an opponent's face, it was bloody effective. And it was easy enough to hide too, slipped up inside the sleeve of an anorak. He was ready. He was ready for the bastard. It was now or never. And he was bloody fucking ready.

It was, for the time of day and year, extremely dark. Since Smith had left Wittenham Clumps, thick low cloud had thrust dramatically in from the west, gobbling up the blue sky until it was all gone. The wind which had brought it had then relented, leaving the grey billowing masses to mark time over Oxford and the countryside around, threatening, though not yet delivering, rain. Smith, suddenly noticing a large lump of stone in front of him, again swung the wheel abruptly first one way and then the other, before slipping down a gear for fear of stalling the car. It was at that moment that the smell hit him. It was the smell of smoke, though it wasn't the comforting smell of wood smoke or the burning of autumn leaves. It was an altogether more unpleasant and acrid odour, an essentially unnatural smell.

He peered in front, looking for its source, but trees now pressed in from either side, scratching at the car and limiting his view. Up front, the track curved away to the right and out of sight, and he pressed his foot down again, briefly spinning his back wheels as they lost traction.

'Shit!' Up front the road was straightening out, forcing its way out of the clinging wood, and leading straight to a dilapidated-looking stone building that Smith assumed must be Dingle Dell Cottage. But his one-word exclamation had nothing to do with the building. Parked in front of it was a vehicle. And it was on fire. 'Bloody fucking shit!' Dark black smoke and blistering orange flames were erupting skywards from it. As he drew closer, the detail of the object started to register and its outline become apparent through the flames and smoke. It was bigger than a car. A van in fact. The sort of van beloved of builders. In fact, a make of a van that Smith recognized only too well. He lurched to a halt and jumped out, forgetting the baseball bat that he had been handling only seconds before. Or not so much forgetting it as leaving it, because the fact was that a baseball bat wouldn't be any use at all in rescuing his friend from the blaze. 'Sam!' he screamed, but he knew there would be no reply. He ran forward, but after three of four steps, the heat of the blaze stopped him in his tracks. Reluctantly, he retreated. 'Sam!' he screamed again. 'Sam!' Because there was nothing else he could do. 'Sam!' Again and again and again he bellowed out his friend's name, and he stopped only when something hard and heavy collided with the top of his head.

If Al Smith had not ducked very slightly before impact, he would almost certainly have died instantly. A sixth sense, a primeval survival instinct, or some undeliberate stumble – whatever it was that caused the sudden lowering of his head – the result was that the metal boating spike which his unseen assailant swung at his head missed the centre of its target and instead struck him a glancing blow on the top of the head. But glancing blows with heavy objects can still inflict severe damage, and before Smith hit the ground he had already entered a world of oblivion. His assailant stood over his inert body for several seconds, but when Smith half opened his eyes and gave a groan, the man, rather than hitting him again, merely smiled. 'Still with us, you bastard?' he snarled. There was no reply. Merely another groan. 'Perhaps this will wake you up?' he continued and he began to pour water over him. 'Hello!' he shouted. 'Hello! Anyone at home?'

Smith groaned yet again and tried to raise himself from the ground with his left arm, cajoled into consciousness not so much by the shouting or the wetness as by the smell. It was a strong, unpleasant smell, as well as being a very familiar smell, and in the circumstances it was a frightening one. His clothes, he realized, were covered not with water, but with petrol. As adrenalin began to pump through his veins, he tried desperately to get himself upright, now using both arms to force his body upwards, but it was a pointless expenditure of his personal resources. His assailant calmly put the petrol can back down on the ground, picked up the metal spike again, and for a second time swung it in an arc through the air. This time, however, he aimed not at Smith's head, but his left knee. He was a strong man, and fury added to that strength: the bar crashed unhindered into its target and Smith went down again in screaming agony.

His assailant sniggered. 'Now you're not going to get any ideas about running off,' he mocked, though the snigger and words were wasted on Smith. Through the excruciating pain, which seemed to rip from the knee right up his side to the base of the skull, all his limited energy and concentration was focused on just one thing – survival – and if survival proved impossible, then at least revenge. He twisted his face upwards in an attempt to see more than just his attacker's legs, but the act of trying to focus merely caused more pain to streak across his head. The man laughed loudly this time, and kicked him hard in the stomach, so that he collapsed again in a heap.

'I didn't mean it,' Smith begged. And then again: 'It was an accident!'

If Smith hoped that these words would somehow stop his assailant, they failed. His attacker aimed another kick at him, this time at his left leg rather than his stomach. Smith screamed again.

'An accident?' his assailant shouted. 'You didn't mean it? What sort of idiot do you think I am. My girlfriend burns to death and you call it a fucking accident. Next thing is you'll be begging me to forgive you, to turn the other cheek. Well, let me tell you, I'm no lovey-dovey Christian. If I believed in a God, he'd be the eye-for-an-eye, tooth-for-a-tooth type. Vengeance is mine, you bastard, do you get it? Vengeance is mine! And you are going to burn, just like her.' With that he bent down, picked up a second can and began to pour yet more petrol on Smith. He was curled up in a semi-foetal position, his left hand on his stomach, the other flapping around the smashed knee. But inside his head, his mind was remarkably clear. He just needed to get the bastard closer.

'It was all her fault!' Smith snarled. 'The bloody bitch started it!' The odd thing was that this was almost true. They had come together in the pub, the six of them on their way back from a peace protest, and the five of themselves on their way home after the game. Sitting at adjacent tables, they had got on all right at first. One of the peaceniks asked about the game; he was an Oxford United fan, and they, it turned out, were all from the Oxford area, but after a bit it got a bit political, and the woman – she had long, fuzzy hair, and circular glasses, and a stud in her nose – started to go on about war, and the army, and how soldiers were the stooges of politicians, and how no one in their right mind should kill people for a living – and that had really wound Al Smith up because his little brother Jo had joined up two years ago, and twelve months later had been blown up by a suicide bomber, so he didn't want to be lectured by any hippie on the ethics of bloody war. 'The frizzy haired bitch started it!'

That got his assailant's attention. The empty petrol can was hurled away, and he stepped right up to Smith, so that his boot was almost touching his face. 'You're lying. You're a lying piece of shit. You drove them off the road. I know that because Sarah told me, and so did Jake just before I killed him. So say what you like, because it won't change a thing. Your time is up, arsehole!'

And then he struck a match. Not that Smith saw him do it – he could see only his legs, and the burning van beyond – but he knew it was coming, and he heard and recognized the tell-tale noise, so that he knew he was too late. Smith's right hand, which had been flapping around his smashed kneecap as if in some vain attempt to assuage the pain, had moved further down his right leg, and had finally located what it sought, a short-handled knife strapped in a leather sheath just above his right ankle. It had then taken several critical moments of desperate scrabbling to pull up the trouser leg and grasp the handle, but then only a second to lunge through the air and strike deep into the man's calf. The match fell pirouetting and reeling through the air, igniting the petrol vapours before it reached Smith's jacket. The man fell to the ground, bellowing out pain. As the flames erupted into his face, he twisted violently to the left, trying to hurl himself away to safety, but two clawing hands had hold of his coat, and like Rottweilers with their prey, they refused to let go.

When the police arrived some two minutes later, the smouldering corpse of Al Smith lay inert on the ground, all life thankfully extinguished. But under its blackened bulk lay the still twitching, and barely recognizable body of Jim Blunt.

It took Jim Blunt six days to die. He was in the John Radcliffe Hospital for almost thirty-six hours before he opened his eyes, and another twenty-four passed before he uttered any sound decipherable as a word. On day four he finally began to form sentences and to show awareness of his surroundings. DI Holden, who dropped by each day to check on his progress, was so encouraged that she brought Detective Constable Lawson with her the following afternoon. In the presence of Lawson and a prickly, protective nurse, Holden conducted a painfully slow interview with Blunt. The nurse terminated the exchange after only three minutes when Blunt feebly waved his questioner away and turned his head towards the window. For the remainder of the day Blunt slept desultorily. At six o'clock he took some soup with surprising enthusiasm, but then fell into a deep sleep from which he never awoke. At

9.05 a.m. the following day he was declared dead by the duty doctor. The transcript of the interview is reproduced here:

Holden:	Do you know who you are?
Blunt:	Yes. James Henry Blunt.
Holden:	Did you kill Jake Arnold?
Blunt:	Yes.
Holden:	Did you kill Martin Mace?
Blunt:	Yes.
Holden:	Did you kill Sam Sexton?
Blunt:	Yes.
Holden:	Did you kill Alan Smith?
Blunt:	Did he die then?
Holden:	Did you kill Sarah Johnson?
Blunt:	Sarah? (There was a long pause.)
Holden	She fell from the top of the car park. Did you push her?
Blunt:	No.
Holden:	Were you there at the top of the car park when she fell to her death?

(*Blunt began to laugh and after several seconds turned towards the window. At the staff nurse's insistence, the interview was terminated.*)

EPILOGUE

They decided to drive as far as the St Clement's car park, and then walk. Not that there was a lot of choice, it being Oxford. It was a clear, cold night, the first one of the winter, and after the rain and endless low cloud of the previous week, it came as something of a relief. For Lawson, the unexpected sunshine of that day seemed highly appropriate: her permanent transfer to Holden's section had been all but sealed (the paperwork was on the Chief Superintendent's desk, awaiting his signature), a small pay rise had been secured, and only that morning she had been allowed to sit in and witness the conclusion to the inquest into Sarah Johnson's death. Life was indeed good.

'A good day at the office, Guv,' she said, as the two of them stood at the pedestrian crossing. Holden turned and stared at her constable with a look of incredulity. She had spoken barely a word since leaving the station. It was not that Lawson had found her silence sullen or gruff, it was just that Holden had brought every attempt at conversation to a gentle but firm closure. But this, Lawson kept telling herself, was a social outing, and therefore chat was essential.

Holden sniffed. 'For you, Lawson, perhaps.' And she stepped onto the crossing as a yellow Mini pulled up to let them over. Another conversation strangled at birth. Lawson sighed silently. Well, maybe there would be people at the private viewing to talk to. A private viewing. It sounded so exclusive. The first she had ever been to, and hopefully not the last. She didn't move in the world of private viewings, and she had been delighted, and touched, when Holden had shown her the invitation: 'DI Susan Holden and colleague' had been hand-written in the most elegant of scripts at the top of the printed card.

'So, would you like to come, Lawson,' she had said. 'Fox laughed when I showed him, and Wilson said he was playing football, which seems a pretty feeble excuse to me, and—'

'So I'm third choice, am I, Guv?' Lawson had chipped in, no longer feeling quite so touched.

Holden had looked at her with irritation. 'It's a question of seniority, Lawson.' She snapped. 'I could hardly ask you first.'

'I was joking, Guv,' she had replied hastily, conscious she had overstepped the mark.

'I don't think so, Lawson. I don't think so at all.' There had been a silence then, cold and hard. Eventually, Lawson had been forced to plead: 'I would like to come with you, Guv. If you don't mind.'

Holden had given a half laugh. 'Look, Lawson, do you think I couldn't have persuaded Fox to accompany me, or Wilson, if I'd really wanted their company? But I didn't want them. I wanted you, because I thought you'd blend in better. Fox is a philistine and would have stood out like a second-hand car salesman in the Royal Enclosure at Ascot. As for Wilson, bless him, well he's not exactly socially adept. Whereas you, I trust, will just merge in. They know I'm a cop, but we are going as enthusiasts of art. You could be my young cousin, or half-sister from a second marriage, or even my innocent young lover. Just so long as we aren't obviously coppers. That way we might learn more.'

'About art?' Lawson had said, eager to make amends.

Holden laughed again, but it was a louder and altogether kinder laugh, cut off only by the sudden need to negotiate the final road crossing. They were now on the approaches to Magdalen Bridge, the ancient eastern entrance to the medieval city. They walked briskly in a finally contented silence, along the slight curve of the High Street until they came to their destination.

The Bare Canvas gallery was certainly not as Holden had seen it when she had last visited it to interview Les Whiting. The garish, abstract, frameless canvases had disappeared. So too had the bright white walls on which they had been displayed, to be replaced by a network of oppressive grey partitions which mimicked the grim walls of the multi-storey car park. The wall nearest the door as they entered had a blue circular plaque on it. Holden expected it to be a copy of the one that she had seen, but it was not. In the middle was a single word followed by a question mark: 'Why?' And round it, in smaller writing, the words 'Ed Bicknell and Ms Johnson invite you to ask the question'.

'Welcome, Susan!' Les Whiting stood before them, arms held wide apart in full greeting mode, a mode which obviously involved dispensing with the formalities of police titles. 'Les Whiting, gallery owner and entrepreneur, at your service!' He bowed theatrically.

'Entrepreneur?' Susan Holden quizzed. 'Is this a new departure?'

'Art has moved on. Think Damien Hurst. Think Tracey Mein. And so the purveyors of art must move on too.'

'This is my colleague, Jan Lawson,' Holden said quickly, conscious that Whiting had ignored her.

'I guessed!' he said, but barely glanced at her. 'You won't believe the Press interest. They were crawling all over the place this afternoon, and getting Anne to pose this way and that. They couldn't get enough of it.'

'Is she here?' Holden asked, curious to know exactly what Anne's part was.

'She will be soon. Ed Bicknell is somewhere. Would you like to have a chat? Honestly, he's like a schoolboy who's raided the tuck shop. Can't believe his luck.'

'So you're all making a killing are you, out of a death? You and Ed and Anne?'

If she had hoped her aggressive questioning would throw Whiting off balance, Holden was disappointed. It merely spurred him on. 'Does it all come back to money for you, Susan? I'm disappointed, I really am. I thought you were smarter than that. It's not just money – though that helps, of course it does. We all need money, even you, Susan dear. It's about being taken seriously. From now on, we will be known, and for that reason alone we will be taken seriously. In this world of celebrity, that's what matters. The unknowns are ignored. Tell me if I'm wrong?'

'Sadly, Mr Whiting, I fear you are right,' Holden said, before moving forward past him, with Lawson close at her back. The exhibition was, as Lawson later told her mother, laid out backwards. 'I'm not sure why. I suppose Bicknell thought he was being clever and artistic, making us take it all in backwards, but the whole thing was too clever by half if you ask me.'

The first images were of flowers: first an old woman, shapeless in her jumper and skirt, walking right to left, in her hand a Tesco carrier with the heads of flowers protruding; she was placed on the left-hand side of the photograph, as if about to step out of it. Next the same woman holding a large bunch of flowers in her right hand and tossing a broken-stemmed one away with her left; then the woman picking up the flowers; then a dog, a rather mangy collie type cocking its leg over the flowers as they lay on the pavement; two youths in sportswear and baseball caps walking past laughing; an old woman with a stick labouring past and not looking; then a small girl, one hand firmly gripped by a woman (an older mother or a young grandmother, Lawson speculated) – the child was looking over her shoulder as the flowers passed all too swiftly by. The final image was of a smartly dressed woman, laying flowers on the pavement, while in the foreground a pair of trousered legs strode by.

'Are they genuine or staged, do you think?' Lawson wondered out loud, but Holden didn't answer. 'Come on,' she merely said, 'let's go and see what's next.'

What was next was a body. In the first photograph, the body was almost incidental. Most of the picture was taken up by a policeman, hand thrust forward, obviously trying to block the photographer from taking shots of the body which could be seen sprawled in the background, taking up but a small fraction of the image, but unmissable because it was the only thing in the picture that was in focus. Holden sucked in her breath and pondered. Either Ed Bicknell was a very skilled photographer, or he was a dab hand at manipulating his images on the PC. In the next couple of photographs, the body again took a subordinate role, this time to the two policemen who arrived and began to cordon off the area. But the remainder – and there were a dozen or so of these – focused unreservedly on the body that only seconds earlier had been a living, breathing Sarah Johnson. She had landed on her back, or at least had finished up on her back, her head twisted violently at an angle. The photographs were displayed in a huge circle, and it was possible to trace anticlockwise the seconds after impact, as blood spread in a gradually expanding arc from the gaping wound that had been her face. The photos were snapped from a variety of angles and heights: one was so close up that the camera might have been laid on the pavement only a foot or so from the head, while another had been taken from directly above the battered head, as if from some miniature helicopter.

'He must be a cool bastard.' Lawson literally felt her gorge rise as stomach juices momentarily forced their way up into her throat. She was trying to imagine herself there at the time, watching this man clinically lining up his photos. Did he delay his 999 call so that he could have more time with the body? Indeed, was it he who called the police? She couldn't remember from the records. Maybe he was clicking away with his camera while some other bystander was ringing for an ambulance and the police. Did he have to ask people to move away from the body so he could have a clear view for all his shots?

'Good evening, ladies!' Holden and Lawson were taken by surprise by the voice close behind them, and turned as one. 'Are you enjoying it?' The voice belonged to Ed Bicknell, an Ed Bicknell who had scrubbed up considerably since Holden had last seen him. The scruffy Che Guevara T-Shirt and ripped jeans had been replaced by a dark brown velvet suit and glistening white shirt, and his hair and beard had been subjected to a very thorough make-over in honour of the media. He was, no question, a man determined to make his mark.

'Ah, Mr Bicknell,' Holden smiled. 'The man of the moment.'

'I'm not sure "enjoying" is quite the right word,' Lawson said firmly. 'Do we really need to see so many pictures of the poor woman? She was someone's daughter, you know.'

Bicknell smiled at her patronizingly. 'Actually, both her parents are long since dead, so I doubt they will object, but nevertheless I take your point. Not that I would agree with you, however. There's no escaping death, not for any of us. We have to look at it how it is – final and brutal. But we all move on after the death of others. If we are very close to someone who dies, it may take us some time, but our own emotional survival demands that we do move on, that we learn to walk past those reminders of death just as in the first part of the exhibition those pedestrians walked past the flowers. But what interests me is why Sarah Johnson jumped. What made her decide that it was better to walk to the top of a car park one fine morning and plunge to her death, than to carry on living? Did that blue plaque really push her over the edge? That's the line the *Daily Mail* will doubtless pedal in its feature in tomorrow's edition, but who cares what the *Daily Mail* thinks? Maybe the blue plaque freed her to be true to her innermost convictions. Maybe it simply gave her permission to jump. Maybe she looked in the mirror as she brushed her hair that morning and suddenly decided enough misery was enough. Watch the news. Read the newspapers. The world is a catalogue of misery. Maybe Sarah saw the world more clearly than we do. Maybe that was the reason why she jumped. Twenty-twenty vision.'

'And maybe,' said Holden, 'we'll go and see the rest of the exhibition.'

He shrugged unconcernedly, and turned away as they themselves moved on through a doorway into a small auditorium. There were several people already sitting in the chairs, and one – a woman's voice – called out encouragingly from the darkness. 'Quick, it's only just started!'

The moving image on the wall was black-and-white and silent: a woman dressing. She was dressing with her back to the camera, so that her face was not immediately visible, but when she turned to pick up a pair of trousers, her profile came into full view: Sarah Johnson. Or rather, as Holden quickly realized, Anne Johnson pretending to be Sarah Johnson. The resemblance was striking, even creepy. For the next ten minutes they sat and watched this woman play out the penultimate scene of her sister's life: staring listlessly into the mirror as she lethargically brushed her hair; trying on six pairs of shoes and boots before reverting to the black ankle boots she had first tried on; writing a note which she then crumpled onto a plate and set fire to; going to the loo and then reappearing after barely thirty seconds; picking up her mobile phone in her left hand and making a call while her right hand weaved an erratic path through the air as if conducting an invisible orchestra; shutting the kitchen window; putting on her coat; staring again at herself, this time in the mirror in the hall; and finally walking out of the front door.

Lawson was nearest the exit, and so it was she who was first to reach the doorway, and she who screeched first and loudest at the figure coming the other way. It was, as logic would have told her, none other than Anne Johnson dressed up to look like Sarah, but in that first moment Lawson was a creature of instinct, not logic, and the woman she saw, dressed in exactly the same clothes as in the film, and looking

238

exactly the same in every respect, really did shock her, albeit briefly. Anne Johnson smiled in obvious pleasure.

'Gosh,' she said, 'I don't usually have that effect on people!'

'You surprised me,' Lawson said defensively.

'That was the idea, actually,' she said unrepentantly. 'It's nice to see you again, Constable,' she added, 'but now, if you'll excuse me, I'd better mix with the other guests.' And she swept away from them.

It was a relief to both Holden and Lawson to discover that the next doorway led into a very different room. In the middle of it, there was a long trestle table, on which stood a selection of drinks. Furthermore, unlike the rest of the gallery, the impression here was of light and space – and also of being watched, for all around on the walls were pictures of people looking. They were, according to the large title on the end wall, 'The nosey-parkers of death'.

'Are they genuine?' Holden asked as with one hand she took a glass of white wine from the woman standing by the trestle, and with the other gestured towards the surrounding walls. 'Were they taken at the time, or faked up later?'

'Does it matter,' the woman replied defensively.

'They look fake to me!' Lawson said loudly, determined to put her embarrassment with Anne Johnson behind her.

'And what is that,' Holden asked, pointing to a PC screen in the corner beyond the table.

'Oh that's genuine,' the young woman said quickly. 'He had a camera set up at a different angle, shooting down the street and taking shots every thirty seconds. It shows people looking at the plaque, and then the dead body, and everyone rubbernecking, but he wasn't very happy with it. When you zoom in to get a closer view, the images lose definition. He needed a better camera really.'

Holden moved forward round the side of the table to get a closer look. Lawson and Holden followed, and for some time the three of them watched in silence, sipping from their glasses, as every fifteen seconds or so a new photo took up position on the screen.

'We haven't seen these before,' Holden said without elaboration.

'No,' agreed Lawson. Though at that moment her mind wasn't really attending to the images that kept appearing in front of her. 'I've been thinking, Guv,' she continued.'

'Don't overdo it, Constable,' Holden murmured back.

'Well, being here makes you think. And there's one thing that I really can't get my head round. In fact, it's really beginning to bug me.' She paused, untypically needing permission to carry on.

'Yes?' Holden said, still watching the PC screen. 'What is it then?'

'Well,' Lawson said earnestly, 'there's one thing that really puzzles me. Don't you think it's an extraordinary coincidence that on the very same day that Anne visits her sister at the crack of dawn, Bicknell sets up his suicide plaque just down the road. I mean, it might be coincidence, but personally I find it hard to believe.'

For a moment, Holden turned to look at her colleague. There was a frown across her face. 'I see,' she said quietly. She continued to gaze in the direction of Lawson for several seconds, before turning silently back to yet another new image on the PC. What she saw, however, caused a dramatic change in manner. 'Look!' The excitement in her voice was palpable. She pointed urgently towards the screen. 'There, Lawson! In the background.' And she moved her finger further forward until it was almost touching. 'Look at the jogger!'

'I see him, Guv.'

'A woman or a man? What do you think?'

'Very hard to identify, Guv. The hood is hiding most of the face. A woman or a small man.'

'There's red piping on the trousers. Oh Damn!' Their fifteen seconds was up, and in the next photo to be displayed, taken exactly thirty seconds later, the jogger was nowhere to be seen.

Holden turned and tapped the woman by the table on the shoulder. 'Do you know how long this runs? When it started and when it finished?'

She puckered her nose as she assessed the question. 'I think it's about a fifteen, maybe twenty-minute loop. Sorry, I can't pretend I've watched it through.'

Holden turned back to her colleague. 'The time, Lawson. It must have been a couple of minutes after Sarah was killed.'

'Are you suggesting that the jogger was something to do with—'

'It's a cul-de-sac, isn't it? The jogger is coming out of a cul-de-sac.'

Lawson strained to remember what the side-street was like. 'I think there are some flats on the other side, so maybe the jogger lived there?'

'But if not, where did he or she come from? From the car park. In which case, the jogger must be the killer.'

'Based on size, it can't be Blunt.'

'Which leaves us with Anne Johnson.'

Lawson looked at her boss. Holden's whole face was alight with excitement, as the implications of what she was saying and thinking surged through her body. Lawson, however, felt uncertain and even bemused by this sudden development. She fiddled nervously with the stud earring in her right ear, as she tried to weigh her next words with care.

'It is possible,' she admitted uncertainly, 'but even if it's correct, proving it may be harder.'

'I know that!' Holden replied emphatically. 'I'm not stupid, Lawson.'

'No, Guv,' Lawson said quickly, and then turned back to watch the still revolving cycle of Bicknell's photographs.

Holden too turned, waiting for the jogger to come round again, but she was irritated to find that her attention no longer fully engaged. Partly that was because most of the photos had nothing to capture her interest, and partly because her mind refused to jettison what Lawson had said earlier about the coincidence of Bicknell's suicide plaque project and Sarah's supposed suicide.

'Lawson,' she said finally, her eyes still on the photos, 'I think we need a copy of these, and I think too we need a chat with Bicknell.'

Lawson turned to look at her boss, but her eyes focused instead some metres beyond her. 'Speak of the devil,' she said quietly, 'here the great man is!'

Bicknell was approaching the drinks table, an empty wine glass in one hand, which he exchanged for a full one.

'Ah, Mr Bicknell,' Holden called across the room. 'We've just been watching this.'

He took a swig of wine, and moved towards them, a large grin across his flushed face.

'Not my best work, I'm afraid.' He spoke expansively, as if he was a photographer with a long and distinguished career. 'Didn't quite get the exposure right, and the shots are too long. In fact, I nearly didn't bother with it, but then I thought what the hell, it's not taking up a lot of space.'

'Can I have a copy,' Holden cut in.

'If you really want to.'

'Tonight if possible!'

Bicknell shrugged. 'OK. I've got a back-up CD in Les's office. Just in case anything went wrong.' And he walked off towards a door at the back of the room.

'We'll come with you,' Holden said, beckoning Lawson to follow.

'No need,' Bicknell said, as he unlocked the door.

'Actually, there is every need. We need a chat with you. Now, sir, if you don't mind.'

Bicknell turned to look at her, suddenly wary at her change of manner. 'This is hardly the time—'

'This is exactly the time, sir' Holden interrupted, her voice low but insistent. 'We need to have a conversation right now, and we can either do it discreetly and very quickly here, or my constable can whistle up a car and we can do it down at the station. But that would, of course, take a lot longer—'

She allowed her sentence to fade to a stop, and waited for his response.

'Not much of a bloody choice, is it,' he snarled, before pushing his way angrily into the office.

Holden waited for Lawson to shut the door behind them, and then reverted to a more conciliatory manner.

'So, Ed, tell me where this idea of a suicide plaque came from? Did someone put you up to it?'

He looked at her in disbelief. 'Put me up to it? What the hell do you mean? It was my bloody idea. Mine, and no one else's.'

Holden considered apologising, but decided that would be being altogether too friendly. 'OK, so what gave you the idea?'

He looked hard at her again, but this time there was no visible emotion in his face, and when he spoke he did so in a matter-of-fact way. 'My father killed himself. He was an alcoholic, you see, a drunk. First he crashed the car while under the influence, and killed my mother, and then, three months later, he walked to the top of a car park and jumped.'

'I'm sorry,' Holden replied, and paused, though only briefly before continuing her questioning: 'Can I ask when you decided to do your blue plaque—' Again she tailed off, but this time it was because she was struggling to find the right word.

'Installation?' Bicknell suggested.

'Right, installation.'

'Oh, I don't know, maybe six months ago, maybe more.'

'Really? So will you tell me why you decided to do it on that particular Friday after a such a gap?'

'Well, I suppose I just kept putting it off and putting it off until I couldn't put it off any longer.'

'So you woke up early one morning and just decided on the spur of the moment to do it, did you?'

'Of course I bloody didn't. I had to prepare for it, didn't I? I had to make the plaque, and organize my cameras and work out exactly the best position.'

'Did you discuss your installation with your fellow students?'

'You must be joking. I didn't want them nicking my idea.'

'So you didn't discuss it with anyone? Not even your tutor?'

'Especially not my tutor. I wouldn't trust him further than I could vomit.'

'So you didn't discuss it with anyone at all?'

For several moments the question hung in the air. Bicknell pursed his lips in thought, before slowly raising his glass and draining the red wine from it. Only then did he look Holden full in the face.

'For the last few months, I've been going to a support group. For people who've suffered loss. In my case, my parents. For others it was husbands and wives, lovers, children, in one case a twin sister. And we talked about how we felt and all that sort of stuff, and how we could properly confront our loss and move on. To be honest, I thought it was all going to be a load of bollocks at first, but it wasn't, and so I kept going back. And I got pally with this guy who had lost his girlfriend in a car crash, and one night we went to the pub afterwards, and I told him about my idea and he was really interested and encouraging, and said I really should do it.'

'And this guy's name?'

'Jim. I didn't know his other name. First names only in the group. But, of course, I recognized him when his face appeared in the papers.'

'It was Jim Blunt?'

'Yes.'

Holden took a deep breath in, and then let it out again, as she tried to maintain a semblance of calm.

Lawson, sensing the situation, took up the baton. 'Can I ask you, sir, if you actually discussed with Jim Blunt the precise day you were going to do it?'

'Oh yes, we discussed it,' Bicknell said. He was relieved now. Talking about it even to the police, was amazingly cathartic and comforting. Outside the support group, he never talked about his parents. Now he spoke almost cheerfully. 'In fact, he suggested that Friday was a good day for him, and he might come and take a look himself after he'd attended some meeting he had first thing.'

At 9.05 the following morning, DI Holden presided over a meeting of Fox, Wilson and Lawson. She herself had arrived in the office at 7.45 a.m., but had felt no sense of impatience or indeed urgency. She knew what she wanted done, and 7.45 was too early to go banging on doors. She was glad, however, of the peace of her office, and took the opportunity to read through the files and statements again, and to make some notes for the interview she had planned. At 9.05, when the three of her colleagues filed in, she briefed the two men on the previous night's developments, and then laid out her instructions for the morning. Lawson would accompany her in locating Danny Flynn. Fox would get hold of Blunt's mobile phone records, and also make a phone call to Dr Adrian Ratcliffe. And Wilson was given the task of knocking on doors.

Holden and Lawson found Danny just leaving his flat. He recognized both of them, and looked at them uneasily. Like many people, he found himself getting uncomfortable when confronted by the police, even when they were bending over backwards to be nice.

'Sorry to bother you, Danny,' Holden said in a voice that she hoped sounded both apologetic and friendly. 'But we really do need your help.'

'Why?' he said. He was genuinely puzzled. It was weeks since the young one had talked to him in the hospital, and he had heard on Radio Oxford the night before that the inquest had decided that Sarah had committed suicide, so he couldn't see what else there was to talk about.

It was the young one who spoke next, her voice calm and barely loud enough to be heard over the passing cars. 'Danny, do you remember that when you were in the hospital you told me how you had seen Sarah visiting Jim Blunt's house.'

'Of course,' he said indignantly. 'I'm not an amnesiac, you know.'

'No, of course not. All I want is for you to tell me what Sarah was wearing that night?'

Danny didn't answer at first. Instead, he busied himself with doing up the zip of his windcheater, and then thrust his hands into his pockets. His face and eyes remained cast down, as he searched for a detailed memory of that night. Eventually he looked up at Lawson. 'She was wearing a skirt, black I think or some other dark colour. And a short jacket or coat. It might have been leather. And she wore boots. Red ones. I remember that clearly.' Danny looked down again, apparently finished.

'That's really clear, Danny,' Lawson enthused. 'Was she wearing any jewellery that you can remember?'

'No,' he said quickly, still looking down. 'I wasn't that close and it was dark.'

'I understand.' Again she spoke gently, and with care, all too conscious of how suddenly her last interview of Danny had disintegrated. 'I think you said last time you saw them kiss, just before Sarah left. Can you tell me a bit more about it. Was it, like, a kiss between girlfriend and boyfriend or maybe more of a hug like between friends?'

Danny twisted his head, first to the left and then to the right, a man enduring the pain of something he'd much rather not remember. 'Not a hug.'

Lawson paused, not sure how much further to press. Holden, sensing this, intervened.

'Danny,' she said. 'I just want to ask you one question. It may seem a bit odd, but I want to ask it anyway, and then we'll leave you in peace. OK?'

He finally raised his head to look at his questioners, and nodded slightly.

'I know you've met Sarah's sister, Anne. They are very alike, aren't they? So what I want to know is whether you're certain the person you saw that night was Sarah. Could it possibly have been Anne?'

'You think I'm stupid,' he said, his voice rising wildly. Lawson recognized the behaviour and knew that they had lost him now, just as she had previously lost him in the hospital. Holden lifted her hands, in apology or surrender, but Danny wasn't looking. He had turned, and was already moving away from them down the Iffley Road, striding out like a competitor in a fifty-kilometre walk. Lawson made as if to follow him, but Holden grabbed her arm. 'Don't bother,' she said firmly. 'We've done enough.'

*

Holden's team met up again in her office at just after eleven that morning. After she had given an account of their encounter with Danny, Wilson was asked to report on his door-to-door enquiries.

'There are eight flats in the side road opposite the car park. I spoke to residents of five of them in person, and managed to contact two others by phone. Obviously, I asked them about their neighbours too, so that I could cross-check the evidence. There are just two men and one woman who appear to jog. A couple who by all accounts always go out together in matching navy blue tracksuits, and a man who admits to running in the mornings before he goes to work, and who says he never wears tracksuit bottoms, merely shorts, because he doesn't like to overheat. He's about five feet eleven, so size rules him out anyway.'

'So, there's no one living there who matches our mystery jogger?' Holden asked for confirmation.

'No.'

'What about you, Sergeant?'

'Interesting developments, I think, Guv.' He paused as he sought to organize his thoughts, but this provoked a glare of irritation from Holden. 'That is to say, Guv, that Blunt twice made phone calls to Sarah Johnson's mobile, on the Sunday and then the Tuesday before her death. The first one took about two minutes, the second about three. I've also spoken to Adrian Radcliffe and he said Anne did have a grey tracksuit.' He stopped, having said all he had to say.

Silence descended. Each of them was temporarily lost in private, yet similar, thoughts. Blunt had known Anne Johnson too. Blunt had known about Bicknell's plans. Blunt. It all led back to Blunt.

'OK,' Holden said eventually. 'I'll say it how I see it, and you shoot me down. The question, first, is quite simple: did Sarah Johnson commit suicide or was she murdered? And if she was murdered, was it Blunt or her sister who did it? Suicide has been presumed because of Sarah's mental health issues. The timing of her death may be explained by Bicknell's blue plaque, or by the distress caused by the early morning visit of her sister with whom she didn't get on. However,' Holden continued, 'a case for murder can equally be made out. First, we have an unknown person dressed in a grey hooded tracksuit leaving the scene of the murder. This person was not a local resident. The side-street from which he or she emerged is a cul-de-sac. Either this person is a genuine jogger who ran into the cul-de-sac – but how likely is that? – or this person was someone who had just participated in or at least watched Sarah's death? From a size point of view, the figure is too slight for Blunt, so my best guess is that it is Anne Johnson. What do we know about Anne Johnson? That she lies when it suits her: she denied being in Oxford at all until we produced cast-iron evidence from the car park CCTV; that she didn't get on with her sister; that her sister, who owned a flat worth a considerable amount of money was planning on changing her will, probably to Anne's disadvantage. This gives Anne motive for murder, quite apart from any sibling relationship problems that the two of them may have had. But to this we have to add Bicknell. Bicknell, we now know, told Blunt all about it, even down to discussing when exactly he should do it. Blunt killed four persons who were involved in the death of his girlfriend, and the fifth one was Sarah. Yet when I asked him if he killed Sarah, he denied it, and when I asked if he was there when she fell, he laughed. We also know Blunt made two phone calls to Anne. He could have met her; maybe it was Anne whom Danny saw kissing Blunt, not Sarah. Personally, I believe these are connections, not just coincidences. How did Blunt find out about who was in the vehicle that caused the death of his girlfriend? Well, from Sarah, surely. Eventually, she had to tell someone, and Blunt seemed a safe man to tell. Only he wasn't. Around the same time, he is put in touch with Anne by Sarah. They speak on the phone, and maybe they meet too and develop a relationship. Blunt also comes across Bicknell, and learns about his plaque idea, and suddenly he realizes he has an opportunity to get rid of Sarah and make it look like suicide. So he helps Anne set up her alibi. She arrives and then leaves from the car park. Probably she parks a distance away down the Iffley Road, pulls a hooded top and tracksuit trousers over her other clothes, and goes back to the car park. She rings her sister saying she can't find her car keys. Her sister finds them hidden under a magazine or something, and heads for the car park. She stops at the suicide plaque – where Bicknell, of course, photographs her – and finally gets to the top, where Anne, perhaps helped by Blunt, pushes her over the wall. Anne goes down the stairway, and goes out into the cul-de-sac to avoid the CCTV, but is caught on Bicknell's other camera.' Finally Holden stopped talking, and looked around for a response. Fox immediately took the lead.

'It's a good theory, Guv. Hell, it's so good, I think I believe it, but the only problem is the evidence. It's all circumstantial. What is the evidence? An intention to change a will? A not very good photo of a hooded person? An alibi that we can undermine, but not disprove. The fact that Blunt kissed and may have had an intimate relationship with Sarah, or was it Anne, and the witness of this is in any case a man with a history of paranoia. Hell, it just won't wash in a court of law.' He paused. 'Sorry,' he added, 'but I have to say it how I see it.'

Holden nodded, and then looked at the others. 'Wilson, Lawson, how about you?'

Wilson looked down, unwilling to enter the fray. Lawson, sensing it, took up the challenge. 'For what it's worth, I'm afraid I think Fox has got it about right. Sarah was murdered, but we can't prove it.'

'Quite,' Holden agreed. 'The only person who knows for certain what happened is Anne.'

'So we need to apply some pressure,' Fox said. 'We've come all this way. We can't just leave it.'

'Look!' said Lawson eagerly. 'Anne doesn't know that we know that she and Blunt know each other. She probably doesn't know that we know about Blunt and Bicknell. Maybe that's where we can apply some pressure?'

Holden pursed her lips. 'OK,' she said eventually. 'let's give it a try.'

'So, how can I help you?' Anne Johnson asked mildly. She sat one side of the table in the interview room, directly opposite DI Holden, arms folded neatly on her lap, her face a picture of unconcern. DS Fox sat on Holden's right, but no one sat on Anne's left. With a quizzical smile she had politely declined the opportunity to have a solicitor present. 'I don't suppose this will take long, will it?' she had said.

'Do you own a grey tracksuit, Miss Johnson?' Holden didn't see that anything could be gained by any pleasantries.

'No!' Anne replied.

'Are you sure?'

'My tracksuit is red.'

'You're sure about that?'

'Yes, I wore it yesterday.'

'Dr Adrian Ratcliffe tells me you have a grey one.'

'I can assure you I don't have a grey tracksuit.' She spoke firmly, even confidently.

'He's prepared to swear a statement to the effect that you have.'

She laughed. 'I gave it away.'

'When?'

'What does it matter? When a charity bag came through the door. It was getting scruffy, so I stuffed it into the bag along with a load of other clothes, and put it out to be collected the next day.'

Holden paused, and then glanced towards Fox. He pulled a photo out of a folder lying in front of him, and pushed it across the table. 'Is this you,' he said.

Anne looked at it carefully, then looked up, a smile across her lips. 'Is that the best you've got? It could be anyone, couldn't it? Well, not you, Sergeant. It's obviously not someone as big as you. But out of the population of Oxford, I guess there would be thousands of possible suspects.'

He stared at her bleakly. 'With modern digital techniques, you'd be amazed what detail we can get from a photo like this.'

Again Anne laughed. She was confident, unshaken. 'I think you're bull-shitting, Sergeant. It's a long-range, out-of-focus photo, and the face is pretty much hidden by the hood.'

'What the hell is so funny?' Holden spat the words out with real anger. 'We show you a photo of someone running away from the scene of your sister's death just two minutes after her death, and you laugh. If it's not you, it could be your sister's murderer. Is that funny? Don't you care that she might have been murdered?'

'Christ, what's the matter with you? She jumped. She was a depressive. She was very down that morning. We had a row. Maybe I was partly responsible for her mood that morning. But she came out, saw that blue plaque, and that was the final straw. Why do you find that so hard to believe?'

'Did you know Jim Blunt?' Holden's sudden change of tack appeared to throw Anne Johnson off balance. Fox, watching her, thought he saw a flash of anxiety in her eyes. But when she spoke, her voice was unwavering.

'Any chance of a glass of water?' she said.

'Answer the question please, Miss Johnson,' Holden insisted.

'Why do you ask?'

'Because we've been checking his mobile phone records.'

'Ah!' She smiled yet again. 'You're trying to trip me up, aren't you, Inspector.'

'Did you know Jim Blunt?'

'I knew of him. He rang me a couple of times. My sister had given him my number. He was worried about her and rang me.'

'You never mentioned that before.'

'I guess you never asked.'

'So did you ever meet him?'

'No!'

'You mean, he rang up twice, because he was worried about your sister, but he didn't want to meet you to discuss her.'

'I told him I didn't want to get involved.'

Again Holden glanced across to Fox. This time he pulled a typed sheet of paper out of the folder, and looked at it for several seconds as if reminding himself of what it contained. Then he looked up.

'On the Wednesday before your sister's death, a witness saw you leaving Jim Blunt's house.'

'I wouldn't even know where he lived.'

'Do you own a black leather jacket.'

'Who doesn't?'

'A pair of red boots, mid-calf in length?'

'Are we talking heels or flats?'

'Just answer the question.'

'I have lots of clothes. I like clothes, and I like buying shoes and boots and anything else that takes my fancy. Sarah did too. We were similar in that respect. I've had to have a major clear-out of her stuff, I can tell you.'

'Do you have a pair of red boots?' Holden spoke angrily now. 'Yes or no.'

'Yes. But so did Sarah. And, before you ask, yes, I got rid of them too. A girl doesn't need two pairs.' She smiled triumphantly, conscious of Holden's rising frustration.

But Holden wasn't quite ready to give up. 'You left them in the same charity bag as the track suit, did you?'

'Wow! You are a stickler for detail. I put the grey tracksuit in a charity bag in Reading, where – as you know – I live. And I took Sarah's clothes to the recycling centre at the bottom of the Abingdon Road. All right?'

Holden struggled with a sudden and barely controllable urge to hit Anne Johnson. She wanted to slap the lying, conceited cow so hard she ricocheted off the far wall. She wanted to grab her and shake her until she could shake her no more. She wanted, above all, to drag a confession out of her arrogant, pouting mouth. She wanted justice and closure for Sarah and for herself, but she knew now she never would.

'Where were you on the Wednesday before Sarah's death?' It was a last throw. 'And please don't tell me you can't remember, because I won't bloody well believe you.'

'Inspector!' she exclaimed in a voice of mock horror. 'I would never allow language like that in my classes. But just to put your mind at rest, I do remember that I was at home. I dare say I was glued to Crimewatch from nine o'clock to ten. I like to think that if I watch it regularly, then one day I'll recognize someone in a CCTV shot, and then I'll be able to help the police solve a crime. Now, wouldn't that be good.'

'Can you prove you were there?' Holden snapped back despairingly.

Again the conceited smile dominated Anne Johnson's face. 'Can you prove that I wasn't?'

Holden made no reply. For several seconds she sat and looked at her adversary in silence. Finally, she stood abruptly up. 'You are free to go home,' she said curtly, and then, without waiting, she stalked out of the room.

THE END

FREE KINDLE BOOKS

Made in the USA
Monee, IL
05 September 2020